My name's Rich. Which is funny, because at this moment I have only 72p in my pocket. I can't afford clothes. I can't afford booze. I can't afford anything. Every single one of my art pencils needs replacing and I can't afford that, either. I daren't even sharpen the bloody things when I need to now. If they get much shorter I'll be holding them with tweezers.

But my drawings—they're good. And now I'm sending them out to try to make myself some money. I've done my research. I've got the names of five little local companies—three advertising, two graphic design. I've written out five really good letters that stop just this side of actual begging, saying, This is a sample of my work and I'll do anything for you, anything at all.

I can hear you saying I haven't got a hope in hell, I'd have better odds if I spent my money on lottery tickets, not stamps.

Yeah, well, maybe you're right, but I've got to try, right? I'm desperate.

Look for all of the books in the Hard Cash trilogy by Kate Cann

Hard Cash
Shacked Up
Speeding
(coming soon)

hard cash

kate cann

Simon Pulse
New York London Toronto Sydney Singapore

First Simon Pulse edition October 2003

Originally published in Great Britain in 2000 by Scholastic Ltd.

Published by arrangement with Scholastic, Ltd.

SIMON PULSE
An imprint of Simon & Schuster
Children's Publishing Division
1230 Avenue of the Americas
New York, NY 10020

The text of this book was set in Ehrdardt MT.

Printed in the United States of America
10 9 8 7 6 5 4 3 2 1

Library of Congress Control Number 2003101653
ISBN 0-689-85905-8

To John, with love

Chapter 1

My name's Rich. Which is funny, because at this moment I have only 72p in the pocket of my worn-out jacket, and no prospect of getting my hands on any more until Friday. I can't afford clothes. I can't afford booze. I can't afford anything. Every single one of my art pencils needs replacing and I can't afford that, either. I daren't even sharpen the bloody things when I need to now. If they get much shorter I'll be holding them with tweezers.

Money. It does your head in. Not having it, I mean.

I saw this bloke on the way home tonight. He was one-handedly trying to park his brand-new BMW convertible in a very narrow space and all the time he was jerking back and forth he was jabbering into this flashy little silver mobile. I stood there, in the shadow of the tree by my gate, and stared at him, and my stomach went into this tight hot knot of hate and envy.

He jammed the car to a stop, not straight, as though it wouldn't really matter if someone took his sidelight off because he could always get another sidelight—or another car—and jumped out. Everything about him gave off money vibrations. His suit, his shoes, the way his hair was cut, the way his body and face was a little bit plump but still shining and toned, like he ate and drank very well but then worked it off at some high-tech gym afterwards.

He went round to the boot of the car and hauled out a classy-looking sports bag, two carriers from one of those late-night top-price delis, and a bunch of lilies. Then he slammed the boot shut, locked it with a noisy remote, and headed off across the street.

I stared after him, and I wanted to kill him. You sleek bastard. You're going to leg it into your smart flat and whip up whatever designer-foody goodies you have stashed in that bag and then some top bird is going to come round and you'll pop some champagne and give her the lilies and she'll end up shagging you with all her silky clothes chucked around the place. And the real pain of it is this is just normal workaday stuff for you. This is life.

And I can't even afford a couple of sodding pencils.

To the rich shall be given all the food all the cars all the booze all the birds yeah even until the ending of the earth.

And the poor had just better get over it.

"Be grateful you've got a roof over your head and food on the table," Mum always says. With a look that implies that I'm an ungrateful git. Which I probably am. I walk up our path and let myself into our skinny little hall that's needed redecorating for five years and more. Every spring, Dad makes some joke like, "Why don't you do it, Richard? You're supposed to be able to paint." And I think maybe I should, but I don't ever get round to it.

"Mum?"

"In here, luv. In the kitchen."

"What's for supper?"

"Spag bol."

"Great, Mum. I'm starved."

"When aren't you? Grate me up that cheese, luv."

We don't have proper Parmesan on our spag bol. We have old Cheddar that Mum gets cheap from the market. It's OK—smells as bad. She does OK with the pathetically small amount she has to spend on food each week.

They're proud of how well they budget, my parents. To hear them talk you'd think budgeting was every bit as good as having money.

Dad walks through the door and looks at me in the raised-chin, challenging way he's used ever since I got more or less sanely past puberty. Dad challenges most people, especially men, and Mum says he could've got a lot further in his line of work if he didn't do it quite so much. But he says it's better to be hard up and keep your pride. Maybe he's right.

"So how was college, son?" he asks.

"Oh, OK. Got bollocked by Huw again."

"Why?"

"Late assignment."

"Good God, d'you ever do an assignment you don't give in late?"

I shrug. "It was a crap topic."

"He's the teacher, son, not you. If he sets you a topic it's because you need it for your grades."

"I don't see what drawing a pile of lemons and crap has to do with anything."

"Nor do I, but if he sets it, you do it, right?"

"Leave him alone, Bill," says Mum tiredly.

"Yeah, leave me alone, Dad," I say. Sometimes I think he just asks me stuff so he can jump on something and lecture me about it. He's on my back the whole time. It does my head in if you want the truth.

"Call Sam for me," Mum says to Dad. "It'll be ready in five minutes." Dad stomps out to the hall to yell up the stairs for my little brother,

Sam, and Mum says, "Work isn't the only reason you're fed up, is it?"

I shrug.

"You still mooning after that girl?"

I shrug again. I could shrug for England, I reckon.

"I don't know, Rich. Why don't you just ask her out?"

"'Cos she'd say no."

"Course she wouldn't. Good-looking boy like you."

"I can't afford to ask her out."

"Good God, you'd think feminism had never happened. Girls don't expect to get paid for nowadays."

"Girls like Portia McCutcheon do."

Mum dips her mouth in the way that says, "She's not worth it then."

Maybe she isn't, but I'll never get the chance to find out, will I?

Sam bursts in talking to Dad about football, just like I used to do, and we all sit down and eat and Dad tells me to cheer up and I hate myself for being so miserable and sour. It's not my folks' fault they're not rich. They're great—well, Mum is—loads better than some of the jerks I see letting themselves in and out of the remote-controlled gates of the posh tenements just up our street. It's just—

My parents are the salt of the earth and, yes, salt glitters, but not like diamonds do.

I had a job two months ago. It lasted three weeks. I worked two nights, sometimes three, in this bar in town. It was brilliant. OK pay, free food, free beer—that's what did me in, of course. I liked the beer too much. And I got totally pissed once too often and got fired, with no hope of a reference. Not that there were any other jobs to go for. Bar jobs are like gold dust in this place.

Sam has a paper round. The little sod's a lot richer than I am and what's he got to spend it on? Chewing gum and hair gel, that's all. The odd trip to lie his way into a 15 movie. I've considered asking him for a loan but, Christ, you've got to have some pride.

Last week Dad said I could do the sweeping up Saturdays at his factory and got very short with me when I turned it down. Pride again. But I mean, *me*—sweeping up?

Anyway, it was OK to turn it down because I've got a plan. Mum still slips me a few quid every Friday, about a fiver, whatever she can afford. And this Friday I'm spending it on stamps. I've already blagged five big A5 envelopes out of the stationery cupboard outside the Art Department. And I've got five sets of six of my top drawings—I managed to photocopy them when the office was empty of all but Charlotte, who thinks I'm a "nice boy" because I don't have excess body-piercing like most of the art lot.

These drawings are—they're good. Even Huw said they're good. "Christ, though, boy," he said. "Look at the pain in these. Look at the barely repressed rage. We should get you some therapy. Mind you, if these scribbles are indications of your inner being, what therapist would knowingly go anywhere near it?"

Ha, ha. Huw reckons he's a real funny man. My pictures are pretty dark though. Monsters and ghouls and nightmares. But they're *strong.* They come off the page at you, alive—more alive than most stuff in the real world. I love them and I loved doing them. And now I'm sending them out to try to make myself some money.

I've done my research. I've got the names of five little local companies—three advertising, two graphic design. With the help of Charlotte I've written out five really good letters that stop just this side of actual begging, saying, This is a sample of my work and I'll do anything for you, anything at all.

I can hear you saying I haven't got a hope in hell. I can hear you saying, You'd have better odds if you spent your money on lottery tickets, not stamps.

Yeah, well, maybe you're right, but I've got to try, right? I'm desperate.

Chapter 2

I get up late the next day and get into college even later, and miss the lecture on Impressionism. Well who cares, everyone knows they only painted that way 'cos they needed specs. I ought to go into the art rooms and do some work but instead I edge past them just about flat against the wall in case Huw spots me and bursts out demanding his Lemons Portrait. By this time it's nearly lunchtime and I can't afford lunch but I think, sod it, I'll go and get a cup of tea to stave off the hunger pangs and just as I'm walking through the cafeteria door I bump smack into Portia.

We're visual people, we artists. And Portia is visual dynamite. Today on her stunning body she's wearing a little short jumper that probably cost about a hundred quid and tight classy jeans. And her hair is black and silky and her face is pointed and perfectly symmetrical like a cat's.

She's with her friend Jenny and she's eating a bag of chips. "*Hi*, Richy," she says. She always says the *hi* kind of half seductive, half sarcastic when she talks to me. I know she fancies me—she flirts with me and teases me but then she walks off because I'm scruffy with crap hair I cut myself and I'm always broke. She's a snob. I hate myself for having such a thing about a snob. But I don't have control over my feelings, do I?

"Hi," I say. "Did you get to the lecture?"

"Yes. Didn't you?"

"No. I forgot to get up."

"*Yeah?*" she smirks, with this sexy kind of overlay in her voice. "Tired were you?"

Jenny giggles. Jenny giggles a lot. It's hysteria brought on by the pride of being Portia's best mate, I reckon.

"Just asleep," I say.

"Well you didn't miss much. They gave out these sheets. Want to photocopy them?" And she waves a thin sheaf of papers at me.

"Thanks," I say, taking them. I know I won't copy them because photocopying is 4p a sheet, but taking them means I have to give them back, which means an excuse to talk to her again.

"Want a chip?" she says, and she dips into her bag and pulls out a chip, then shoves it straight into my mouth. God, it's a turn-on being fed by her. And *God*, it tastes good. My stomach kind of seizes with wanting more. I chew it slowly, making massive eye contact with her, and she pouts up at me and says, "Hasn't he got great cheekbones?" Then she actually reaches out and strokes my face. "We should draw him."

I get an immediate groin-clench. Just from that contact. And Jenny giggles again, as though she knows.

"Any time, girls," I say, all smooth.

"Yeah? Life classes?"

In life classes, the models strip off. Right off. "You bet," I say. "Long as I get to do you the week after."

Portia laughs, and glides off on her way as though she's already wasted far too much time talking to a total no-hoper, and as she glides past a bin she dumps her bag of chips in. I'm behind her really fast and I pick up the bag of chips just as she's gliding out of the door and can't see me. The chip bag's nearly full and it wasn't up against anything manky, only a couple of Coke cans.

I stand there and stuff them in my mouth and tell myself I'm not really low and disgusting, picking things to eat out of litter bins. These are the chips of the woman I'm obsessed with, so it's like an erotic thing, a stalker's thing.

They taste *great*. How could she leave them?

That's how she stays so fit and thin I suppose. I'm feeling quite chuffed with myself, thinking that was quite a hot little interchange, when some gossip I'd repressed surfaces to the front of my brain. This gossip is that Portia's got a new boyfriend. Only a few people have seen him, but he looks about twenty-five and he's got a Golf GTI he picks her up from college in.

Shit. I finish the chips and mooch over to the counter to buy a cup of tea. Then I carry it over to an empty table by the window. The cafeteria's right by the college entrance, and from here I can look out on the concrete steps and the rubbish blowing about and the students walking in and out. I stare out and tell myself I'm a fool to even think about Portia, I'm a fool to starve so I can buy stamps to send off drawings to flashy companies who'll bin them soon as look at them, I'm a fool to—

"*LOOK*, you skiving little work-shy bastard, it's bad enough you skip my classes and never give anything in on time but when I'm reduced to tracking you down at the trough it really has gone beyond a BLOODY JOKE!"

Oh, shit. Huw. He sits his stocky form down right in front of me, leans menacingly across the table, and glares from under his beetly black brows.

"Two weeks late, Richard boy. Two weeks. All

I want is a little still life, a couple of little yellow lemons. Is that too much to ask? Is it? You flunk this, and you're on very thin ice."

"It's stupid, drawing fruit."

"No one's denying that, boy. No one's denying that. All you have to do is prove you can do it as well as those trip-to-hell visions you come up with, and I'll never ask you to draw as much as a goosegog as long as you live."

"My mum didn't have any lemons."

"You've had *two weeks*!"

"She never gets any."

"You could've bought them yourself."

"Huw, I'm so skint I—"

"Look, lad, I don't want to listen to your excuses. It's not just the lemons, it's your whole bloody attitude. You can't cherry-pick what you do and what you don't do. I let you bend the rules too much as it is—late work, sloppy work—'cos some of your stuff's so brilliant it can carry the crap. But I'm getting tired of it, OK? So stop acting like such a bloody little prima donna and get down to *work*." He pauses, draws breath, and I consider saying, "How come you always call me little when I'm about a foot taller than you?" But I don't.

He's pulling a white paper bag out of his pocket. "Now, I knew you'd come up with some lame excuse about not having any, so I've bought you some lemons along, OK? You have *got to do* a still life. For Christ's sake just *do it*." And he throws the bag down on the table.

"Thanks, Huw," I mutter, as he pushes his chair back from the table and stands up. I feel really ashamed. I pull the bag towards me—it's the wrong shape just for lemons. I pull it open and inside there are two lemons and two pencils, a 2B and an F. Just the ones I need for a still life.

I jump up. "Huw—thanks!" I shout after him. "*Thanks*, mate!" But he just flips an acknowledging hand in the air without turning round, and stamps out of the door.

I draw the lemons as soon as I get home. I feel kind of superstitious, what with Huw buying me them and what with tomorrow being the day Mum should give me enough cash to post off my drawings. I prop them up as best as I can, but the stupid things keep rolling about, and then I can't get the outline on them, and I rub out so often it looks mucky, and then the light changes, and my shading's rubbish, and in the end I tear my sheet of paper up in a stress and lob the lemons in the bin.

Half an hour later I come back, fish them out, and start again. By this time all the warm feelings of gratitude I've been having towards Huw have evaporated, and I'm ready to ram the poxy lemons down his throat. But I make myself finish. One just-about-good-enough fruit still life—*sir*!

The next day I wake up early, and my head is full of calculations about how much Mum might have left out of her week's money to be able to part with some of it to her firstborn son. I'm thinking—how much meat did she buy, how much bread, did she get anything extra like Guinness for the old man. Which is all very sordid and demeaning, but I can't stop myself. And then I go down to breakfast and I'm all smiley and amenable, and she says, "Have you got any plans for tonight?" And I say, "No, I'm skint," and wham, before I know it there are six one pound coins chinking down on the table beside me and I scoop it up quick before Dad comes in and I say, "Thanks Mum" just at the exact same time as she's saying, "You will try and get a job of some sort won't you, Rich, have you thought of filling shelves?"

I say I'll think of it and I think of it for exactly two nano-seconds as I leg it up to my room and collect my five big, white, carefully addressed envelopes. Then I go down to the Post Office and get them weighed and hand over £4.90 for the stamps and the girl says, "Put them through this window at the end. You don't want to bend them, do you?"

"No," I say, and I have this huge desire to kiss

each envelope as I lay it down, kind of good luck on its way, but I don't of course.

And then that's it.

Now I wait.

With only £1.52 left, I can predict already that my weekend is not exactly going to be a scorcher.

God, if this art thing doesn't work out I will be humble. I'll sweep the floor at Dad's factory—I'll clean his sodding *toilets* if I have to. And when I've finished that I'll stack shelves. And maybe get a paper round too. I'll have no life. I'll just do lots of little jobs all paying about 50p an hour and I'll be really grateful.

If this doesn't work out.

Please let it work out.

I hurry back home and make myself a sandwich—two staleish crusts and some peanut butter—to take into college so I don't faint from lack of sustenance. I'll eat it somewhere where people can't see me—the bogs if I'm desperate—because there's something so naff about bringing in a little packed lunch. Especially my kind of packed lunch. And I'll let myself buy one cup of tea.

Not going to think about next week, when I'll be completely broke. Not going to think about the weekend. Concentrate on those white envelopes. Channel energy into them.

All in all, I'm on a high as I run up the college steps. I think about yesterday, about Portia really giving me the eye, and the chip. I think about her saying she'd like to draw me, the way she touched my face. I stroll into the art room and open my folder.

"Well?" barks Huw. "Have you managed to draw those bloody lemons, boy?"

"I have," I say smugly. I hand over the picture. Huw looks at it unenthusiastically. "What, Huw? It's OK, isn't it?"

"Yes. Just. It was like pulling teeth to get you to do it and somehow, lad, you've managed to evoke that sensation here. However."

"Huw, it's two bloody lemons. How am I supposed to make them look?"

"They're fine, Richard," he sighs, opening his desk drawer and filing my picture away. "I suppose I could even say you've captured their sour essence."

"Yeah, well," I say sulkily, delving into my bag, "I brought them back in case you need them." And I bring out the two lemons and hold them out to him. They're looking a bit dull and bruised by this time.

Huw pulls the corners of his mouth down. "I'm not the gin-and-tonic type, lad. Bin them."

I grin and take aim, and the lemons smack into a waste paper bin for the second time in their short lives. Then Huw fixes me with one of his beetly looks and says, "Now—the portrait. You have a week left before you're two weeks late with that."

"What portrait?"

"You know perfectly bloody *well* what portrait. Get some gullible friend to sit for you and produce a life-like portrait. And I mean *life-like*. None of your twisted abstractions, lad. It has to be a recognizable *face*. If you can't get anyone to sit for you—and frankly I'd be surprised if you did, no one wants their name under your psychotic doodlings—do your mam's profile while she's watching TV."

I smile cheerfully and say, "Sure, Huw. It'll be in by the end of next week," and I'm half way out of the door before he can haul up his jaw again. I reckon I'm on a winning streak today and I have had an IDEA!

Chapter 3

It's nowhere near lunchtime and I was going to make myself wait until then to go and get my one cup of tea, but I know Portia usually has a coffee around eleven and there's a chance she'll be in the cafeteria. . . .

She is. She's holding court at one of the middle tables with Jenny and another girl whose name I don't know. There is no way I'm going to sashay over there and take on three of them. But they have a kind of hopeful finishing-off look about them, so I mooch over to the counter and examine all the gross delicious-looking pastries on offer, and wait.

My luck's in. A couple of minutes on, and the three stand up, cackling loudly about something, and Jenny and the other girl go on ahead while Portia lags behind a bit, putting her purse into her bag. Smooth as an oil slick, I intercept her. "Hi, Portia."

She's not as playful as she was yesterday. She returns my "Hi" a bit frostily.

Go on, jump in, I think. You've prepared for this moment. "Portia, you know what you said about drawing me . . ."

There is no way anyone could prepare for what happens next. There is no way anyone should have to go through it. Portia takes a step back from me and lets her mouth drop open in comic amazement. "Oh *MY GOD*!!" she shrieks, right at the top of her voice range. "I *DO NOT BELIEVE* I'm hearing this! That was a *JOKE*!!"

Jenny and the other girl have spun round. Everyone within hearing range—which is everyone in the cafeteria, and possibly in the whole college—has craned round to look. "Look, don't get so excited," I say, all kind of smooth and dominant and I'm-in-charge-here. "I know it was a joke. It just—gave me an idea. I thought we could pair up. For this portraits project."

"OH MY GOD!!" she screams again. "Jenny—Richard thinks I want to *DRAW HIM*!"

I want to grab her by the throat before she shrieks anything else, but I say, "OK, OK, forget it. This is not personal, Portia. I just thought—"

"Without his *CLOTHES ON*!"

I begin to really hate her. "Portia, for Christ's sake. Stop making such a big deal of this, OK? Of course we'd have our clothes on. Taking them off was your idea."

"I *BEG* your pardon?"

"Oh, shit. I mean your *joke*. I didn't mean—look, I just fancied drawing a girl, OK?" In desperation, I wheel round on Jenny. "What about you, Jen? Have you done your portrait yet?"

Boy, does that change Portia's mood. She practically shoulder-barges Jenny out of the way and says, "Look, I didn't say I wouldn't sit for you. It's just—I've done mine. Jenny and I did each other."

Well, there's a surprise. "Can I see?" I ask, and I kind of sag in relief as the two girls simultaneously flip open their posh folders and the attention is off me at last. They whip out two creamy, gooey, girly sketches. Jenny's one of Portia is a particular riot. Talk about idealized. It even has a Christ-like aura of light playing round its hair. Portia's one of Jenny is kind of wishy-washy nice-nice. Between them, the two pictures tell the story of the friendship rather well.

"God, they're brilliant," I say.

"You think?" says Jenny.

"Yeah. Really good." I could lie for England.

"I s'pose I *could* do two portraits," Portia

ponders. "Huw's been nagging at me lately, telling me to stretch myself."

"That is *so* stupid," pipes up Jenny, loyally. "You want to do *clothes* design—where does *stretching* come into clothes design?"

"Lycra?" I joke, and the two girls look at me blankly. I've noticed this before, that Portia isn't exactly bright, I mean. She often doesn't get my jokes. Plus she has this two-dimensional view of things that can make talking to her a bit flat. But like I say, I'm a visual person, and also possibly highly shallow when it comes to birds, so what goes on inside her head doesn't bother me that much.

"Think how pleased Huw'd be if you did two," I say. "You could do a big thing of the contrast. You could do me in charcoal, or . . ."

"Like—all rugged?"

"Well . . . yeah."

"I don't see you as rugged, Richy."

Fine.

"Look—I don't really think so—OK?" she says, starchily, as she puts her sketch of Jenny back in its folder. A mobile phone starts ringing from the depths of her bag. She fishes it out, answers it in a voice utterly different to the one she was using on me, and swans out of the cafeteria.

I leave it a minute and skulk out after her.

Well, my idea for the big pull backfired big time, didn't it? I can feel everyone's sniggering eyes boring into my back.

I probably won't go back in for my tea, later.

I probably won't go in the cafeteria ever again.

I sulk through the day, make it to five-thirty. The weekend is officially here. I hate the start of the weekend. All the shit that comes with being broke—grinding you down, holding you back—it's far worse at the weekend. As I scuff down the college steps I think about those five white A5 envelopes processing somewhere through the guts of the Post Office system, and I'm filled with desperate hope and need and greed and most of all the lust for hard cash. Money, money, money. It's the key to all the doors of all the places you want to be. It makes you look good, gets you laid. Money is as powerful and exciting as a drug; it fills your head and stakes your claim in the world.

It also lets you buy the odd half-pint in the local and without it, believe me, no one wants you around.

"Hey, Chris!" I shout. Chris is my mate and he's five steps ahead of me. "What you up to?"

"There's a party, Jim Blake's place," he calls back. "Want to come? We're meeting up first at the Rose and Crown."

"Oh, right. I'm a bit—"

"Skint. When aren't you, Rich?"

Great. I'm predictable as well as poor.

"Look—come to the pub late," Chris said. "I'll buy you a beer. We're taking some cans to the party. It'll be OK."

"Thanks, mate," I say. Chris is a good bloke and right now I want to kill him because it's so easy for him, being a good bloke. He gets this humungous allowance from his folks. He told me once that they think it's his job to be at college and they want him to concentrate on that and not do other jobs just to get cash. That's the kind of parents to have I reckon.

I go home pretty deflated, steeped in the fact that my idea to pull Portia through a mutual sketching session fell so spectacularly flat on its arse. I'm humiliated by that and I'm humiliated by not having any dosh to go out this evening and I'm humiliated by all the hope I've been pinning on the five big, white, useless envelopes, and I'm just generally humiliated by life in general.

I go upstairs. Our house is so small and crappy I have to share a bedroom with my stupid little brother. The third bedroom got turned into a bathroom when the house was hauled into the twentieth century sometime around 1976.

I hate having to share. It means I have to look at hideous posters of footballers and naff pictures of the latest sappy girly groups. And me a visual person. It's a bit like making an animal lover sleep in an abattoir I reckon. The only thing I quite like is the glow-in-the-dark cosmos that Sam stuck all over the ceiling a year or so back. It's kind of calming.

To add insult to injury, we've got bunk beds. I've got the bottom one, and it's too short for me now. When I pointed this out, Mum looked so stricken at the thought of having to find the cash for a new bed I told her it didn't matter because I always sleep curled up. Which I have to now, obviously, so I wasn't lying. Sometimes I jack-knife down on my bunk and I imagine what I'd do with the room if it was all mine. Just paint it out dark blue, paint the floor white, scrawl all over the crappy IKEA shelf units so it looked like urban decay, hang my clothes on a pole in the middle. . . . Then I get to imagining a better, bigger room, split-level, with huge floor-to-ceiling windows and skylights and stuff. I'd do it all white, with some neatly placed unpleasantries like a bed straight off a porn set and maybe some gargoyles trickling water. I quite like bad taste, you see. I like vulgarity. But you need to be rich to be vulgar, because you can do it properly then, with style.

Being poor cramps my style.

In the end I get off my bed and go into the

bathroom and halfheartedly spruce myself up for Friday night. I have a wash, then I put the jeans I wore to college back on and I find an old white shirt of Dad's in the back of his wardrobe that he won't mind (or more to the point, won't notice) me borrowing. As I pull on my battered old desert boots I get this wave of revulsion, this wave of longing for something better. I've tried to give up thinking about clothes, wanting them, but I can't, it's not in me. I only go for the arty scruffy look 'cos I've got to. My old jacket is like my pelt. People wouldn't recognize me without it I reckon.

I head off for the pub about nine-thirty, late like Chris suggested. I have absolutely no enthusiasm for it because nothing's going to happen, but it'd be even more depressing to stay in, wouldn't it?

When I get in the pub I go straight over and order a half of draught before I even look for Chris and everyone. I can't walk over to their table with my arms hanging loose and empty, it's too shaming, waiting for Chris to finish his drink and include me in the next round. Once I've got my half in my fist and literally only coppers left in my pocket, I scan the room for Chris, and I spot him over in the corner, with five other people, two of them not-bad-looking birds from the Drama Department. The Drama Department is famous for the looks of its birds. Trouble is, they also have voices they like to exercise, running them up and down the scale, full volume, and arms they like to make lots of theatrical gestures with.

Still, who am I to be in any way picky? Beggars can't be choosers.

"All right, mate?" says Chris, as I sit down next to him. He clocks with approval the beer I'm drinking very, very slowly.

"Sure. You?" I say, and I nod at the two girls and the three other guys, most of whom I know by sight if nothing else. The guys either side of the two girls shift up very slightly closer to them, and the one on the left leans his forearm on his girl's shoulder.

Crass, I reckon. Like dogs marking territory. But it cheers me up a bit because it means those guys reckon that I, Richard Steele, am a Threat—despite my terrible haircut done at the bathroom mirror with the kitchen scissors and my sub-Oxfam-shop clothes. So I smirk a bit into my slow beer, and throw myself into the conversation.

Which limps and lurches along until about ten-thirty when we get up to go. We drop into the off-licence to pick up some beer and Chris acts like I've already given him my wad of cash, which means he has to put in twice as much as the others. He's a good mate, and it shames me, and

I can't even thank him. We get to the party and—I don't know, I just can't be bothered. It's like my life is pissing me off so much I don't want to live in it anymore. Around midnight, I walk out and get on the late bus home. Only I have to get off again, don't I, and walk, because I don't have enough for the fare.

I wake on Saturday even before Sam starts rolling about and groaning and dangling his skinny little legs down from the top bunk in front of my face. This is unheard of for me, but I know why I've done it. The white envelopes will arrive today, slap, slap, slap, down through the letter-boxes in the graphic design studios and the ad men's offices, and it's just possible that some keen geezer will come in to graft away over the weekend, and he'll open one of them up, and he'll see my drawings, and . . .

Possible, not probable. It's *probable* no one will open them till Monday, which is what I planned. But because it's *possible,* I already feel this scary little jump inside, and when the phone goes at about ten I nearly leap out of my skin.

By midday I can't bear it anymore and I have to head out for a walk. I can't keep still at home. Now it's happened, now I know those envelopes have been delivered, I can't think about anything else but my drawings in some art-director's hands. It's not just a supid Steele half-baked plan anymore, it's out there, real.

And I want it, so much. I want someone to pull my pictures out of the envelope and think, "Yes. Serious talent here. What we've been looking for"—I want it *so much* it's as though I can actually see it happening. As though that's real too.

I walk to the end of our road, past the posh gated tenements, and I pick up my speed until I'm out onto the dusty outskirts of the town, walking alongside sad little allotments and rubbish-filled spaces. All I can see in my head are those envelopes and my drawings, and some guy gazing at them. . . . Stop *obsessing*, I tell myself—that way madness lies. Or at least a suicidal downer when it doesn't come off. Which it won't, I tell myself, it won't—after all, what are the odds?

If I'm jumpy at the weekend, I'm psychotic on Monday. I'm nervy, prowling, going out when I can't stand the silent phone anymore, coming back, demanding "Anyone ring?" and feeling that sick, smashed feeling when the answer's "No." Then Tuesday. Then Wednesday. And the phone doesn't go, not for me anyway, not with anyone who matters. And by this time I have to face the fact that my envelopes have been opened and the contents almost certainly binned. Rip, look, chuck, over in five seconds, just like that.

I haven't quite given up all hope, but what was once a great hungry greedy roaring beast is now a little starveling dying fading maggoty nothing.

I think, Come the end of the week, *I'll* phone *them*—I'll phone every one of those companies and ask them did they see my pictures. Only just the thought of that makes me feel like throwing up. Having to cope five times over with "Who? What? No. No. Sorry."

I'm just—*sunk*. I'm so down I hardly speak to anyone, I don't try and stalk Portia, I listen to Huw's tongue-lashings and don't come back at him. No one asks me what's up. Shows what a misery I am most of the time I guess. Then, finally, Wednesday night Mum tells me I'm looking ill and I mutter something about thinking I've got a virus and I go to bed early and just stare up at Sam's phoney cosmos as it glimmers and swims in the dark.

Thursday, I say I feel really bad and I'm staying home. I know I shouldn't, I should make myself get up and move and interact with people and get my mind off it, but I can't, I just can't. Mum puts her hand on my forehead and peers worriedly into my face. "You're not hot," she says. "D'you feel sick?"

"Yes," I say. "Very."

So they all leave me to it, letting themselves out of the house one by one, shouting goodbye, leaving me in silence.

And at eleven o'clock in the morning, the phone goes.

Chapter 4

"Hi, yeah, er—who am I calling?"

What? I think, heart thudding, and I say, "Richard Steele."

"Right—yeah—the kid from college—yeah—er—sorry—hang on—*Camilla*! We need them *today,* not tomorrow, or next fucking week—*Jesus*!"

I'm in hell, waiting. This could be *it*—or it could be a mad insurance salesman—or a—

"Sorry," says the voice. "Jesus. It's like a fucking circus here. I forgot who I dialled for a minute there."

"Richard Steele."

"Yes. Yes. I'm Nick Hanratty. From Abacus Design. Your sketches . . ."

My blood's pumping so hard in my head I think it might explode, splatter my brains out across the hall table.

"They're good. I was impressed. I *really* liked the nasty bat one. Your mother worry about you?"

I force myself to laugh, although my throat's swollen up so tight it comes out like a squeak. "Yeah. A bit."

"Well, look. You want to come down to my office, have a chat about them?"

"Yeah. *Yeah*. When you say have a chat, do you. . . ?"

"Look, no promises, obviously. Nothing definite. Just, I think we might be able to use you."

"What, one of the pictures?"

"Well, no. Doubt it. They're too weird, too dark. But I like your style. All that energy, it's great. Kind of . . . *neo-adolescent*, if that's not an insult. Raw, you know. Young. And we have this client right now wanting raw and young."

This is crazy. At the same time as I'm crowing and grinning and bursting with excitement over what he's said, there's this . . . *grief*, almost, inside me, that he doesn't want to use one of my pictures just as they are, that he didn't pull them out and think, That's brilliant. That's amazing. That's *it*.

"So when can you come down?" Nick Hanratty's saying.

"Any time. This afternoon?"

I'm waiting for him to say, "Got to look at my

diary, what about a week next Friday," but he says, "Great. Not before three, OK, or I'll still be out for lunch. Any time after that. Just buzz along, and we'll have a chat."

How come it's so simple? How come? How come the difference between happiness and *death* is "Come along sometime after three"?

He gives me the address, which I know anyway of course, and describes how to get there—it's in one of the old wool mills along by the canal. Luckily, I can walk it. Walk it? I'll *fly*.

I have two and a quarter hours before I set out on my journey. First thing I do is put on an old rock track, Led Zeppelin, and turn it up to top volume, and mime this pumping, macho stomp of triumph round the kitchen and up and down the hall. Then I go and have a shower because I realize that in my depressed state I'd forgotten all about washing for the last couple of days. Then I find another of Dad's neatly ironed worn-collared white shirts in his wardrobe, and select my least disgusting pair of jeans from the pile on the floor. Then I stand in front of the old battered pier-glass in Mum and Dad's room and think, *Shit*.

No way round it, I'm unimpressive.

Still, I'm not going to worry too much about how I look, or how I come over, or *anything*. He wants raw and young, he's got it. Poor, raw, and young. And I'm so pent up I reckon I won't make sense when I talk to him, I probably won't even be able to *talk*, I'll just gibber at him like a crazed ape. But it doesn't matter. It's my art he wants, not me. It's those babies he's got on his desk he likes—not enough to say, "Yes, we want that one," but enough to say, "Let's talk."

I go downstairs and check my watch. Just over an hour to wait. I realize I'm *starving*. Major, gut-tearing starvation, because I've been too pitiful and sad to eat my usual troughs full of grub over the last few days. I'm not pitiful and sad anymore, though, I'm ravenous. I'm a hunter off out on the kill, and I need *food*.

I ransack the fridge. All I can find is a dish of leftover stew that I vaguely remember Mum producing last night. I decide to eat it cold as it's too much hassle to heat it up, and I add a big dollop of Branston pickle to spice it up, and find a crust of bread to dunk in it. Then before I tuck in I drape a tea-towel round my neck as a bib. It's one thing to look a bit impoverished and scruffy at an interview; quite another, I reckon, to look stew-spattered.

I finish my meal, I even rinse the plate, and it's still nowhere near time to go. So I spend the time pacing round about the house just enjoying feeling like I feel, kind of excited and triumphant and anticipatory and *alive*.

Then I leave the house. I'm still far too early but I reckon it'll give me time to make sure I've got the right building and stuff. Plus, I make myself walk slowly. Well, I try to, but my feet want to bound.

It takes me maybe thirty minutes to get to the canal on the edge of town. There are about eight old defunct mills ranged along it, all four storeys, most with big double doors on the top floor where the wool would have been winched up straight off the canal boats. They're reckoned to be fine old Victorian buildings, and there was a move at the end of the seventies to restore them and turn them into a trendy canal complex of offices and flats. The scheme never quite got off the ground, though. The eighties' recession was biting before the place was even half full, and the car parks were left half gravelled, the hanging baskets withering.

I quite like the seedy, derelict air the whole place has now, though. There's something wonderfully sinister about old dark buildings looming over a canal—maybe that's the reason why the yuppification never quite came off. If you walk here at nightfall you can see rats running along the edges, and plopping into the water. Maybe that's another reason it didn't come off.

I walk over the old canal bridge, and make my

way to the third mill from the town side, like Nick Hanratty had said. Round to the side, and there's a big impressive front door, with two completely embarrassing stone lions posing either side. They're kind of upmarket garden centre and whoever put them here had no *style*. All that saves them is the fact that they've been graffitied on. One has a moustache and a monocle, and the other looks a bit like Marilyn Monroe.

This is the place, though. A battered copper sign next to a dodgy-looking intercom says *Abacus Design, Please Ring*. So I ring, and wait, then ring again. And then a weird crackling comes down the intercom, a bit like Martians trying to make contact.

"It's Richard Steele," I announce, feeling like a prat.

The intercom crackles again.

"To see Nick Hanratty?" I whine.

Another spew of crackling, and this time the door joins in with a deep kind of whirring noise, so I grab the huge handle and turn it, praying, and sure enough the door swings open, and I step into the cool, square, lofty hall.

Ahead of me is one of those ornate, wrought-iron lift cages, with broad stone steps to the side. All round me on the floor are piled huge cardboard boxes, and to my left is an open door with

"Litchford Knitwear—Clothes Distributors" written on it.

I'm about to knock on the Knitwear door when I see a little purple sign propped against the window behind the lift. It says *Abacus Design* and it's pointing up. So I run up the stairs, and the next floor seems completely empty, but there's another little *Abacus Design* sign on the window ledge, with the arrow going up, and when I reach the next floor, I know I'm definitely there.

Glossy-looking art boards are stacked round the door, which is open. I can hear some pounding music coming from inside, and at least three people are shouting—not angrily, just as though shouting is how they usually communicate.

I peer inside, and I get a shiver just looking round me. It's terrific. They've washed white and purple over the old brick walls, and painted the pipes and radiators toxic lime green. There are flashy phones and computers on big desks, and huge boards propped up everywhere, covered with sketches, diagrams, photos, images, colour, colour, *colour*. . . .

Huw's art rooms have a grey, dusty, tired look. His rooms say, Art for grades, art to pass exams.

This place says, Art for money. Lots of money.

"Hi!"

Someone's spotted me in the doorway. It's a

girl swivelling on a stool in front of a console, with three orange clips in her spiky hair.

"Hi," I reply, nervously. "I'm—er—Richard Steele. I've come to see—"

"NICK!" she shrieks. "Your student's here!"

Then she stands up and comes over to me, giving me a nice grin. She reaches out, takes my arm, tugs me into the office, saying, "I'll show you where he is."

We walk past about three people doing fascinating stuff on boards and screens, and into a glassed-off bit at the end. Nick's inside it, behind a desk piled with stuff. I know it's Nick because he's yelling into a phone and I recognize his voice.

He's kind of brown-haired and ordinary looking, with a soft, blokeish-looking face. You wouldn't look twice at him if you walked by him on the street, but in a pub or at a party—well, he'd demand your attention then. He's vibrating with energy, charged like a dynamo. He's a little too old for the deeply trendy gear he has on, but somehow it looks OK because of this energy. As he speaks he gesticulates madly, as though his hand action is going to get conveyed down the phone line too. Maybe it does.

I take in a deep, deep, shaky breath, and then he spots me. "Richard—hi!" he says, his hand first palm-out towards me, next waving me into the chair opposite. Then he dives back in to the receiver and says, "Yeah—yeah—Thursday, no problem—and I'll get them to go with the new designs and—" Right behind his left shoulder on the wall there's a big blow up of one of the Tarot cards, the one where a man is falling off a tower struck by lightning. It looks dead sinister. I can't remember what it means if you get dealt it, but I bet that's dead sinister too. I'm still staring at it as he jabs the phone down.

"Don't get freaked by that," he grins. "It's just a reminder of how bloody vulnerable we all are in this business."

"As if we need reminding," the orange-clip girl calls out, from outside the door.

Nick reaches across the desk, grabs hold of my hand, and squeezes it. "Thanks for coming in, mate," he says. I smile, and my lips have gone so dry I have trouble getting them back down over my teeth, but he doesn't seem to notice. He draws a folder towards him and pulls out my drawings. I can't help noticing that he has pinky-silver nail varnish on the nails of the hand he didn't grab me with.

"Now, your stuff," he says. "Like I said—brilliant. Scary. Tough. These guys look like they actually have blood pumping. They're great."

"Thank you," I croak. I remind myself to breathe. Everything in me is on hold, on tenter-hooks.

"These clients I told you about—"

"The ones who want raw and young?"

He stares at me. "I said that?"

I nod anxiously. "Yeah. . . ."

"That is *exactly* what they want. What d'you think of alcopops?"

I shrug. "Well—it's a little girl's drink."

"*Right*. Soft image, yeah? Trying to play down the booze side and up the fruity juicy side so the parents won't freak."

I nod again.

"My clients—they do Sling—and they reckon they've overdone it. Made it too soft, too pink. They want to remarket it, repitch it. You know, the way that energy drink was got away from the hospital room and on to the sports pitch?"

"Lucozade?"

"That's the one. Similar makeover needed here. Lose the fruit and the fun, the whole soft girly giggly this-is-safe-really image, gain sharpness, style, a touch of danger, but still youth, still kids, still refreshment, not the whole boring boozed-out-of-their-sad-skulls adult world. I'm seeing a black bottle, ink blue maybe, see-through, and this etching effect—this creature, *your* creature—kind of a psychotic Bacchus only not wine, wine's middle aged—and just the name, Sling, and then a *completely simple* in-your-face ad campaign—if they can run to TV we can animate, no reason your stuff can't animate, you could even get in there and work on some of it?"

There's a moment's silence and I realize that the last thing he said was actually a question, and I need to answer, despite the fact that I'm about ten minutes behind trying to work out what he's on about. "Um," I go. "Sure. Yeah."

"My client is obsessing about the youth thing. Youth impact, youth input. That's why I want to wheel you along to our first meeting. Your drawings and you—an authentic teen presence. You're OK. I was afraid you'd be some kind of a dork but you're OK. What more can the bastard want? A free meal, that's what. You up for dinner? Beginning of next week—Wednesday maybe?"

I gulp. My head's reeling. "Sure," I breathe.

"Right. Now—I've got some stuff here about their product . . . somewhere . . . here . . . no . . ." He's ripping open drawers as he speaks and burrowing in like a frenzied dog after a bone. "Shit—where IS it? *Camilla? CAMILLA!?*"

Fifteen seconds later the orange-clip girl sticks her head long-sufferingly round the door. "Yeah?"

"That stuff from Marley-Hunt—the alcopop stuff—where did—"

"You said you were taking it home with you last night. To look at."

"Shit. So I did. OK. Home time." He leans over the desk, focuses on me like a lighthouse. "Rich—come back with me, and I'll give you this stuff—you need to check it out, know what the product is—maybe come up with some ideas –"

I gawp. "Draw some stuff, you mean?"

"Not necessarily. No time. We'll show him these, and go from there. . . . Hey . . . one other thing." He hooks out a silver key from a wooden bowl that, judging from the spray of ash, gets regular use as an ashtray, and unlocks a tiny drawer right at the edge of the desk. Then he pulls out a thick, rubber-banded wad of money. Then he kind of bounces it across the desk at me.

I stare at it, disbelieving.

"Don't take this the wrong way, mate, but you need some new clothes for this dinner. No one expects a student in designer gear—just maybe a little less hickey, yeah?"

I swallow. My hand wants to reach out and seize the bundle of money, but it's welded to my side. "Look on it as expenses," Nick goes on. "OK? Non-declarable, natch." Then he laughs. And I find myself croaking something stupid like, "Are you sure?" and he laughs again, and says, "Look, darling, if it all works out, that little bundle is just the very smallest down payment on what you could be making."

I stare at him, face blank. I feel like the whole

of my body is being flooded with something strong and sweet. Then my hand slowly detaches itself from my side and trembles its way across the desk and closes round the fat, thick, delicious, dirty-edged wad of money.

Chapter 5

Seconds later Nick's grabbed a black leather jacket from a hook on the back of the door and is propelling me out of the office. I stow the bundle of notes in my jeans pocket and it wedges there, tight and fantastic, straining my seams like the biggest hard-on in the world.

I follow Nick out into the hall and watch him yanking open the clanking iron gate of the lift, and four things line up together in my shell-shocked brain, freezing the pleasure.

The money. Nick's place. The nail varnish. Nick calling me darling.

Suddenly alarm bells are going off. It's all been too easy, and if there's one thing I've learnt in my seventeen years it's that in this world nothing's that easy. How could I forget?

Nick hauls me into the iron cage, saying, "I love this lift. It's so *camp*."

"Camp?"

"Camp. Haven't you seen *Rocky Horror*?"

"What?"

"You know. The film. Where that nervous jock couple are front of screen, and a lift just like this one *sli-i-des* down behind them, and you just see these *amazing* platform shoes, then the fishnets, and the corset, and then the guy himself. . . ."

"Oh, I remember. He sings, doesn't he . . ."

"*Sweet Transvestite*. God, he's beautiful. I love that film. It's a classic."

I've edged about as far away from Nick as I can now; I'm practically grating myself like cheese through the bars of the lift cage. I'm praying fervently that the stupid thing doesn't break down 'cos the last thing I want is to be trapped between floors with Nick. It's not that I'm a homophobe or anything, it's just that I don't want to have to deal with—anything. You know. *Anything*.

We head out of the huge mill door, into the watery spring sunshine. "I like the lions," I gabble, waiting for some comment about nowhere being safe from the graffiti artist.

"Yeah, well," says Nick. "Mine's the best one."

"Yours?"

"The glam one. Mark did the posh one. What d'you think?"

I swallow. "Oh, yours," I say. "Yours is the best."

"I think so. Anyone can draw a monocle on a lion, darling. It takes skill to give it lip liner. When it hasn't exactly got lips."

"Yeah," I say. "Right."

"And eyeshadow."

"The eyeshadow's great."

"They're bloody horrible lions. We had to do something."

"I agree," I say, and we turn the gravelly corner, and Nick unlocks the most beautiful old Lotus Elite I ever saw. I'm not really a huge car person, but I reckon some appreciation of motors comes along with being male, and I could certainly appreciate this one.

Except that now I'm going to have to get into it, on my own, with him.

"Isn't she *gorgeous*?" Nick says, caressingly. "I got her for fifteen hundred. Only took another twelve hundred to do her up. Barb says she's not safe, though. Especially not with the kids in the back."

"Barb?" I ask. *Kids?*

"Yeah. Barb's my wife. You'll meet her in a minute."

Chapter 6

The drive is terrific. I sit there and enjoy the speed, and the wind zipping through my hair, and laugh to myself about thinking Nick was trying to buy my body. We drive into the centre of town and pull up outside one of the big old substantial houses that a wool-mill owner probably lived in a century ago, so it's kind of appropriate that Nick lives here now.

He parks, very askew, in the front drive and as he lets himself in the big front door he's already starting up a stream of talk: "Barb? *Barb!* You seen that Marley-Hunt crap I brought back last night? Where are you, Barb? Come and say hi to Richard. He's the hotshot mentally disturbed artist; I showed you his sketches, remember? *Barb?!* You there?"

The door at the end of the wide hall bursts open, and through it race two incredibly thin, pointy-faced black dogs, barking and wuffing. "Aw-right, tinribs!" crows Nick, as they mob him. "Have you been good, then? Where's your mum then?" The dogs turn their attention to me, sniffing and checking me out. They've got big eyes and long noses, like friendly rats, and as I pat them I can feel every bone along their backs.

"How come they're so thin?" I ask.

"'Cos they're lurchers," says a down-to-earth voice.

I look up, and there's Barb. She grins at me, and I like her immediately. She's got wild, short, hennaed hair, and a sinewy, strong-looking body, and bare feet. She's wearing a tight T-shirt, and raggedy old jeans, and earrings that look like they've been put together in a metal-work class.

"Lurchers ought to be thin," she says. "Fat would slow them down."

Nick grabs her and lands a noisy kiss on the side of her mouth, then he turns to me and ruffles my hair. "Meet Rich. Isn't he great?"

"Great," she says. "Needs a haircut."

"Give him one, doll. He's coming to the big Marley-Hunt dinner next week."

"Oh, God, the poor kid. He'll be bored to tears."

"Nah, he won't. He'll get pissed, won't you, Rich? Where're the kids?"

"Freddie's at Ben's for the night, Scarlett's upstairs."

"Cool. Let's get the kettle on."

I find myself kind of swept along through the hall with the dogs weaving round my feet. Everything in the hall—walls, ceiling, cornices, banisters—has been painted sea green. It's stunning, and kind of surreal. We reach the kitchen at the end (huge again, ochre-yellow this time, lots of shiny chrome), and Barb pulls out a white wooden chair from the black wooden table, reaches her hand up to my shoulder, and propels me onto it.

I don't have much choice about sitting down. She's really strong. I watch nervously as she pulls a towel down from a rack, opens a drawer, and takes out some wicked-looking shiny scissors.

"Er . . ." I begin.

"Your sketches are something else," she says, pleasantly. "Real talent there."

"Er—thanks."

"Nick was dead chuffed with them. Weren't you, pooch?"

"*Dead* chuffed. I just hope that bastard John Hunt will be too. *Where* d'you say the file is?"

"I didn't," says Barb. I swivel in my seat and notice she's got out a big black screwtop jar, and a spatula, and a roll of tin foil. "It's on the side—

there." She points at a glossy red folder.

Nick swoops on it, and Barb deftly wraps the towel round my neck, tears off a strip of foil, and shoves it into my hair.

"*Er* . . ." I say again, more high pitched this time, but Nick has pulled out a series of photos and is waving them in front of my anxious nose. Which has just picked up the acrid and unmistakable smell of ammonia.

"See?" Nick's saying, insistently. "This is the old Sling bottle. Soft, floral, fruity. Health and fun, yes, but too nice, too daytime, too . . ."

Something wet lands on the foil, and so presumably my hair too, and I feel it being scraped about. And at that point I crack. "What're you *doing*?" I wail.

There's a shocked silence, then Barb's face comes round from the back and peers into mine. Then it shoots upright and glares angrily at Nick.

"Nick, you wally, you haven't even *asked* him have you? What you said when you came in—I assumed he *wanted* his bloody hair cut! I assumed that's why you've brought him here! Jesus, you are the absolute bloody sodding limit you really are—the poor kid must think I'm *mad*."

Too right, I think. Totally barking, both of you. Nick meanwhile has clapped a theatrical hand to his forehead. "I *did* ask you, didn't I, Rich? You do want your hair cut, don't you?"

"Er . . . well . . . I . . ."

"Barb's *ace*. She's a professional. A stylist with style. She does all ours."

"Um . . ."

"Trust her, mate, OK?"

"Er . . . OK," I mutter. "Er . . . thanks. But what are you . . . what's that . . ."

"I'm just putting in a few bleach-spikes," Barb says, matter of factly, and dumps a second spatula's worth of ammonia-smelling gunk on my scalp. "Not strong ones. Lift your mousy colour a bit. Then short but not too short, yeah?"

"Trust her," says Nick, again. "Trust *me*, mate, you're privileged."

Trust? What choice do I have?

So I sit through Barb daubing and foil-scrunching, then I wait while she leans against the counter checking her watch regularly and we both listen to Nick ranting on about his ideas for a TV ad campaign for Sling. Then suddenly I'm being tipped forward face first into the kitchen sink and Barb's shampooing me off. Next I get mauled by a towel, and then the wicked scissors come out, snip, snap, snackety snip, and my hair's falling like chaff on the ground. And all the time Nick is keeping up this non-stop jabber about how he envisions the new image of Marley-Hunt alcopops, and expecting me to answer, and come up with my ideas, while all I can do is try not to cringe as my mind's eye sees Rich Steele with a nancy-boy bleach-streaked poncy multi-layer haircut.

"There!" says Barb suddenly, and whisks the towel off my shoulders. *"There!"* She sounds pleased—proud even.

It's OK, I tell myself, it's OK. Soon as I get home I can shave it all off.

"Barb, that is *brilliant*," breathes Nick. "God, he looks good, the bastard. *Too* good. Where's a mirror, doll? Show 'im."

They both look vaguely about for a hand mirror, while Nick says, "What Barb does is—she reflects *you*. When she cuts hair. She reflects the real *person*."

Oh, brilliant. So Barb actually thinks I *am* a bleach-streaked poncy multi-layer nancy-boy. "No mirror?" I croak.

"Can't find it," says Barb, scrutinizing me again. "Run up to the bathroom, top of the stairs, first left. You know—you look a bit pasty."

Well, *thanks*. It's probably terror—terror of what you've done to my hair.

"It's the hi-lighting brought it out. You need a tan. Hey—in the bathroom cabinet there's some of Nick's pseudy tanning cream. Rub some of that in. Take it away with you. It costs a fortune but it's worth it 'cos it looks completely real."

"Thanks," I say, and then I stand up and

escape from the kitchen and down the hall and race straight up the stairs. I grab the handle of the first door on the left but it won't budge. And as I rattle it in anguish, a shrill, dignified, reedy little voice calls out, "I *shan't* be a minute!"

Five full minutes of agonized frustrated waiting later, and the door swings open, and this . . . *vision* appears. A girl of about ten, huge beautiful eyes, hair a black wavy waterfall down her back. She's draped in this great sheet of soft red velvet and on her head she has a wonderful glittery tiara.

"Sorry," she says to me, a bit frostily.

"No, I'm sorry," I gabble. "I'm sorry I tried to barge in."

"I *always* lock the door," she announces primly, then she turns and sweeps off like a queen. And I stare after her, overcome with this need to paint her, to do her all surreal and gothic in dark, thick oils, all red and black and luscious and . . .

I remember my hair and screech through the door and practically head-butt the mirror.

Oh, yes. Oh, yes. Oh yes oh yes oh *yes OH YES*!!

I've got cheekbones. I've got strong eyebrows arching like James Bond. I've got bold sexy eyes. I've got a haircut that's neither bleach-streaked nor multi-layer poncy but just *shaped*, and careless, and active, with jags of light in it, and oh

God I love it, I never knew you could love a haircut this much.

I love myself. I twist and turn this way and that in front of the mirror, just loving myself.

You wait, Portia McCutcheon, I think. You just *wait*.

Then I open the cabinet door and get out Nick's high-priced tanning cream, and read the instructions, and I think how normally I'd never do anything as poncy as applying fake tan. Then I remember what Barb said about how real it looked, and I wash my face and take a deep breath and rub some of the cream in *evenly and thoroughly*, just like the label says. I smirk at myself again in the mirror, and start shoving the tube of tanning cream in my pocket to take it home with me, like Barb told me to, and as I do that it butts up against the wad of money.

Chapter 7

The money. I'd almost forgotten the *money*. I sit down on the edge of the huge white claw-footed bath and draw the roll slowly out of my pocket. I take off the rubber band and drop it on the floor. Then I lick my index finger and start counting. I get to one hundred. I get to two hundred. I get to three hundred. Then I stop at eighty. Three hundred and eighty pounds.

It's a fortune.

All the notes are used, old even, and I love that. It makes them more authentic. Each one of these notes has been used again and again to buy clothes, drinks, food, fun, and now they've all come back like little homing pigeons for me to send out into the world again. In exchange for whatever I want. I feel like a prince, I really do.

You always see people in Newspaper Bingo adverts and so on chucking great fistfuls of money into the air and letting it fall down round them like confetti. Well, I have no desire at all to do that. There's no way these babies are leaving my *hand* let alone getting thrown around—Jesus, some of it might go down the pan, for a start.

I count the notes again, gloating like a miser. Only misers don't spend like I plan to in the very near future. *Yes*. Three hundred and eighty pounds. I pick the rubber band up off the floor and snap it round the wad of money, shove it back in my pocket, and go downstairs. As I move I can feel it in there, like something alive, like a presence, and I feel absolutely great.

I walk into the kitchen and without really planning to I'm heading towards Barb, gurgling, "Barb—what can I say—it's superb, it's brilliant, you're the best barber I've ever had!" I've got my arms kind of splayed open and like it's the most natural thing in the world she walks into them and gives me a hug.

"You look terrific, darling. Doesn't he look terrific, Scarlett?"

I look up, over Barb's head, and see the little red-and-black Madonna seated at the table. She examines me, expressionless, then pipes, "Quite attractive, yes."

Nick and Barb laugh, and Nick says, "OK, drinks time."

"Oh, Nick—it's barely six o'clock," moans Barb.

"So what? We're celebrating. This kid is saving my skin, I tell you. Even if that idiot Hunt doesn't want to go with Rich's style and my ideas, he'll have to admit they're bloody good and I haven't let him down even though I've only spent half a day or so on the whole bloody project."

"Oh, Nick, that is so *typical* of you. When are you going to stop doing everything at the eleventh hour?"

"When I'm six feet under, doll. Now—Rich—what d'you want with ice in it?"

"Ice?" I echo.

"Ice. Crushed ice." And he heads over to the huge silver fridge in the corner of the kitchen. I say fridge, but it looks more like an upright sci-fi coffin—the kind of thing you get frozen in, and then ejected into outer space.

"Blackcurrant and strawberry please, Daddy," says Scarlett.

"Coming up, sweetheart," says Nick, and he grabs a fancy glass, and pushes a button on an alcove set into the front of the fridge. Immediately there's a loud grinding noise and both dogs start barking. Then from the alcove comes a great spurt of ice shards, most of which miss the glass.

"Bloody *thing*," moans Barb. "The pressure's up too high—it must be!"

"Nonsense," retorts Nick, squirting various cordials into the glass. "It's a precision machine, this."

"Stupid bloody thing," Barb repeats, looking at me for support. "He bought that just so he could have ice in his silly bloody cocktails—look at the room it takes up! It throws the whole kitchen out!"

"She'll shut up when she's got a margarita in her hand," murmurs Nick smoothly. "Margarita OK for you, Rich?"

I have a real yen for a beer, but I daren't ask for one, because you can't put ice in it. "Great," I say, and soon I'm sipping this exotic syrupy stuff over mounds of shattered ice. It's OK once you've had a couple of mouthfuls. Quite nice in fact.

"He's not the one doing the sodding cooking!" Barb's still grumbling, and Nick laughs and puts his arm round her and force-feeds her margarita, until she's laughing too. Then he says, "Talking of *cooking*, Barbie, I'm starving," and he pretends to eat her neck.

Scarlett turns to me and says, "Mummy and Daddy are always being silly like this."

"Yeah?"

"*Yes,*" she says, emphasising the "s" loudly. "*Yes*, they are."

I ought to hate the kid but I can't. She's so self-contained she's fantastic.

"Stay for dinner, Rich?" says Barb. "Stir-fry. Ready in twenty minutes especially if you help chop."

"Well I . . ."

Nick shoves a knife in my hand. "Come on, darling. Have a heart."

So I stay. I stand next to Nick and we chop peppers, and celery, and fancy-looking mushrooms, and Barb heats up oil in a huge black wok and throws everything in, including a big bag of big frozen prawns, the kind that cost a fortune. Nick opens up white wine and insists on grinding ice into the glasses because he says it's not cold enough. Scarlett solemnly lays four places round the black table. And all the time we're laughing and joking and messing around, friendly and easy, as though making a meal is fun and not a chore. As though *life* is fun and not a chore. And I know I'm there as a bit of an audience for them, a bit of a sounding board, but it doesn't matter. I feel like I've known these people for years.

"You asked Rich to come round on Saturday?" Barb asks, after we've been eating for about five minutes and our forks have slowed a bit.

"Saturday?" repeats Nick.

"Oh, my God, you've forgotten, haven't you.

You've asked about thirty people round. You've organized a bloody *party*. And you've *forgotten*."

"Barb, keep your hair on. Thirty people is not a party. It's just a few drinks."

"Is it hell. We've got to do food, you know we have."

"All right, all right. It's not a problem. Rich—come to our small party. Bring some mates."

"*Nick*—are you *mad*? He's a *teenager*. You don't tell *teenagers* to bring mates, or you get your house trashed."

"*A* mate. Bring *a* mate, Rich. Can you come? You ought to. I know we're ancient old crusty fogies to you, but there might be some people here it'd be good for you to meet. . . ."

Oh my God. Richard Steele. Networker.

"Yeah, I'd love to come," I say. "What time?"

When we've finished eating Nick and I have a top-speed flick through the Marley-Hunt folder and I get an idea of the kind of company they are and where they are "design-wise," as Nick says, and Nick talks some more about where they want to go. Around ten o'clock, it seems judicious for me to say I'd better get home. Nick offers me a lift but he's so pissed by this time I decline, firmly, and leave.

I walk it—I want to. It only takes about thirty minutes. I spend the first fifteen minutes mentally goggling at my amazing fortune, at the fact that I might well get paid megabucks for having something I've dreamed up and drawn plastered on a leading alcopops bottle. What was it Nick said? "That little bundle is just the very smallest down payment on what you could be making."

Then I walk through the town centre past all the shut up shops and I spend the next fifteen minutes looking in the lit-up windows thinking—I can buy that. And that. And that. I tell myself first thing tomorrow morning I'll be back. With my little bundle.

When I get home, the house is in darkness, and it smells, like it usually does on a Thursday night, of greasy shepherd's pie and cabbage. It goes through my mind to wake everyone up and tell them my brilliant news and show them my hair and everything, but in the end I don't bother, I just go upstairs to bed without waking anyone.

Chapter 8

The next day, I'm awake a good ten minutes before I hear Dad's evil little alarm clock go off on the other side of the wall. I stretch my legs out as far as they'll go, so I've got them jammed against the end of the bunk bed, with my head butting up against the wooden board at the top, and I lie there bracing my muscles, enjoying being too big. Then slowly, gloatingly, I let all the events of yesterday kind of unroll inside my head, from the first phone call to the drunken stir-fry dinner, and I'm kind of amazed, and disbelieving, and ecstatic, and terrified, all at the same time, but mostly disbelieving, I'm like, Did all that really happen? Then I turn over and pull out the fat wad of money from under my pillow, and I think, Yep, it did. It really did.

I wait while first Dad and then Mum trudge in and out of the bathroom and go downstairs, and then I beat Sam to it. I'm nervous that my hair'll be all crudded up overnight but it looks brilliant, even before I flick water on it and run it through with my hands. My skin's got some colour in it, too, from the tanning cream—for a moment I'm tempted to go and fetch it and rub a load more in, but I think, No. Keep it subtle.

I wash quickly and go downstairs, wondering how long it'll be before anyone notices my hair. On the way down all I see of Dad is his back view hurrying out the door, determined not to break his record of never being late for work, and I shout "Bye" just as the door slams. In the kitchen, Mum's freaking because Sam's football kit, left on the boiler overnight to dry, is still wet, and she's simultaneously aiming a hairdryer at the waistband and burning the toast and she doesn't look up, just says, "Where were you last night, Rich? You might've phoned, told me you weren't coming in to eat."

"Sorry, Mum," I say. "Events kind of—over-took me, you know," and I'm waiting for her to say—What events? What happened? but she doesn't, so I sit down in a bit of a sulk and pull the economy cornflakes towards me and tip myself out a great big bowl.

"You're out of bed early," she says, scraping the burn off the toast into the sink. "For a Friday." Fridays, classes don't start till late, and I have been known not to get up till midday.

"Yeah," I say, "stuff to do," wanting her to say, What stuff? But she's out the door shrieking up the stairs to Sam so in the end I just finish eating and pour myself the dregs of tea out of the pot and grab my old jacket and go.

As I walk into town I feel like my brain is schizophrenically split in two. Half of it is making lists, as in: Essential Items. 1. Smart trousers. Can I get away with posh jeans? Probably black. 2. Shoes. Classy, smooth, stylish, durable. Definitely black. 3. Shirt. To make statement or rather understatement. Not black. Terracotta maybe. Or blue—subtle weave. And while this careful listing is going on the other half of my brain is doing an insane, noisy war dance: YO! YO! YO! Money, money, money!! Spend, spend, SPEND!!

I'm battling hard to keep the crazy half under control as I walk into my first shop, a shoe shop. I've lurked round this one before, checking out what it has to offer, and I reckon it's on a perfect mid-point between cheap, trendy crap at the bottom end of the market and those specialist places with laughable prices at the top end. I go up to the racks and scan my eyes over them—and there it is. My ideal shoe. That's the good thing about being a visual person, the right stuff just shouts out to you like it's lit up by a neon sign. It's a simple black loafer with style and class and a sole that will last, and it says the wearer is a bit rugged, needs a shoe that'll keep up with him. I pick it up and glance around for a shop assistant to get my size before I've even checked the price on the sole. Eighty quid. That's OK. Shoes underpin the whole look, they have to be good. And I'll still have three hundred left.

A thin, weaselly-looking shop assistant saunters over and stares not so much at the shoe in my hand as down at the beaten up, totally embarrassing old desert boots on my feet.

"Can I help?" he asks, all supercilious.

"Yeah," I say. "These. Size ten. Please." He hesitates just long enough to be insulting. I bare my teeth at him in what could be a smile and resist a strong childish impulse to yank out my roll of tens and twenties and jab it into his face. Then he saunters off—slowly—and I sit down and pull off my boots and I'm faced by two ratty non-matching socks, one with a hole where my big toe juts through. Shit. Why didn't I make my first stop a sock shop? Too late. The weaselly guy is laying down a white, tissue-rustling box in front of me, and peering at my feet like there's no way he wants them inside his perfect new shoes.

Tough it out, I think. Nothing else to do. I grab the loafers, jam them on, stand up, and take three steps over to the slanted mirror they've got against the wall.

They look brilliant. They make my old jeans look like total kak but that's OK because my old jeans are on death row anyway. I walk slowly across the carpet, like I'm considering the fit, but I already know the shoes are perfect and I've got to have them. I sit down, and enjoy the weaselly guy hovering for a bit. Then I slip them both off and drop them back in the box, and say, "Yeah—I'll take them, thanks."

The weaselly guy picks up the box and makes his way over to the till, but he's clearly reluctant to ring anything up until he's seen the colour of my money. I enjoy making him sweat a bit longer, then I stroll over to the till and pull out my roll and peel off four twenties, blam, blam, blam, blam, and the till clocks up so fast it risks burnout.

And then I'm swinging out of the door, with my first carrier bag clutched in my hand.

Next stop—jeans. I've decided on jeans, black ones, 'cos they'll last and I can wear them everywhere. I don't go for poncy designer, just basic class, and in the changing room I can't resist it, when I've found the exact fit I leave them on and take out my new shoes and try them on too. Brilliant. Together they look brilliant and my legs look pretty long and hot too.

In fact, I think—eyeing myself in the mirror with the curtains squeezed tight shut—my body is not bad. OK, it could do with a bit more action, a bit more direct work on the pecs, but all the footy training I did before I discovered sex shaped it up well, and the occasional games I still get into at college keep it more or less toned.

And now, at last, my body's getting the gear it deserves.

I square up to the mirror one last time and think, You wait, McCutcheon. You'll regret being so snotty to the old me once you see how hot the new me's turning out. Then I pay for the jeans. Forty quid. Now for the shirt.

This is the scary bit. It's OK to go all understated with jeans and shoes but if you go understated with your shirt too you risk no one noticing you at all. I browse through several shops, but nothing grabs me. Again, I'm avoiding poncy labels where you have to pay to advertise across your chest, but I still want something with style. To put off making any kind of decision I buy a three-pack of plain black socks—no room for major choices there—and then, because once I've found this shirt I'm going to look so good I'll slay Portia, she won't stand a chance, two pairs of sharp-looking dark blue boxers. Now I'm totally kitted out. Apart from the shirt.

I head away from the main shopping centre,

down a side street, and walk by a classy-looking men's clothes shop with a "Closing Down Sale" sign in the window. That's enough to get me inside, and once I am I can see exactly why it never made it as a business. It can't make up its mind whether to be cutting edge or an old man's outfitters. There are racks of fuddy grey suits, and nasty ties, and there's even a shelf of old geezer's hats, but over by the door there's a pile of hopeful-looking Ben Sherman–type shirts, with a thirty per cent off card swinging just above them. Almost immediately I lay my hands on this oaty-coloured one, real good quality, with a hazy, lazy kind of weave running through it. It's great. It's not *the* shirt, it's not the one to wear to the posh dinner where I'll convince them to use my art and make me seriously wealthy, but it's great, and it's my size, and it's thirty-five quid, and I hand three tenners and a fiver over without hesitation and without trying it on.

Outside the shop, I do a quick maths check. I've spent a hundred and eighty-nine pounds, which means I have a helluva lot left, which means I can afford lunch. I'm very hungry.

It is absolutely bloody brilliant to swagger into a sandwich bar and go up to the glass counter and just point out what you want without having to scrounge around in your pocket for bits of change and do desperate money-to-menu calculations in your head as you order. In fact it's so brilliant I go a bit insane, and I order so much stuffing for my baguette the lid slides off as I carry it over to a table. I eat it though, every bit. Then I hit the streets again.

I'm overcome by a strong sense of unreality as I tour the mall at the far side of town, laden with glossy carrier bags like a bimbo on a credit card spree. It's like I've entered a parallel universe, where I'm me and not me. I mean, all this *energy* I'm putting out, this purpose, this *determination*—and for what? For clothes, that's what, just *clothes*. There's something a bit sad about it. Something suspect. But that doesn't stop me launching myself into a big, expensive department store and making a swift tour round the men's department.

And that's where I see the shirt.

It's a kind of petrol-soaked blue and it costs seventy-five quid. That in itself should be enough to make me ram it back on the rack and walk on by. But I don't. I shake it out and walk over to the mirror on the wall and hold it up against me.

I look at my reflection and I don't notice the shirt because I'm too busy staring into my own eyes. I've got these weird greeny-blue eyes that can look sexy and interesting (I've been told) but retreat into wishy-washy dish water if they're up against a colour that's too strong for them. That's why I borrow my old man's white shirts so much. Look, I'm visual—I can't help myself.

Anyway, with this shirt on, my eyes jump up about three gears. They're, like, *lasering* out of the mirror at me. It's all in the colour. I hate it when guys with baby-blue eyes wear baby-blue shirts because it's so corny and obvious, but *this*—this is *class*.

"Would you like to try that on, sir?" says an oily voice. Funny how having a stack of posh carrier bags up next to you changes the attitude of these shop guys.

"Er—I'm . . . er . . ." I hold it up against me again.

"That size looks right for you, sir. The changing rooms are over there."

And before I can think I'm half stripped off behind the plush maroon curtains and I'm sliding the shirt over my shoulders.

Oh, God it feels good. The cut, the fit, the material . . . And I look fantastic. I look like a prince. I take it off again and march out of the cubicle and push it into the salesman's hands.

"No good, sir?"

"It's great. It's just—"

"It *is* expensive," he agrees mournfully, and turns to replace it on the rack.

I take off with all my carrier bags shifting and banging in my hands, and do a fast tour of the shop, and I'm thinking, Immoral. Wasteful. Only an idiot spends that much on a shirt. I think of my Dad's face if he knew I was even thinking about buying it. I think of what my Mum could do with seventy-five pounds. Then I think about the Big Dinner. I think about looking and feeling just exactly right as I sit there, pitching my art to the big alcopops guy. I think about getting the commission, and all the money I'll earn if I do. And then I march straight back to the shirt rail, grab the shirt, and pay for it. Three twenties, a ten and a five. And the salesman smiles conspiratorially as though he knows I've made the right decision.

Chapter 9

It's two-fifteen. And there's no way I'm going straight home, not now. I'm going into college. I'm going to *strut*. If I hurry, I'll make the three o'clock History of Art lecture Portia always goes to because she seems to think that lectures matter. And then I'll be there for that loitering around, what's-going-on-this-weekend session round the college steps.

And then—*maybe*—I'll give Portia a second chance. Maybe I'll ask her to Nick and Barb's party.

At college, I head straight for the locker I share with Chris down in the basement, right by the men's bogs. I open it up and put my fantastic shirt inside, right at the back where it's safe. Then I put the other shirt in, and the socks and boxers. Then I lock up and head for the bogs, where I struggle awkwardly into my new jeans and put my loafers on. Then I check my reflection in one of the nasty smeary little mirrors above the sinks, and smirk. I was right to keep my (Dad's) white shirt on. I'm looking pretty bloody brilliant as it is, what with the haircut and the tan. A total transformation might be just too much for some people to take.

I lock up my old gear, and head for the lecture room only five minutes late. It's looking pretty packed down at the front, so I lope up the steps, two at a time, all charged up by the jeans and the shoes. I slide into an aisle seat at the back and scan the rows for Portia. There she is, third row from the front on the other side of the room, turned to the lectern. I can see her gorgeous profile quite clearly. All soft lines and strong lines, both together. Drawn by an angel. She's taking a few notes with a glittery pen, then she sticks it in her half open mouth, presses it against her lip—*Jesus*. Does she know what she's doing to everyone watching her? OK, OK—*me* watching her.

The lecture slumps on, and I gaze at Portia scribbling notes. Jenny whispers to her, and Portia kind of tips her head back to hear, and her neck arches, and her mouth smiles, and I'm—I'm in a *mess*.

The lecture's over. What was it about, anyway? I'm now engaged in military-type forward-planning tactics—shuffling papers, letting people past me, moving down an aisle, stopping to check the contents of my bag, all to make sure I'll exit at the same time as Portia without anyone having the least suspicion that that's what I'm doing.

"Hi, Richy!"

All *right*! She's there, bottom of the steps, and she's smiling at me, one of her elegant sorceress eyebrows raised.

"Oh—hi," I say, casual as hell, hefting my bag onto my shoulder. "God, that was dull, wasn't it?"

"Mmmm," she says. "I had trouble keeping awake." Then the line of students at my back shunts me forward and Portia and I are side by side, moving out to the corridor. She's looking up at me sideways as we shuffle forward, and my neck's prickling like crazy.

"What've you *done*?" she suddenly squeals. "Your hair—it looks *faa*-bulous!" We're outside the door, and she's stopped, looking right at me, so naturally I stop too. "I *lo-ove* your hair!" she goes on.

"Oh—thanks," I say, all indifferent, as though the reason I hadn't got around to getting my hair cut properly for about three years was because I was the type of guy for whom haircuts were totally unimportant.

"No, *really*. You should keep it like that. You look *cute*."

I put all my psychic control into not going beetroot. Inside I'm crowing. "Thanks," I repeat gruffly.

"No, really. You look really good. And *smart*. Listen, Richy, I was thinking. That portraits project. You done yours yet?"

"Na," I say, heart banging hard.

"Only—look. If you still want me to sit for you I will."

Oh, God, she's changed her mind because I look *smart*. She said she'd *sit* for me. Oh, God, it's happening.

Money's making it happen.

"I didn't mean to be mean the other day—you know, when you asked," she goes on. "I just had a really bad headache and I was pissed off with my mum."

"Yeah?" I say, sympathetically. "Why were you pissed off?"

"Oh, *God*. *Everything*. She's always on at me to clear up and babysit my little brother and stuff. She wants me to do all this work and she absolutely flips if I say I should get paid for it. She's so *tight*—I mean—I just can't live on the allowance she lets me have. She's such a bitch. Really. She's . . ."

I'm not really listening to Portia. I'm watching

her mouth make all these soft, squashy shapes as she speaks and imagining running my tongue up under her lips and along her teeth.

". . . *and* I unstacked the dishwasher at least three times last week, but according to her I do nothing and I'm totally selfish. I'm just sick of it, I really am. It really does my head in."

"I bet it does," I murmur. I think about putting my hand supportively on her arm, but I don't.

"I wish I could afford to move out. She should have someone like Karen Black as a daughter, all drugged up half the time, then she'd realize she's lucky to have me."

"She would. Yeah."

"*Anyway*. When d'you want me to sit? Or lie down. Or any position you want I s'pose really."

Portia—don't *do* that to me. I won't be able to *walk*. "Er—well. Huw's screaming for it already. What about the start of next week?"

"Tuesday? Tuesday afternoon? I'm sure we can find an empty room somewhere. . . ."

Oh, *God*. An empty *room*. "Tuesday'd be great," I say, and I'm just about to summon up the balls to ask her if she's got any plans for tomorrow night when her mobile goes off like a siren. She pulls it out, shrieking, "Oh, *GOD*, that'll be Tony. He said he'd pick me up early!" Then she dashes off, screaming, "*Sorry-sorry-*

sorry!" into the phone and calling, "*Bye-eee!*" over her shoulder.

I'm left floored with disappointment. And then Jenny, who'd been hovering like a handmaiden all through our conversation, sidles past me murmuring, "She's not really into Tony, you know. She's just *using* him."

Chapter 10

This news from Jenny is such an instant fix that I swagger like a gunslinger along to the lockers, collect my new clothes, then head out of the main college doors and down the broad steps. Inside my head a corny old song is reeling about: "Just a matter of ti-*ime* . . . I can wait bay-*beeee* . . . for you I can wait." It's so bad I have to be making it up rather than remembering it, but who cares. I spot Chris, who as usual doesn't look that keen to see me just before a cash-intensive Friday night, and I bound cheerfully over to him, because this time it's different, this time I've got my own cash.

"Blimey, Rich," he says, "what you done to your hair?"

"Got it cut. Like it?"

"Yeah. Suits you. God, have you got—you've got *streaks* in it, you big tart!"

"Admit I look brilliant. Go on, mate. Don't let envy get in the way."

"Well, yeah. I mean—you looked so shit before it wouldn't take much but—*yeah*, it's cool. And what's all this?" He jerks his head at my glossy carrier bags. "You turned shopaholic or something?"

"Right in one."

"So where d'you get the money?"

"You won't *believe* where I got the money, mate."

"You nicked it, didn't you. Jesus Christ, Rich—"

"I did not nick it. I was given it as the first very small instalment of what I can hopefully expect if things turn out the way I really really hope they're going to."

"You've lost me."

"Well, come on. I'll buy you a drink and explain."

Chris acts out fainting with shock at this, of course—me buying him a drink for once—but soon we're in a swishy, early-opening bar and we've got a bottle of designer beer in front of each of us and I've told him the whole story. He listens, and he's pleased for me, and we have a real laugh, then he says, "It's great it's got this far. It really is."

"It's gonna go further. It is. It's got to."

"Yeah, but—"

"Yeah but what?"

"It might not, Rich. From what you've told me—this Nick character, he's grabbed you to save his arse, like at the eleventh hour, and—"

"He liked my stuff."

"Of course he did. It's brilliant. It's just—it might not fit with this alcopop guy's poxy marketing ideas. It might be too off the wall for him. But just 'cos it doesn't happen this time, that doesn't mean it's no good, or that it'll never happen, or—"

"Oh, shut up, Chris. Doom-merchant. It's gonna happen, I tell you! Want another beer?"

We have two more beers each, all paid for by me, which feels better than I know how to tell you, and I invite Chris to the party Saturday night at Nick's. He's dead pleased—says he wants to go on to Sarah Connell's house party afterwards because he's after her mate Natalie, but he can get nicely tanked up at Nick's place first at the same time as checking him out for me.

"He's kosher, Chris, he is, mate. I thought he was a bit dodgy at first—actually I thought he was queer—"

"After your body?"

"Yeah, well he—"

"Rich, you think everyone's after your body. Fantasy land, mate—they're not. How you shaping up with that snobby bird you keep shadowing?"

"Portia McCutcheon? I'm not *shadowing* her, what you talking about? And it's going well. She's going to sit for me."

Chris's eyes go round in admiration. "*Hey!* Life study?"

"Nah—portrait. But I thought I could tell her I want to bring out her natural side, you know, maybe get her to wear a low-cut top . . . and I'll draw her so she's *gorgeous.* I mean, just a straight study would make her look gorgeous, but I'll make her look totally *magic,* so she's totally blown apart by my image of her, you know, like Kate Winslett was on the *Titanic*, you know when she said how erotic it was being drawn, and Portia'll be so *grateful* she—"

Chris is shaking his head. "You sad obsessed git. Watch you don't drool too much over the drawing paper."

After that I decide to go home and announce my amazing good news to my loving family, only twenty-four hours late, and eat supper with them. We often have fish and chips on a Friday night if there's enough cash left in the kitty, and this Friday night we were definitely having them because I was buying, wasn't I?

Mum gives a kind of shriek when she finally

clocks my hair, and I'm halfway through telling her everything when Dad walks in with Sam and I have to start all over again. Mum and Sam are beside themselves with excitement. Sam keeps squawking, "On the telly? You might be in an advert on the telly?" and Mum keeps saying stuff like, "Oh, God, I'm so *proud* of you, Richard. You mean it was that scary picture of the bat he liked? Doesn't his hair look wonderful, Bill?" and gradually it enters my brain that, amid all the fuss, enthusiasm from Dad is not exactly gushing like an oil well.

"What's up, Dad?" I say. "Don't you think it's good?"

He considers me, heavily. "Yes, of course it's good, Rich. Well done. It's just—well, it worries me a bit."

"*Worries* you? Why, for Christ's sake?"

"Because I've never heard of that kind of money being handed over like that, no contract, no nothing, just 'Here you are, buy yourself some clothes.'" He pauses, looks at me like I'm one step up from a rent boy.

"Well, I need to look smart at this dinner, that's all. No big deal."

"That kind of money is a big deal."

"Not in the ad world it's not."

"Oh, it's the *ad world* now is it? Getting the jargon too are you?"

"Oh, for Christ's sake, Dad, why are you being so—"

"I'm not being *so* anything. I just don't want you to lose sight of what your real job is, with all this *ad world* stuff in your head. Your job is to do well at college, get the right grades, go on to art school. Not get pushed off course by some *ad man's* promise."

I'm ferociously, tearingly angry with him when he says that, with the scorn he lays on the words *ad man*. Which is Nick, I suppose, isn't it. I don't understand it, I don't understand my own rage.

What I do understand is I can't stand being in the same room as him for one more second. "I'll get the fish and chips, Mum," I grit out. "OK?"

And I'm out the door.

I walk at top speed to the chippy, and when I've got the hot vinegary-smelling parcel in my hands I veer off into an off-licence and buy four cans of Guinness. I don't know why I do this. Maybe I want to make the peace with him, make him smile. Maybe I want to force him to say thanks to me. Anyway, I get them, and I hurry home, and the first ten minutes is taken up by Mum telling us to wait till the frozen peas are done and then doling out the fish and chips and the four of us taking the first five or so hungry mouthfuls.

The Guinness is just sitting there, at the end

of the table. I jerk my head at it, look over at Dad. "Don't you want one?" I mutter.

"Yes. Thanks." He reaches over, unhooks one from its plastic loop.

There's a loud silence as Dad pours out his Guinness. Mum finishes off her mouthful of fish and starts up, soothingly, "Well, this is lovely. Thank you very much, Rich luv, this is lovely. I really like fish and chips on a Friday and I don't know we could've run to it this week, what with Sam needing a new school jumper and everything. . . ."

"Didn't you find that jumper?" asks Dad.

"No," grunts Sam. "I went to Lost Property twice. It wasn't there."

There's another silence. I look round at the cramped room with its shabby wallpaper, thinking what a contrast it is to Nick's house, trying not to hate it. Then Mum says, "When d'you think your important dinner will be, luv?"

"Sometime next week, Nick said. Beginning of next week."

"What does Mr. Morgan think of it all?" Dad suddenly asks.

"Who, Huw?"

"Yes. Your *teacher*." He lays solemn emphasis on the word *teacher*, like I was a trainee Trappist monk or something.

I shrug, finish my mouthful. "Haven't told

him yet. Haven't seen him to tell him."

"Well, when you do—I'd be interested in his opinion."

"'Cos you don't think my opinion's worth shit, right?" I blurt this out before I even know the thought's in my head.

"I didn't say that, Richard. Of course your opinion's worth something. But you're only seventeen. You're a bit young to know how to judge people. This is a good bit of luck, this Nick person phoning you up like that, wanting to take you off to have dinner with a client." He pauses, picks up his glass of Guinness, drains the last dregs. "But don't imagine that's everything. Don't imagine that's your future all sorted. Someone who'll pick you up fast'll drop you fast too."

I get out of the house pretty soon after that, go down to the Rose and Crown. I don't have to make my beer last this time so by ten o'clock I'm well tanked up, and I'm buying drinks not just for Chris but for quite a few other people too. I'm aware the wad in my pocket has shrivelled down quite considerably but I'm don't want to depress myself by counting it.

This time next week, I tell myself, I'll have my own bank account. This time next week I'll have my own credit card. A whole fucking *pack* of credit cards.

Chapter 11

I'm quite pleased when Chris phones me at seven-thirty the next night and says—"This party tonight, Rich. What'm I s'posed to wear to it? I don't have to look all posh do I?" I'm quite pleased 'cos that's usually the sort of question I'm asking Chris.

"Nah," I say. "Just your usual gorgeous self."

"And do we have to bring anything? You want me to get some beer?"

"No, no beer. Beer is banned. You don't serve it with ice."

"Wha-at. . . ?"

"You'll find out. See you at eight, OK?"

I already know what I'm going to wear—the oaty shirt that cost me thirty-five quid. The first time I wear the fabulous seventy-five quid shirt will be at the Big Dinner. Call me superstitious, call me an idiot, but I'm saving its first outing for then.

I feel great as I shower and get dressed. New boxers, new body wash, new everything. And my hair's lost that newly shorn look—it's looking even better than ever. I just wish Portia was coming with me instead of Chris. To make use of it all.

We turn up at Nick's doorstep about quarter to nine, having had a swift half on the way to rev us up a bit. I'm feeling weirdly nervous. I'm fighting this bizarre anxiety about Chris letting me down. Normally it's me letting Chris down. But Nick and Barb—they're different. They're off the wall. And they *like* me, they like the weird side of me. I guess I'm scared Chris will be just too nice and conventional for them or something—make them think they were wrong about me.

I knock, and Scarlett opens the door to me. This time she's got a black lacy evening dress on, with cobwebby-looking sleeves. It's way too long, but she's hitched it up over one arm, revealing two skinny calves and silver Dr. Martins. Her black hair's hanging long and loose like before, and she's got a pair of pointed cat's ears on her head. Each cat's ear has a non-matching dangly very sparkly earring attached to it.

"Hey, I like those," I say, pointing at the cat's ears. "They're brilliant."

For the first time, I see Scarlett smile. It uplifts her whole face. "Thank you," she says. "I made them today."

"You like to wear stuff on your head, don't you?"

"*Tiaras,*" she corrects me. "I love them. I collect them."

"You do? How many you got?"

"About ten."

"Wow. Can I see them sometime?"

"Sometime," she says. "But I have to open the door to people at the moment."

"Course you do," I say, and Chris and I shuffle past her. As we dump our coats over the banister Chris mutters, "Blimey. Weird kid. But come back in five years, eh?"

"Shut up. *Paedophile.*"

"Lighten up, mate. She's going to be a scorcher, that's all. D'you see her *eyes*?"

A small messy boy cannonballs past us, scattering crisps from a bag. "That's Freddie," Scarlett announces, from her position behind the door. "My brother. He's here tonight. *Unfortunately.*"

I make my way through the kitchen doorway and there's Nick, stationed by the huge fridge, shouting at the top of his voice to the people gathered round him. They're all smoking, drinking, laughing, shouting back, and every now and then everything's drowned out by a sudden burst of ice-grinding as Nick mixes up another cocktail.

•

I have a full-on anxiety attack, which I hide behind a phonily relaxed smirk. Notice me, Nick you bastard, or my mouth'll crack off.

Beside me, Chris is silent, waiting. It's all up to me. I take a step further into the kitchen and, at last, Nick looks up and grins. "Rich!" he calls.

I'm saved. I'm flattered he's acknowledged me. "Hi!" I call back. "This is—"

"You want a beer?"

"Yeah, great, but I thought you—"

"I'm getting pissed off making cocktails. Have a beer." And he opens the door to the big fridge, pulls out a couple of bottles, and tosses them to us—*one*, *two*.

Oh, Jesus. Social death if I drop it. But I don't, and neither does Chris. Nick has gone back to the conversation he was having, and we stand there like idiots with our unopened bottles. "We s'posed to use our teeth?" hisses Chris.

"Here, gimme those." Barb appears at my elbow, takes the beers and flips the tops off at top speed with an opener she's got chained to her waist. She's got a very low top on and she's wearing a completely amazing necklace round her neck. It's a kind of pearl choker, rows and rows of pearls, but these aren't pretty-pretty nice-nice pearls like a WI member might wear. These pearls are slightly sinister, strung in wavy rows like flotsam left on the shore. These pearls look alive, like they might hatch at any minute and release tiny alien life forms. Barb catches me goggling and says, "Like it?"

"Yeah," I say. "Brilliant. I've never seen anything like it before."

"I don't suppose you have, the price it was. Nick bought it for me."

I look at her. She's got all this glitzy makeup on and she's freaked her hair up somehow and she looks stunning. "Who's your friend?" she says.

"Oh, sorry—yeah, this is Chris. Chris, this is Barb. Nick's wife. She was the one who did my hair."

Chris mutters hi, all awkward, and Barb says, "Hi, Chris! Welcome!" Then she smiles at me and says, "I kind of expected you to bring a *girl*-friend, Richy."

"Yeah, well I might have done, only—"

"She was going out with her boyfriend," finishes Chris, and the three of us laugh, and Barb says, "Well, watch your backs. Lots of predatory women here. Hey—you hungry? Let me show you where the food is."

She turns and starts pushing her way through the crowds in the kitchen, and Chris is hissing at me, "Hey, did she *mean* that? About the women? *Jesus. Great!*"

We follow her into this huge, long, massive-windowed, wonderful room, empty of just about everything but people. It's the sort of room that has wooden doors halfway to divide it into two, but these doors are wide open, and at an angle between them there's a yellow sofa the size of a boat. It's about the only bit of furniture here, and we're walking on bare boards. Ahead of me in the wide fireplace there's a large stone satyr's head. He's grinning wickedly and he's covered in fairy lights, all twinkling away.

"Blimey," I breathe. "Haven't you gone to a lot of effort."

Barb looks at me wryly. "What d'you mean?"

"Well . . . for the party. Clearing all the furniture out . . . and those lights . . . and . . ."

"Rich, this is how the room *is*. All the time. For now, anyway."

Blimey, I say again, silently this time. Barb jerks her head indicating left, and we follow her out into a little old-style conservatory that looks to be absolutely filled with food. In the centre is a big table covered in dishes of paté and cheese on boards, and baskets of bread, and platters of yummy looking little savoury tarts and roll-up things, and these skewers crammed with chicken, and bowls of dips and complicated salads, and pricey rice dishes with prawns and green bits. Freddie's circling it like a baby shark, snaffling up the best bits. Round the edge, on the broad windowsills, in among the plants and burning candles, are bowls and bowls of posh-shaped crisps and nuts and olives.

"Oh, *wow*," I mutter. I'm so impressed with everything it's just about rendered me monosyllabic. Then I make an effort and say, "That looks fantastic. If I'd known you were going to lay on all this I'd never've had those beans on toast."

Barb laughs. "You help yourselves. There's loads." And she disappears back into the main room, shooing Freddie in front of her.

Chris turns to look at me, grinning. "Jammy bastard," he says, with only the thinnest edge to his voice. "In with the in crowd."

"Yeah, well, we'll see," I bluster. "Come on, grab a plate. People expect us to gorge—we're boys. They'd be disappointed if we didn't." And we start sampling everything, really tucking in.

"Get us another beer, Rich," Chris says. "Go on."

I don't want to make a foray into that intimidating kitchen again, but I figure it's down to me to keep Chris supplied with beer as I was the one who dragged him here. I put my nearly empty plate down and sidle back through the kitchen door. Nick's still holding court by the fridge, talking non-stop, and when I draw up next to him he just flings an arm round my shoulders, opens the fridge door with a flourish, and practically shoves me inside. I find myself nose to nose with a whole army of beer bottles, so I grab two, duck out from under Nick's arm, mutter thanks, and make my escape.

It's only when I get triumphantly back to the conservatory, which is starting to fill up with people after food, that I realize I haven't got the tops off the bottles. I shrug at Chris and say, "Use your teeth?"

"Oh, no!" A woman with wild hair half out of a plait looks up from the food table. "You mean to open those beer bottles—oh, *no*." She hikes a bag down from her shoulder and starts to rummage in it. "I'm sure I've got something—yes. Here. Never travel without a corkscrew, that's my motto. It's got a beer thingy on the other end."

I look at her hands as she passes the corkscrew over. They're caked with white dust, like she's been buried in a chalk pit, and the nails are bone white, cracked and broken. They remind me of Huw's hands, when he's had the whole weekend out in his workshed, pummelling clay and hacking at stone.

"Do you sculpt?" I ask.

She looks taken aback—then she looks down in dismay at her hands. "Um. It's that obvious, is it? Yes. Clay mostly. I wash it off but—well, it's ingrained now. No point when I'll just be back at it the next day or so."

"You could wear rubber gloves," says the man at her side.

Her face contorts with disgust, and he bursts out laughing. "Only joking, precious. Got to feel the clay. I know. She gets off on feeling the clay more than she does me."

"*Aw,*" she mocks, then she reaches a dusty white hand up to his cheek and strokes his face. Portia, I know, would have a blue fit over the state of her manicure, but I find her hands oddly moving. I want to ask her what kind of stuff she does, but Chris has handed back the corkscrew and she's turned her attention back to her man, so I don't.

By now Chris and I have cleaned our plates of their third refills and we're feeling well stuffed. "I suppose we should move out to the main room," I say reluctantly.

"Yeah," he agrees unenthusiastically. We dump our empty beer bottles down by the side of the food table, and shuffle out.

"It's not all old people here," mutters Chris, nudging me, nodding towards a promising-looking duo standing the other side of the fire-place. They're talking to a stoop-shouldered chap whose hair is long at the back and non-existent on top so it looks like a rug sliding off his head. No competition there, I think.

One of the girls has her profile to us—she's

about our age, gentle looking, prettyish, nothing exceptional, with soft brown hair fringing round her face. It's hard to see her shape because she's wearing this loose top and trousers. But the one with her back to us looks really sharp. She's got a terrific body and no qualms about showing it off. She's wearing this hot top, really nipped in at the waist, and tight trousers, and she keeps flipping back her shoulder-length blonde hair.

"Nice arse," mutters Chris.

And then she turns round.

All I can say is I hope to Christ my jaw didn't actually drop open in horror like it did inside my head.

She has to be fifty, fifty at least. Deeply glamorous, but *old*. I feel absolute shock, like these vampire films when someone young with young hair dressed in young clothes suddenly withers up and ages in front of your eyes.

Jesus. I was eyeing up her arse and she's, like, she's my *mother's* age.

"*Hi—i—i!*" she says, coquettish as all hell. "Where did you two spring from?"

"Oh, we're just—we've been eating," says Chris, brilliantly, thumbing back at the conservatory.

She draws in a theatrical breath. "Oh, we're not going in there. Are we, darling? It all looks too scrummy and tempting."

I realize this is some reference to dieting and wonder whether I'm supposed to say something about *her* not needing to worry, good grief *no*. But she's off with, "So how do you know Nick and Barb then? Sorry, I'm just so nosy. I have to slot people into my picture of things."

She has this gushy, hideous, up-herself voice. I look over her shoulder and notice that the guy with the back-sliding hair has seized his opportunity to slope off, and I feel something akin to sheer panic. "I . . . er . . . Nick might be using some of my stuff. My drawings. For a client. For alcopops."

She widens her eyes like I've just told her the secret to existence. "How *wonderful*. You're an artist! Hear that, darling?" and her red-nailed hand reaches out to the girl at her side and tightens like a claw round her wrist. "He's an *artist*! Bonny loves art, don't you, darling?" Then, before Bonny has a chance to do anything but look acutely embarrassed, the vampire-woman husks out a little laugh, flips her hair back again, and says, "Oh, I'm being *so rude*. This is Bonny, my daughter. And I'm Tigger. I was called that when I was a little girl 'cos I was so *bouncy* and it just stuck, you know? I'm still bouncy. It's just *me*." And she flips her hair again and smirks at us.

Beside me I can feel Chris just wanting to *run*.

I send psychic messages letting him know that if he abandons me now he's toast. And then I have a conversational brainwave. "I'm Rich, and this is Chris," I bleat. And then I follow it up with, "How do you know Nick and Barb?"

"Oh, we go back *yonks*," she brays. "I've got my own company, he uses me all the time. I'm a props stylist, for food shoots. He uses me all the *time*."

"Props?" I prompt.

"Yah. As in dishes, platters, anything to do with styling food for food shots. You *know*—there might be a call for a country scene, all wickerwork and earthenware. Or something crisp, light and white. Or seriously uppercrust, all silver and linen. I provide *everything*—it's every bit as important as the food itself."

I reckon it all sounds pretty pathetic—I mean, what does it involve? Shipping along a tablecloth and a couple of plates to an ad shoot? So I can't think of a single bloody thing to say. But then Chris, my saviour, blurts out, "You must need a lot of storage space. For all your stuff."

Her face lights up. "Darling, do I! Luckily I've got a *hu-uge* attic. Tigger's Attic. That's the name of my company. Sweet isn't it? And up there we've got shelves and shelves and shelves, all absolutely groaning. But even so, d'you know—" she loosens her hand from her daughter's wrist and—terrifyingly—reaches forward and attaches it to mine—"I'm always on the look out for new stock. One never has enough to satisfy everyone. And if someone phones up wanting something I just feel I haven't *got,* I'll just go straight out and hunt it down in the shops or the markets. I can't bear to fob someone off with second best. They rely on me, you see, for style, for design, for the whole *feel.* I can't let them down. That just wouldn't be *me*, would it, Bonny darling?"

Then thank God she detaches her claws from my arm, and reattaches them to her daughter's. "I *have* to find the perfect thing," she gushes on. "It has to be *right.* I can't just fob someone off with something that'll just sort of do—it has to be *perfect.* People say I'm stupid, I'm too much of a perfectionist, I'll wear myself out. But that's too bad, that's me, isn't it, Bonny darling? I'm not happy unless I'm doing a first-rate job, unless I'm giving absolutely one hundred per *cent.*"

There's a sort of sickened silence. And then Chris, the bastard, checks his watch and says, "Rich—I ought to go. I promised Sarah I'd be there by ten."

"Oh you're not *going*!" wails Tigger. "We haven't found out what *you* do yet!"

"Business Studies, Computing and Maths," Chris says dampingly. "At the same college as Rich. I really do have to go." Then he says,

"Bye—nice meeting you," and turns, and just *walks off*, the bastard, and I kind of hover, jumping from foot to foot like I'm desperate for a piss. Then I call out, "Hey Chris, did you—?" only of course he's through the crowd, heading for the door, so I gasp, "*Sorry*, I have to ask him—" and hare off, like what I have to ask him is so important I don't even have time to finish my sentence.

Out in the hall, I just about get him by the lapels and smack him back against the wall. "You *shit*. You can't leave me here alone!"

"I can, mate. Look—I've had a great feed, and a few beers, and it's been interesting, seeing the weirdos you're hooking up with nowadays, but now it's time to go."

"But *Chris*—"

"Come with me if you don't want to stay!"

"I *can't*. I've got to—I've got to *network*."

Chris lets out a great derisive snort. "Well, I *haven't*. See you, mate. You'll manage."

"But that hideous woman—she's probably waiting for me—"

"Yeah. Nice ego she has. Poor daughter. No wonder she's so wet."

"D'you see the way she got me by the wrist? Reckon she does that 'cos people try to run away when she's talking to them."

"Yeah. God, Rich—is it all worth it?"

"What?"

"Putting up with this shit—just to earn a bit of money?"

I watch him find his jacket on the banisters and then walk through the door. "Thank Barb for me will you?" he calls back over his shoulder.

And then a trilling voice behind me goes, "*There* he is! We thought we'd lost you!"

Chapter 12

Tigger bounds over to me, hauling Bonny along behind. “Look after my baby for me a minute, will you, Rich?” she squeals. “Only I must collar Nick about something. He’s been after me to prep a shoot for him next week and he’s so naughty he won’t finalize things until absolutely the last minute. . . .”

“Yeah, I’ve got to find Nick too. . . .” I wail—but she’s off. Disappeared into the kitchen.

I turn to Bonny. We stare at each other bleakly for a second or so, then I crank out, “Can I get you another drink?”

She glowers. “You don’t have to *look after* me. I’m fine.”

“No—look—*I* want another beer. Come on.” And I head into the kitchen thinking, Follow me, don’t follow me, your call. I couldn’t give a stuff.

But by the time I reach the fridge, she's beside me. "Beer?" I say.

She nods, and I pull out two bottles, and this time I spot a bottle opener on the edge of a worktop and I flip the caps off really sweet, hardly spilling a drop, and hand her one.

We both slide our eyes over to where Tigger has got Nick cornered on the other side of the kitchen. They're engaged in a kind of full-out verbal competition—both shouting and laughing and not listening to the other one. "I s'pose you're going to tell me how fantastic she is?" Bonny suddenly demands.

"Who—your mum?" I ask. "Fantastic" is so many light years away from what was just going through my head about Tigger that my face kind of freezes over.

"Yeah. Everyone goes on about how fantastic she is, how great she looks for her age and everything, how she's more like my sister."

I shrug. It seems a bit harsh to say she looks like a lipsticked lizard in a wig, so I just mutter, "She doesn't look a bit like your sister."

Bonny's whole face brightens. "I've seen you before," she says.

"Yeah? You don't go to Haverstock College do you?"

She shakes her head. "No. Lady Sarah Manning."

Oh, I think. That figures. LSM is a posh all-girls' school, twenty miles from here.

"Don't pull that face," she says. "We're not all classy nymphos you know."

"Did I say you were classy?" I rap out and thank *God*, she laughs, and we find ourselves being propelled by the sheer crush of people back into the living room again.

"So where d'you see me?" I ask.

"Oh, I dunno. Around? Your hair was different then. Not so —you know—boy band."

"Oh, *fuck*! Sorry. I don't look like that, do I?"

"Yep. Haven't you noticed the line of twelve-year-old girls, trailing you wherever you go?"

I grin at her. "No. There's that ten-year-old over there—" I point over at Scarlett, dancing solemnly on her own in the corner—"but she thinks I'm an idiot."

"Blimey," mutters Bonny. "If *she* starts trailing you, I should get the garlic out."

I laugh, then I look at Bonny, and I realize she's funny. This is not a trait I've come to expect from girls I go after. Not that I'm *after* Bonny, no way but . . . well. Anyway.

"Actually, I know her," Bonny's saying. "I think she's brilliant. Morticia as a kid."

"Morticia? Oh—yeah. *The Addams Family*."

"Did you like the films?"

"Yeah. Not as much as the old TV programmes though."

"Me neither!" Bonny's smiling at me. "I used to watch them all, on Sky. And *The Munsters*. I loved *The Munsters*. I loved the beginning, with all the leaves blowing out from *inside* the front door."

And we jabber on, going through all the horror stuff we can think of, the cornier the better. We're both into the film visuals. I say I'd like to get involved in special effects, only it's all computer now, and she says she'd like to do makeup, which isn't. We fetch more beer from the fridge and we have a brief disagreement over *American Werewolf in London*, which she says is one of her favourite films and I don't rate much, preferring more schlock horror stuff like *Night of the Living Dead*.

It's a great conversation. I can't remember when I last had such a fun one. And she's—I don't know—*glowing*. Her eyes are just locked on my face. You can't help but be flattered.

And then suddenly we're both being hooked through an arm and banged together like floormats and Tigger's squealing, "Well, *you* two seem to be getting along!" Then she clocks the bottle in Bonny's hand and says, "Oh, darling, not beer! Think of the calories!"

Bonny doesn't answer, and Tigger says,

"You'll just have to do lots more lengths at the pool tomorrow, yes?" and then she giggles, and points at the twinkling satyr in the fireplace. "I just *lo-ove* Barb's idea of interior design," she says. "Think she's trying to set a mood? We all know what satyrs are good at, don't we?"

I have this vague recollection that satyrs run around with stonkers on them the size of felled trees, and I say, hurriedly, "I think it's brilliant, what she's done. I love this room."

Tigger glares at me. "Well, Barb's got the time to play, of course. She doesn't work. Just a bit of *hairdressing* occasionally." The vitriol in this is so sudden and violent and unmistakable, it's like she's spat acid in your face. Then she kind of hikes her face up into a smile again and says, "I *must* find Lois. She'll kill me if we don't have a chat." And she teeters off.

I turn and look at Bonny. She's suddenly looking deflated; all the glow has gone. "You go swimming with your mum then?" I ask.

Bonny nods. "We've got membership at this really posh health club," she mutters. "Mum's always going on about the fees, but she says it's worth it. She works out there just about every day, and she goes on at me if I don't come with her."

"And parties? She makes you come to her parties too?"

"Well—she thought I'd enjoy this one. She

comes clubbing with us sometimes."

"With *us*? With you and your friends?"

"Yeah. Sometimes. My friends all think she's great, one of us, they say they wish their mums were more—"

"If my old man ever tried to come to a club with me, I'd have the bastard committed."

Bonny laughs, a real, opened-mouth laugh, and then, because I've had quite a bit of alcohol, I blurt out, "I don't want to be rude or anything, but actually I think your mum's a bit of a pain in the arse."

Oh, *shit*. There's a nasty silence, and I mutter, "Look—sorry. I shouldn't've said that. It's just—she seems to take a lot of space, you know? Like she needs to have an awful lot of attention? I mean—Nick takes a lot of space but it's different with him somehow, he can't help it, and he's, I dunno, *nice*, you know, I mean—he means well, he doesn't . . ."

Jesus, Rich, shut *up*! When you're in a hole—stop digging!

"Sorry," I bleat. "Sorry."

Bonny is looking weird. "It's OK," she says in a little choked voice. "She can be a bit . . . over the top. I know. It's just she . . . she works so hard at everything. She can't bear women who just . . . give up. And she wants the best for me. And everything."

I am not going to agree with this, because I just don't think it's true. And then I'm saved from having to make some kind of answer by Nick yelling at me from across the room. "Rich! Here, mate! Come and meet someone!"

I apologize to Bonny, and scarper over, and Nick enfolds me into his armpit and pushes me towards a big, fat guy with a big, fat cigar in his mouth.

"Luke, meet Rich. Boy wonder. Only seventeen and already more gifted than you'll ever be."

Fat guy Luke ejects the cigar from his mouth and grins like an alligator. "Pleased to meet you, Rich. You do storyboards?"

"Don't you try and poach my infant prodigy to sketch out your poxy storyboards," Nick erupts jokily. "This lad is an original. Seriously—I'm dragging him along on Wednesday night to meet the Marley-Hunt crew. Alcopop account."

Luke sucks in a big breath. "Right. Yoof market, ay?"

"Yeah. Except we don't call it *yoof* anymore. That went out, like, about twenty years ago. You should learn that if you want to break into anything that isn't immediately pre-geriatric." Nick turns to me. "Luke's hoping to do some young stuff. Which will be bloody hard for him, as you can imagine."

I laugh nervously, but Luke laughs too, a comfortable, successful laugh, and says, "Maybe you can give me some advice, Rich. You'll have to show me your stuff."

"Not yet he won't," says Nick. "He's my baby. Maybe later, OK?"

Luke nods, takes a deep drag, and engulfs us in a cloud of cigar smoke. Immediately, Nick pulls out a packet of Marlboro Lights, and lights up. Then he thrusts the packet at me and says, "Sorry, do you—?"

I shake my head. Not getting hooked on fags is probably the sole good thing I can lay at the door of being permanently skint. Nick and Luke chunter on about the way the ad scene is going, and I try and look alert and interested and above all highly employable. Then Nick calls over a tall woman with hair like a white helmet, who he tells me is in films, and then a bloke who's in publishing, and I stand there silently, and smile and listen and smile.

It's not a conversation though. Lots of stuff is said—loudly, emphatically—but nothing actually follows on from what's gone before. Far as I can make out they could say everything they're saying in a totally different order and it would make just as much sense as it does right now. Name drop, anecdote, name drop, I'm-doing-this, he's-done-that. It's like a tennis match with four balls. Nothing connects. Nothing develops.

The group shifts and changes, people wandering off, others joining, and I stay put next to Nick. I'm not sure if I'm networking exactly but I'm hanging on in there. All the beer I've downed is beginning to take an effect, though, and I'm trying not to sway on my feet.

From the corner of my eye I can see Tigger, perched in a girly, leg-crossed way on the arm of the giant yellow sofa. A really good-looking guy is sitting at the end of it, below her, and Tigger's pitching into him big time, swaying about, bending over him, laughing, stroking his shoulder. Bonny's standing behind the sofa, alone, looking bored and uncomfortable in equal measure. I feel really guilty, somehow. After a bit I detach myself from Nick's group, wander out to the kitchen, and pick up two more bottles of beer, meaning to join Bonny and hand her one, but when I get back, she, Tigger, and the good-looking guy have all disappeared, so I drink both of them myself.

I don't see them again for the rest of the night, which lasts another one and a half hard-working hours before I feel I can say thanks and goodbye and weave my way home through the dark streets. I reckon I've done all right. I'm not sure about the point of it all, but I've done all right, I've held my end up. I drop my key as I try to fumble it into the lock and as I pick it up I knock over three empty milk bottles and find myself wondering if I'll ever run into Bonny again.

Chapter 13

Sunday is a wipe-out. I wake up with a dry mouth and a thumping head and legs that feel like lead from that long stagger home. The sun's blinding in through the curtains. Sam, thankfully, has disappeared downstairs to glue himself to moron TV.

I don't want to move but I know if I don't get some water I haven't a hope in hell of feeling better. So I lurch along the landing and open my mouth under the tap, and slurp up as much water as I can manage. Then I lurch back to my bunk, and crash, and I start trying to count the number of bottles of beer I got through last night, which sends me off again more efficiently than counting sheep. The next thing I know Mum's shaking my shoulder gently and waving a mug of tea in front of me saying, "Rich? Rich? Sunday lunch in less than an hour, luv."

I turn over and look at her, all blearily, and she says, "You had a good time last night, then."

"I was working, Mum. *Net*working."

"Yeah, yeah. Go and have a shower and *clean your teeth*, for God's sake, and then let's try and have a nice lunch, OK? And try not to argue with your dad. He's pleased for you, really he is, this chance you've been given. He's just—you know—worried it might all backfire, or you might forget about your college work and not get—"

"Good enough grades," I finish for her. "I know."

She half cuffs me, half ruffles my hair, and hands me the tea, and as she's walking out the door I say, "Mum? Any chance of washing my new shirt and jeans for tomorrow?"

"Leave them in the machine," she calls back, and disappears downstairs.

I drink the tea slowly, then I shunt myself out of bed and along to the bathroom. The shower makes me feel better, and I stand under it for ages, turning it colder and colder 'cos I reckon that'll help the hangover. I'm waiting for Dad's shout up the stairs—"Turn that bloody shower off—water costs money to heat you know!"—so I can yell back at him that it's *cold*, but it doesn't come. Then I go back to my room and pick up my new jeans, and I stand there knowing I've got to take my money out of the pocket 'cos the jeans are going to be washed, and when I take it out, I've got to count it.

And then I do take it out, and I do count it.

Oh, *shit*. I don't believe it. Two notes left, one tenner, one fiver, and a few coins. Seventeen pounds and 76p. Seventeen pathetic pounds and 76p. Out of that fat wad, that *roll* of three hundred and eighty pounds. I feel like I've been punched in the stomach. I tell myself, It's OK, it's OK, it went on clothes, but even with my raddled totting up I can only make the clothes I've bought come to two hundred and sixty-odd quid, so I should have over a hundred left, over a *hundred* . . . I collapse down on the edge of the bunk, and my head's so bent it comes nowhere near the top one.

Seventeen pounds and 76p. My money's just bled away. *Haemorrhaged* away.

My mind races, trying to justify it, trying to account for it, trying to make this sick feeling go away. The lunch I bought Friday, and tea and stuff at college, and that posh shower gel, and the *fish and chips* and Dad's Guinness, they made a hole in twenty-five, and the beer, the *beer* I bought for everyone, rounds and rounds and rounds of it. . . .

I think back to Friday night, Chris saying, "Christ, Rich, let me get *one* round in at least," and me saying, "No, no, it's OK," because it felt so good not to be waiting and drinking slowly and scrounging for once, it felt so fucking good to be able to get my money out and lay it on the bar.

I hold myself together over lunch. It's lamb, one of the cheaper cuts of course, shoulder or something, so it's pretty fatty and it smells really rank, and the mint sauce Dad ladles everywhere smells acrid, like sick. But I get some down, and Sam finishes off my potatoes. Then I tell Mum I'll have some apple tart later, I've got some English homework to do, and I escape up to my room and sit there in a mawkish daze over *Macbeth.*

It starts to get dark mercifully soon, and I crawl back into bed. My head's started to really hurt again. As I sink into the pillow I think—only three days till the Big Dinner, only three days till I'm rich again. But this time I don't believe it, I don't believe I can bring it off.

Despite passing out around nine Sunday night, I still oversleep Monday morning, but I know I feel better, even philosophical, as I slither into my new washed jeans that Mum, bless her, has laid over the chair by the desk. The money's gone, too bad, I enjoyed it, and now I'll just have to make *sure* I make more, won't I? Then I pull down the oaty shirt that Mum's ironed and hung up on the picture rail, and I'm wondering whether to wear it today or save it for when I'm supposed to be drawing Portia on Tuesday. . . .

Drawing Portia.

Jesus, I'd almost forgotten I'm *drawing Portia*!

The fast, fierce uprush of excitement in my guts is closely followed by an enraged spurt of regret that I've spent all my cash and I can't take her out to dinner after I've sketched her. Shit, shit, *shit*, why didn't I think of that, why didn't I *plan* for that, why didn't I set some money by? It would've been the perfect opportunity. I'd've told her I wanted to say thank you, and she'd've been hungry, late in the day, and—*shit*. What can I do with seventeen pounds and 76p? "Coming for a burger, Portia?" Somehow I don't think so. *Why* did I have to blow all that dosh being Mr. Bountiful in the pub?

My mind's racing as I set off for college. I'm wondering if I could get some kind of an advance out of Nick. Or a loan off Chris, only I really, really don't want to do that.

It's Huw, first session. Which is a punishing way to start the week. He always tours around, furious at having to be back in college after a weekend of freedom, telling you how shite you are, how your work is worthless and how you have to put more effort in to compensate for your total lack of natural talent. I'm late, as usual, as I steam through the door, prepared for his robust

Welsh tones to assault my eardrums. Instead it's Portia's silvery voice I hear, from her place at a table by the window.

"Richy—hi! I've found a room for us for tomorrow!"

About ten male heads swivel round and ogle me, and I enjoy the wash of hatred and envy from them. They're thinking she's referring to some secret sexy tryst place, and I don't enlighten them. I just call back, "That's great!" I want to add "babe" but I reckon that's pushing it. She meets my smile, bends over her work again.

Oh, *Jesus*, I think. I need more *money*.

"Stop flirting and get down to work, you useless little bastard." Huw's at my elbow, hassling me before I've even got my jacket off. "Your portfolio looks like something the cat's sicked up on. And before I forget, your *mam* left a message for you. Urgent."

He waves a green office slip at me. I take it, and read: "Your mother phoned; can you go round and see Nick Hanratty at Abacus Design before six today for last minute chat."

Last minute chat. That's OK, isn't it? That's positive. That's not, Sorry, deal's off.

"*Abacus Design*, ay?" Huw's sneering. "What do they want with you?"

"Huw—you read my message!"

"Course I did. So what're you up to, then, ay?

You prostituting your meagre talents to an ad company?"

I tell him the story. I'm trying to be nonchalant but I can't keep the excitement out of my voice, or the pride. Or—I realize with irritation—the need to have Huw approve of it all. Be really impressed with me for once.

But Huw's shaking his head before I'm even half way through. "*Arglwydd Mawr!* You kids. You're so damn impatient to . . . *get on*. What guarantee have you got that they won't just steal your designs?"

"But Nick's got me *involved*. He wants me *there*, at the dinner. Kind of the voice of youth."

"The voice of—? God help us all."

"I just—I trust him, Huw. I'm not going into this with my eyes closed."

"So you're going to be sketching labels for fizzy drinks. What a load of cock."

"Look, if it makes me money it—"

"Waste of your talent, lad," Huw says, and he turns his back on me, and drifts off. I feel this huge need to pick up a paintpot, scissors, anything, and chuck it hard as I can at the back of his uncaring head, but I don't, I look down at the drawing I was supposed to be finishing, and I decide it's crap. So I pick it up, and I rip it up—one, two, three—into eight little jagged bits, and then I start over with a clean sheet. I draw all morning without looking up, hardly, not even at Portia, and what I do is great, it's brilliant, all dark and searing and twisted and mean, and I shove it in the cat-sick portfolio and think, Up yours, Huw.

Chapter 14

I leave college early and arrive at Nick's office at two-thirty. He looks so surprised it's clear he's forgotten he's asked me to turn up. Then he says—"Rich! Yeah. Rich. Hi, Rich. Wednesday night. All booked. Harvey's. You know it? Outskirts of town."

Know it? In my household Harvey's is a byword for ostentatious waste and trendy showiness. "Great stuff," I say. "Looking forward to it."

"You come round to my house—sevenish? Then we can arrive there together."

Inside, I sigh with relief at not being forced to arrive at that citadel of intimidation all on my own. Nick's so loud he's the perfect guy to hide behind. "Sure," I say. "Sevenish. Nick, was that all you—"

"No. No, I got you down here for a purpose."

He picks up a few loose papers from his desk, looking like he's trying hard to remember what that purpose was. "Um—yeah. Marley-Hunt. I know we chatted it through the other night, but I just wanted to get our ideas straight, talk through any more ideas you'd had. . . ."

We spend the next twenty minutes or so discussing how we're going to impress the Marley-Hunt barons, how I have to come over as straight up from the street and plugged direct into mainstream teen culture. I practise keeping my face straight while I come out with teen-culture-type phrases. Then Nick says: "Basically, we'll busk it—we don't know what they're going to ask. Just hope they love your stuff, that's the main thing."

"You showing it to them then?"

"Yeah. With you. More impact."

I can feel all this fear seeping into my guts, fear for Wednesday, fear for the judgement on my drawings, fear for my life being decided over a couple of good bottles of wine and a few plates of tarted-up pasta. But that doesn't quite stop me remembering the plan I've evolved on the way over here, the plan that will let me take Portia out.

"Nick," I begin, "that fat guy at your party, you know he asked if I did storyboards . . ."

"Yeah. Cheap git. Some of 'em use students, keep the rates down."

"It's just—I know you gave me that money and all, but I've—"

"Spent it. OK. You want to do storyboards, you do them for me, darling. Two hundred a roll?"

"Two hundred—?"

"Quid. Yeah."

"I want to do storyboards," I gasp.

Five minutes later I'm in the super-trendy back office at a sloping desk and I'm thinking—Nick's great. He doesn't have to pay me that. He could offer me half that, and I'd jump at it, and he knows it. He's a really nice bloke.

Then Nick's assistant, Camilla, plonks a load of sheets of paper divided up into TV shapes in front of me and rests her hand on my shoulder and runs through what I have to do. "It's gotta be class, Rich, it's gotta be good. It's the storyboards that sell the idea. Now. A thirty-second ad needs up to thirty frames sketching out the action. Here's the ad breakdown." She plonks down another sheet of paper, with a great list on it. "OK, usual boring trying-to-be-funny domestic ad for crap ready-made food. Everyone nearly throwing up round the table, then son feeding stew to dog, then Dad mulching it into the garden, then Mum getting mad, then daughter coming home with Chiccy Bits—"

"Chiccy Bits?"

"Crap ready-made food. *I* didn't name it. Mum cooks it—everyone in ecstasy—dog looking depressed."

"Why?"

"'Cos he won't get any more throw-outs, will he? Get in the mood, Rich."

So I do. Camilla's said how important it is to make each character stand out, so I give the Mum these upturned Edna Everage specs and a dirndl skirt, and the little boy a Dennis the Menace sweatshirt, and Dad a big bald head, and make the dog a cross between a werewolf and a pig. And I give myself the intense pleasure of making the daughter a cartoon Portia with porn-star lips and in-out shape. I take my first sketch into Nick for the OK, which he gives, saying, "I like your style, it's in-your-face, ad people love that. Keep it clear. Keep it simple," and I go back to my desk.

And then suddenly it's quarter to seven and Nick's at my elbow wanting to lock up and I've only done four frames and a bit, which is not very bloody much at all, is it?

"Can I take it home with me?" I whine.

"No. You cannot. One of the things about storyboards is they have to be crisp and appealing and not look as though they've been dragged about on buses and left about on floors. But I don't need it for ages yet—you can come in any time and plough away at it."

I sit silent.

"You didn't think you'd finish it today, did you?" Nick demands.

I laugh like I'm laughing at the very idea, although I'd thought exactly that.

"Don't worry," Nick says. "You'll speed up. When you get the characters off."

"It's not that. It's—"

"You need money now?"

I nod, try to look like a spaniel.

"Look—you can have what you've earned so far," he says grumpily, and he pulls out his wallet and peels off three tenners. "But just this once, OK? I don't get bloody paid in advance, why should you?"

I'm vibrating with gratitude as we head out of the door and he pushes the lift button, and I'm babbling about how great his offices are, how much style they've got.

"Yeah," says Nick. "They're cool. We were lucky to get 'em really. People don't want to be down near the canal 'cos it smells a bit in the summer, and there's this rat thing, which can be a prob if you're a rataphobe."

The lift clanks up towards us and Nick yanks the wrought iron gate open. "There's another floor, too, above this one. We had to take it on—they wouldn't split the unit. Didn't want too many companies based here. Planning and traffic control and disease regulation and all that bollocks. Want to see it?"

I shrug and grin and nod, because with that thirty quid in my pocket I'd like any suggestion put to me, any at all, and we step into the cage and Nick closes the iron gate on us and pushes the up button instead of the down one.

"We just use it for storage," he says. "You know, props and stuff. It's a hell of a mess. The company that had it before us back in the seventies, the MD, he fitted it up as a shag pad."

"A *what*?"

"A flat. You know. To bring girls to. His wife and kids were stuffed into this big house in the country, and he used to stay over at the office to save commuting. Only you don't put *shag*-pile carpet down and mirrors everywhere if you're just concerned with not commuting, do you?"

The lift rattles to a halt, and we step out. There's no doubt we're on the top floor: the ceiling slopes inwards with the roof, and the window behind the lift is small and circular, not big and square and impressive like the floors below. Old storyboards and great sheets of hardboard and bulging paper-filled rubbish sacks are piled up everywhere—we practically have to battle our way through to get to the entrance door.

"The key's on here somewhere," Nick mutters,

rattling out a bristling fob of keys and peering at it. "Yep. This is it. I think." He fits it into the door and it turns, but the door won't budge. So he sets his shoulder against it and shoves, and slowly, the door's forced open. "Haven't been in here for a while. We leave everything piled outside."

The first thing that hits my eyes as I follow Nick through the door is the stacks of yet more art boards everywhere, mounds and mounds of them. And the second is the completely amazing mindblowing window at the far end. It's grimed and grey and filthy, but it goes all the way from the floor to the ceiling, and it's huge and arched, like a cathedral window, broken up by strips of leading into large elegant squares.

"Great, isn't it?" says Nick, catching me gawping. "They replaced the wool doors."

"The wool doors. . . ? Oh, *right*. What they'd haul the wool through."

"Yeah. When it was a working mill. That window opens flat against the wall just like the doors did . . . look, I'll show you."

He makes his way through all the crap to the window, unbolts it, and swings the two great arched halves of window back.

And I'm dazed, breathless, with the low sun and the wet air that rushes in towards me, like finding myself suddenly flying.

"Oh, *wow*," I say weakly, happily. "That's . . . *wow*."

"Great view, eh? Look—careful, there's no ledge. See that hook there, and that? Pulley system. They'd haul the wool up from the canal, and start processing it up here. You always process stuff from the top floor down. Forget why. More efficient or something. It would go down a floor with each stage and end up being made into cardigans on the ground floor."

I'm not really listening to this historical explanation. I'm looking at the great space of sky in front of me, eyes scanning over the rooftops.

And Nick's off across the floor again, kicking aside strips of rat-eaten, rose-pink, shag-pile carpet. "It must have been a great pad thirty years ago. He had the whole of this far side partitioned off, turned into four rooms. He's even had grotty little windows knocked in—high level slitty jobs."

I follow Nick, peer past his shoulder and see a box-shaped room painted deep depressing red, with dull, dirty mirrors all across one wall and the low sloping bit of the ceiling. "This was the bedroom," Nick grimaces. "Tacky."

There's a huge mattress on a wooden platform, kind of a deluxe futon, and a long-dead palm fossilizing in the corner in a lime-green tub. Under the strip of slitty windows hang three smaller lime-green tubs with a few desiccated twigs protruding from them. Below the windows an old suitcase is lying open on the floor with nothing inside it. After the space of the main room it's all pretty horrible. "How could he tuck himself away in here," I say, "when he could be out in front of that fantastic window?"

Nick smirks. "Turn you on, does it, darling? Here—here's the bathroom." He's backing out of the bedroom, opening the next door along. We step into a skinny little room with a dark-purple basin, bog, and creaky-looking shower cubicle. "Aubergine," Nick says. "This bloody horrible aubergine stuff was dead popular back in the seventies."

I look down into the bog. It's full of water. Three fag ends and two dead wasps are floating under a thick layer of dust. "Does it work?" I ask.

"Think so," says Nick, cranking the handle. Nothing happens. "Maybe the water's off. Come on—the kitchen."

This is even more basic. We peer in at two electric rings, a narrow formica breakfast bar and an even narrower cupboard and Nick says, "I guess eating out was part of the whole seduction package."

"What about the last room?" I ask.

"Ah. That's where we *started off* storing things. Don't even open the door. Now come on, let's go."

"Don't you ever think of using it though?" I ask, as we judder down in the lift to ground level. "Turn it into a flat again, rent it out?"

Nick shrugs. "Too much hassle. And you couldn't charge much 'cos it's above offices and it's by the canal."

"But what about for you to use, or—?"

"What you saying, man? You think I want to cheat on my wife?"

"No. Course not." The lift smacks to a stop, and Nick checks his watch and groans.

"*Bloody* hell. I've got to fly. I should've picked up Freddie from his mate's half an hour ago." And he's off across the car park, gravel spurting from his shoes, calling back, "Wednesday, seven, my place, yeah? And *look smart*!"

Chapter 15

I've moved into the fast lane I have. In the next forty-eight hours there are two mega life-altering things happening to me; two major events to get hyped up about and worry over. I decide to concentrate my main angsting on drawing Portia because that comes first. And if that goes as well as I hope it will, I'll be in a brilliant state for Wednesday night, won't I. All confident and successful and tanked up with energy and ready to *sell*.

Before getting into bed that night I check I've got good paper and pencils and I think about how I'm going to do Portia; I project ahead about how I'm going to be able to focus on *drawing* when she's sitting/standing/*lying* there right in front of me. Then I practise looking cool and mean in the mirror; then I rub some more of Nick's fake tan cream onto my face. I go off to sleep fantasizing about taking over Nick's top floor flat and making it with Portia in front of that cathedral window like we're flying in the sky.

"I'm *stiff*. Honestly, Richy, my back's *killing* me. You going to be much longer?"

My session with Portia is not going like I hoped it would.

"*And* I'm cold. Can you pass me my jumper please?"

It's not going well at all. We got through the first ten tension-ridden minutes with her shifting position every five seconds and me looking at this absolute beauty in front of me and trying to draw with a hand that'd turned into a turnip. Then we both relaxed a bit and she divided her time between complaining at me and answering her mobile phone.

I don't feel a bit like I imagine Rossetti did with that fabulous redheaded bird he was always painting. I feel on edge, inadequate. And my sketches are crap. I've done three so far, really fast, really shite, nothing I can use.

"Can't I see what you've drawn?" she moans. I look down at my sketch pad, shake my head furiously. She'd hate it, I know she would. I've made her mouth kind of . . . *sagging*. Like nothing's going on in her head. Like—

Oh my God. I've made her look like a dope

addict. I've made her look like a coke-head. Where did that come from? I didn't mean to do that. I *can't* show her.

"I'm just doing quick sketches, OK?" I bluster. "I'm going to finish it off later. There's so many . . . *sides* to you, Portia. I can't cover it all."

"Yeah?" she says suspiciously. "What sort of sides?"

"Oh—you know," I mumble. "Different sides to your personality and all."

"I thought you were drawing my *face*," she says, then she sniggers, and I realize she thinks she's made a joke, so I laugh too.

She's sitting on a chair with one leg slung over the other and her arms behind her head. It's the most horrible phoney contrived pose and apart from the way it shows her chest off, I hate it. I'm dying to ask her to stand up, but I can't find the courage.

Her mobile goes again, and she twists to answer it. I move round a bit too, and I've got her fabulous face in profile. Her hair's falling just right. "Don't move!" I hiss. "Hold that!"

"Oh, God, yes, that's *Rich*," she squeals into the mobile. "He's still at it. He's done about a million sketches of me already. I'm *exhausted*."

I'm drawing like my pencil's on fire. I have to get her before she moves. I sketch in the mobile, the way her hand's clutching it to her face like the Rossetti girl clutches flowers. I get down her look of animation, absorption. I get her wonderful mouth, talking. Her eyes, half hooded, intimate. Her hair fanning out dark on her neck.

It's the best one yet, easy.

Oh, God, it's *her*.

She rings off and I breathe out, "Just a bit longer, Portia. Hold it just a bit longer." She smirks, but luckily I've got her mouth down perfect already. I'm shading away now, honing it, getting her hand just right with its pretty nails that have a touch of the talon about them.

I stop, hold the paper arm's length, and say, "OK. You can look at this one if you want."

She trips across the room towards me and takes hold of the picture. She studies it and I study her face, which is suddenly crossed by a scary little quiver of irritation.

"H'm," she says.

"H'm?"

"Well—it's OK. The *nose* isn't quite right. You've made it too—it's almost *hooky*."

I take the drawing back from her. "Hooky? It's not hooky."

She snatches the drawing back, peers at it again. "It is. More than my nose is. You've made me look like a witch or something."

She's wrong, it's brilliant, it's *her*, but I know an opportunity when it pitches up in front of me and I'm not about to blow this one. "OK, sorry," I plead, humbly. "Let me have another go. I'll get it right next time. Now I've warmed up."

"Oh, Richy, I'm *tired*."

"I know. I know you are. You've been great. But just *one* more—you could lean. You could lean against that wall there. I'll be really quick, I promise. And then I'll take you out for a huge meal, OK? I'll take you out to dinner."

"I don't know if I'm free for dinner."

"No. OK. I just want to say thank you—for all the time you've given up. A drink maybe?"

She sighs, then she shrugs, and says, "How d'you want me?"

I get her back against the wall before she has a chance to change her mind. I've got her half-profile this time, looking down, hands hanging, hair falling forward. She looks so incredibly sexy I forget to pick up the paper for a minute or so and she goes "Ri-*ich*!" Then I crouch down on the floor and draw, looking up. It's wonderful. I have to make sure I make her face look the way Portia would want it, but for the rest of her I'm free.

It takes twenty minutes. She's sliding down the wall by this time, sighing with every out-breath. "OK, *finished*," I announce, and I hand it over.

"H'm. That's OK. Better. I like the way my legs look so long."

"You're a great subject, Portia."

"You could've defined my eyes a bit more. They *disappear*."

"I can do that. I can do that later."

She studies the portrait a moment longer, then she hands it back. She's still not very impressed, I can tell. My vision of Portia is clearly not the way she wants to see herself. I feel this flash of anger, of regret, and I think—why couldn't I have glammed it up more, made her look like a star? I'd meant to do that, but somehow the drawing just took over.

"So—what about dinner?" I repeat, desperately. Don't let it all just slip away, *please*. "I thought we could go to Allesandro's."

She looks at me, considering. "I love Allesandro's. It's so cool."

Well, hoo-*ray*. I've got *something* right.

"So you'll come?" I croak.

She looks at me again, while my heart thuds, balanced between joy and grief, waiting to know which way to tip.

"Oh—*OK*," she says.

Chapter 16

Once she's decided to have dinner with me, Portia comes over all flirtatious. She links her arm through mine as we walk out of college, which makes my thudding heart pump even harder, and tells me she really shouldn't be doing this. Then she stops and says she has to make a call.

And out comes the infernal mobile again. "You like it?" she simpers, waving it under my nose. It's all glittery with stars and moons and stuff. "I did the cover myself. One of those nail varnish kits. It's so *cute*, don't you think?"

"It's great," I gush. "God, that's clever, doing it yourself. Ones like that cost—"

"Thirty quid or so in the shops," she finishes triumphantly, and punches in a number.

I'm filled with a kind of sick admiration for the pleasure it gives her—the glittery mobile as fashion accessory. Portia is going to be a Fashion Editor, there's no doubt about that. I can see them now, the editorials she'll pen. *This week's must-have item is a PVC bra with detachable straps for those bare-shoulder days.*

"Mum?" she's saying. "Hi. Look, when Tony turns up—tell him I'm working late at college, OK? Tell him I have an assignment to finish. OK? What? 'Cos I don't want to, OK. . . ? Look—if I phone him he'll go on at me and I just—*what*? Why is that your business. . . ? OK, OK, look—just tell him, will you? *Honestly!*" And she flips the phone off.

I'm half-horrified by the casual way she's bullied her mum into lying for her—half-delighted she's done it to be with me.

"He's getting really possessive," she says, and she slips her hand through my arm again.

"Who? Tony?"

"Yeah. Thinks he owns me. I can't bear it. I mean—yeah, we're together, but Christ, I have a life too, yeah?"

"Yeah," I say encouragingly, because that life might be about to include me.

"I mean—last week. We just wanted a girls' night out. Me, Jenny, Chloe, the gang. And he got a real strop on. Thought I was going to be pulling the whole night."

"And were you?" I ask, before I can stop myself.

She shrugs. "Two or three guys. It was a *club*!"

Then she swivels her wonderful cat-face round and looks at me. "You got a girlfriend?"

"Nah," I say, all Jack-the-lad, and I squeeze her arm up against me. "Can't bear being tied down."

"Right!" she enthuses. "It's so corny, all this you-belong-to-me stuff. I mean—he buys me stuff. And I *lo-ove* that—I love a guy to show he cares, you know? But it's like, it all comes with a price tag. Like he can't just *give*. Like if he buys me earrings or something it's like he expects me to be extra-special *nice* to him all evening!" Her voice rises with indignation.

"Um," I say.

"He's on the phone to me the whole time. It's a total drag. What are you up to, how was your day. It's a *drag*."

"I guess he's just really keen on you," I say. I'm practically feeling sorry for the poor sucker by this time.

"He's checking up on me! I can guarantee, five after eight, he'll phone me, check I'm really working at college. When you think about it it's kind of pathetic."

"Why don't you turn it off?"

"What?"

"Your mobile."

She looks at me like I'm certifiable. "I'd miss all my calls!"

"Yeah, but they could leave messages, couldn't they. And you wouldn't have to talk to Tony with—you know. Me sitting across the table from you. When you're s'posed to be in college."

She shakes her head, bemused. "Richy—that's really not a problem."

We arrive at Allesandro's. It's pretty enjoyable, walking through the door with Portia attached to my arm. Allesandro's is one of these totally fake Italian places where all the energy and effort has gone into the decor and the atmosphere rather than the food because everyone's supposed to be so hip and into fab conversations that they don't actually notice what they're eating. I'm deeply glad that my hunch has paid off. I thought old style-queen Portia would love it and she does. She looks around, checking who's there, making sure they've clocked her and admired her. Then she melts as a smooth waiter with a fake overdone accent shows us to a fake rough-wood table in the corner behind three huge terracotta pots with bundles of sticks sticking out of them.

"It's so . . . *Mediterranean*!" she hisses at me. "I love it!"

Mediterranean my arse. And I bet the waiter comes from Wolverhampton. But if it pleases Portia it's more than cool by me.

I hand her the parchment-coloured menu.

"Have whatever you want," I say. "Honestly. I'm so grateful, Portia. You're the best subject under the sun, you really are."

"Yeah?" she dimples. "Why?"

Oh, shit. I've got to answer. Because drawing you's the next best thing to shagging you?

"Because—you're an original, Portia. You're so different, you—"

"You saying I'm weird?" she bridles.

"No. No, I'm *not*. But you're not conventional, you know? You've got something the others haven't. You're not out of the mould, like the others are."

These woolly old clichés seem to satisfy her. She smirks, and scans her eyes down the menu. "Mmmm. Mussels. I *ad-ore* mussels. And *pa-asta.* Can I have both together? Yes. Mmmm. Seafood *pa-asta.*"

She pronounces the "a" in pasta long, like the "a" in arse. I check the price by the seafood pasta, and smile at her encouragingly. "White wine, Portia?" I say. I'm sophisticated all right. I know you have white with fishy stuff.

"Yum," she says. "And let's get some green salad, too."

Oh, great. The best part of four quid for a bowl of rabbit food. But I smile, again, and the waiter slimes over. I order the house white, and a plain tomatoey pasta for myself, which will leave enough money for her to have a posh dessert or cappuccino or something, then I sit back and let myself have the profound groin-stirring pleasure of just looking at her. I've got her here, I think triumphantly. I've got her here *at last*. And then her evil mobile goes again. At least three other people on nearby tables clutch at their pockets thinking it's theirs, and Portia answers hers with a grin of triumph, like she's won in some popularity contest.

"Jen-*neee*! Hi-*i*! . . . No, I'm not. . . . No, of course I'm not. I just told Mum to tell Tony that . . . What? I'm with Richy! . . . Yeah! . . . Yeah! . . . We're at Allesandro's. . . . I know. I *know*. . . . Don't be silly! . . . Jennifer, don't be *silly*." She's looking slyly over at me as she says this, and I set my face into a chiselled manly half-profile just in case Jenny's discussing her getting off with me.

"It was OK," she's saying. "Well—they weren't brilliant but he's going to work on them. Now—have you *heard* yet? About Annie and Jim? . . . Tell me, *tell* me!"

The next five minutes are taken up by her squealing into the mouthpiece, and saying stuff like, "She was never right for him!" and "God—what a bitch!" while I sit there like a lemon, trying to look relaxed and lovingly indulgent when I really want to reach over and ram the stupid phone down her throat.

Why am I so strung up about her? She's rude. She's an idiot. She's just a total turn-on too. She's imprinted into me, that's what it is. Like she's in my DNA. She's woven into my sexual DNA. I've got no *choice*.

"I have to go, Jen—the wine's here!" she squawks, and snaps off the phone and smiles at me, and I'm enslaved again.

The waiter posily slops a bit of wine into my glass, and I go through the cringe-making ritual of snorting into it and tasting a bit and saying fine, fine. Then he pours for Portia, and fills my glass, and as he disappears I raise my glass and say, "Here's to the most beautiful model I've ever drawn."

"Oh, Rich," she dimples. "You say such *sweet* things!" She leans forward, chinks her glass against mine. "I think it's great when a guy can say nice things. You know—when he's confident enough in himself. Tony's, like, really uptight. It's like getting blood out of a stone, getting him to give me a compliment."

I smile, shake my head, like I can't understand how Tony's not showering her with compliments every waking minute, and she goes on, "It was fun, sitting for you. I mean—I know I grumbled a bit but—"

"You were *great*," I lie. "A real sport. Honestly. I kept you there far longer than I should've done."

"Oh, you just wanted to get it right," she says, lowering her eyes at me over the rim of her glass. "I admire that. And anyway"—she takes a pouty little sip of wine—"you're making up for it *now*."

Oh, yes, oh, *yes*, this is going really well. This is going *so* well. This is—

Blaaaaa! The fucking mobile rings again. And without so much as a regretful glance at me, Portia whams it to her ear. "Matt-*ie*! Hi-*i*! Where are you?. . . You're in the bath?! Oh *honestly*!"

Oh, *great*. The next caller'll probably be on the *bog*. I sit back and glug down half a glass of wine, while Mattie and Portia exchange mind-numbingly dull gossip. Portia keeps saying, "I know, I *know*," and I think, If you *know*, how come Mattie keeps telling you? Then our plates of food are put in front of us, and Portia manages to say goodbye to Mattie. She lays her mobile down equidistant between uson the table, where it squats like a silvery glittery poisonous toad.

I decide to have another go. I jerk my head at the phone and say, "Seriously, why don't you turn it off?"

She looks at me uncomprehending. "Why?"

"Well, it's—you know. It keeps interrupting." She's still looking at me as though I'm mad. "Us talking," I go on. "You know. If you turned it off they'd leave messages wouldn't they?"

She shrugs. "Yeah, but they'd be *cold* messages. I need to know what's happening when it *happens*."

Like when one of your friends takes a dump? I want to say, but I don't; I start stabbing my fork into my food instead.

"*And* I'd have to call them back," Portia adds, disparagingly. "So I'd have to *pay*."

That settles it. The phone stays on. But another refill of wine each and we're beginning to mellow again. Portia's making the devouring of her mussels into this whole erotic show, with lots of licking and sexy little *mmmm* noises. I'm so entranced I just about forget to eat myself, and when she holds out a half shell towards me, I slurp off the mussel, making sure I get a good suck at her fingers too, even though the thought of eating a mussel with all its guts and everything still inside it makes me want to barf.

"I *lo-ove* seafood," she purrs.

"You know what they say about it, don't you?" I risk.

"An aphrodisiac? Yeah. And in my experience, it's *true*."

Oh, boy, I'm getting hot here. I start doing frantic sums in my head, wondering if I can afford to order another bottle of wine and still get her a pudding, and I smile at her, and she smiles back—and then *Blaaaaa!*—the mobile shrills out for the third glorious time.

But instead of picking it up, Portia checks her watch. "There, you see! It's five past eight—it's Tony!"

Blaaaaa!!

"Oh, *God*—I knew it!" she squawks. "I told you he'd phone on the dot!"

Blaaaaa!!

"Portia—" I hiss, urgently.

"Honestly, he's so predictable!"

Blaaaaa!

"Portia—*answer* it!" Everyone at the surrounding tables is glaring and craning round, and a waiter's coming towards us.

Blaaaaa!!

"Honestly, Rich, I get so sick of it, I—"

Blaaaaa!!

"Portia—get the fucking PHONE!"

There's an icy pause, then she scoops up the mobile just before its seventh ring. "Tony—hi . . . Yeah, I know. Sorry about that . . . I forgot this *assignment*. I just had to get it done . . . I know, I know . . . Well, I did try but then I couldn't get through and by the time I went to try again I knew it was too late and I knew you'd've left so I phoned Mum . . . Look, I've said I'm *sorry* . . . I had absolutely no choice, OK? I'd much sooner be with you than stuck here in this bloody library flogging away . . . Yeah, well, I'm disappointed *too*, baby. . . . You should be sorry for *me*. . . . OK. OK. Tomorrow night. Bye, darlin' . . . Look—I can't talk now. . . . Phones are banned in here, that's why. . . . I've got to *work*—I've only done half of it. . . . *Bye*. You too, baby." Then she makes these wet kissy noises and flicks the phone off, and I'm left sitting there stunned by the incredible smoothness of the deceptive act I've just witnessed.

She glances up, catches my expression. "*What?*" she says defensively.

I hold out my hand. "Gimme that," I say.

"What?"

"Gimme that goddam phone. I'm turning it off. If it rings one more time I swear I'll smash it, OK?"

A little smirk is flickering at the corners of Portia's mouth. "Woah. Mr. Tough Guy."

"Just hand it over, McCutcheon."

And she does. I swear it's even given her a thrill, me coming on all macho like that. I slightly ruin the pose by having to ask her where the off button is, but then the deed is done, and we get back to eating.

Wow. I'd've expected her to lay into me about swearing at her and grabbing her phone, and instead she's gone all girly and sweet. All *right*. I fork some more spaghetti into my mouth, grinning at her, and she smiles back. I decide I daren't risk the financial outlay on another bottle of wine, so I slow my drinking down, and fill her glass up for the third time. Then I come out with the seriously impressive line I've been waiting to say all night. "You ever been to Harvey's?"

"You kidding?" she says. "Harvey's costs an arm and a leg. I'd *lo-ove* to go there. I've asked Tony to take me for my birthday, but—"

"I'm going there tomorrow night," I say, casual as all hell.

"What? How? Who with?"

And I'm off. I tell her all about my drawings, and Nick, and Marley-Hunt, and Sling, the brand of alcopop needing a makeover, and her eyes grow huge and satisfyingly round with being totally impressed by me. Then I'm into why I want it to work, why I don't only want money for money's sake, but 'cos it'll set me *free*, and I'll be able to fund a gap year before art college, and I really think she's listening, and she's *with* me, understanding what I say, so maybe she's not all that shallow after all, maybe underneath she's really OK—when I notice she's drawn back and she's looking pained.

"What's up?" I ask.

"Nothing. Just you're spitting quite a bit, that's all."

I feel like I've just been smacked in the face. "Oh, shit," I mutter. "Sorry. I—*God.*"

"It's OK," she says peevishly, dabbing at her nose with a napkin. "Carry on."

Carry *on*? When I've just been totally humiliated? I fill in the silence by downing the last millimetre of my wine, and then I clear my throat quietly. And Portia reaches out across the table and puts her hand on mine. "Hey—don't be offended, Rich. Look—I shouldn't've said anything."

"No," I mutter. "You should've just sat there getting drenched by my saliva, right?"

"Oh, come on. Loads of people talk with their mouths full. Just forget it, OK?"

I try to smile but my mouth won't make it. Half of me hates myself for getting so into talking I didn't realize I was spraying her, but a *good* half of me hates *her* for pointing it out.

I'd never, ever point something like that out. I swear I wouldn't. Ever.

"What chance d'you think you've got?" she says coaxingly. "Really? Of this whole thing coming off?" And she kind of strokes my hand a bit.

She's good, is Portia. At coaxing and wheedling; at bringing someone round when she's pissed them off. But then she must get a lot of practice, what with the way she treats Tony and all.

"I dunno," I mutter. "I can't tell. I just have to wait."

"I bet they want you. You're good. God, wouldn't that be brilliant? Wouldn't that be *ace*?"

I can feel myself thawing. "Yeah," I say. "It would."

"You'd be rich," she coos. "You'd be *famous*."

"Well, not famous. But I'd make some money. And it's a start, you know? It's a beginning." The waiter arrives and scoops our plates up, handing out two glitzy dessert menus at the same time. "What d'you fancy?" I say.

"Oh, I *shouldn't*."

She does though. This great creamy gooey meringuey sundae that takes me right up to my financial limit. I sit and watch her as she toys with it, scooping out the chocolate bits and crushing the meringue and leaving most of the ice cream. I'm totally absorbed watching her pointy tongue flicking in and out of her mouth, which is just as well as we've completely run out of conversation. I grovel a bit more about how glad I am she sat for me, and then there's a silence as my mind races, searching for a new topic. Then Portia drops her spoon peevishly in the half-full sundae glass and says, "I ought to go, Rich. I oughtn't to be too late."

I have this sudden desire to snatch the glass up and finish off the sundae, but I tell myself it wouldn't look attractive. So I just nod and smile and beckon the waiter.

When the bill arrives I read the *Total* line and get a full-on stab of panic. I haven't got enough. I'm, like, over three quid short. Trying to look relaxed I scan the list of orders, praying for a mistake—and then I see it. The gratuity line, adding on six pounds sixty. And the tiny tiny practically-needing-a-microscope line saying:

You are not, of course, obliged to pay the 15% gratuity that we have added on for your convenience.

Convenience! You call nearly giving someone a heart attack *convenience*! But I'm saved. I pocket three pounds and lob down the rest of my cash, which gives them something like an 80p tip, which is all they deserve after scaring me like that, the bastards. Then I hustle Portia out rather rapidly.

"Thanks for coming, Portia," I say. "Can I see you home?"

"Some of the way," she says. "*Tony*'s probably waiting for me. Staking out my house."

I know where she lives, and I know we can get to it through the park, which is still open this soft spring evening, with its shady paths lined by little romantic fake-Victorian lamps. I put my arm round her shoulders as we start walking, and she doesn't shrug me off.

"That was a lovely meal, Richy," she purrs.

"Glad you liked it."

"You didn't have to, you know. Take me out, I mean."

"Portia—I wanted to!"

She simpers out a little laugh, and tucks herself tighter under my arm. All *right*. We're turning through the park gates. I steer her to the left, 'cos I know the spot I'm aiming for. I'm feeling all mellow and a bit slurry from the wine, I'm feeling all kind of now-or-never, like it's the best chance I'll get. We veer away from the broad main path, and alongside some low hanging trees, and I kind of swivel round in front of her, and bring my other arm up to her shoulder.

"I wish you weren't with Tony," I say.

She looks coolly up at me. "Well, I'm not right now. Am I."

She's finished speaking but she's left her fabulous mouth open. I bring my head down and before I can bottle out I fasten my mouth to hers and start kissing her.

And—*hallelujah*—she lets me.

Then she kisses me back. And *God* she's good. She's got a little, soft, muscular tongue, following mine. After her crushing comment about me spitting over dinner part of me's waiting for her to pull me up on my snogging technique, too—tell me I'm dribbling or something. But she doesn't. Her hand's sliding up the back of my neck, raking into my hair. She's *into* this.

After a while she pulls back and takes a breath and says, "Wow."

"Wow," I echo. I can just about hear what I say above the pulsing in my head.

"Are you that good at everything else?" she smirks.

"Try me," I say—oh, *God,* try me here, *now*, in those bushes *THERE.*

"Maybe I will, sometime," she says, and I go to move in on her again but she pushes me off. "I have to *go*, Richy. I *do*."

I'm not going to beg, not like I did about drawing her. If I start begging I'll get carried away—I'll get down on my goddam *knees*, I'll do anything to neck with her like that again. I take hold of her hand all kind of slow and significant, and we walk off, along the path back to the main road.

She makes me say goodbye to her at the top of her street. All the way between here and the park I've been singlemindedly planning how I can get another snog out of her. Determination is half the battle I reckon. I lurch round to face her again, then I get hold of her by the elbow, and say, "I wish you didn't have to go."

"Well, I *do*." She's edgy, eyes swivelling for Tony's car.

"Will you come out with me again?"

"Oh, come on. How can I? I mean, this wasn't a date—this was—"

"OK, if I get that account—will you come out with me to celebrate?"

She smiles up at me. "Where?"

OK, Portia, message understood. "Harvey's of course."

"You bet," she sniggers. "Now I have to *go*."

"Goodnight, then," I mumble.

She looks up, surprised she's got away so easily, and I bring my face down fast, and *all right*, she's hooking her right arm round my neck, and we're off on another really fierce snog.

I think she's the kind of girl who gets off on danger. She pulls back, squeaks, "*God*, he'd *murder* me—" and goes in for the kill again. It's too much, too much. It's fantastic. Then she yanks away, and rushes off, like we're in a spy movie or something, and she does this *really really* corny thing of waving her hand without looking back, as though she's certain I'll be staring after her.

Which I am of course.

Every inch of the way.

Chapter 17

All the way home I can taste her mouth, and I'm grinning, I can't stop myself, I can only just stop myself from continually punching the air in triumph. I knew it. I *knew* all Portia and I needed to do was connect physically. Kind of *fuse* that chemistry between us. Maybe now we've done that, and maybe now she thinks I've got money coming, maybe I'll be in with a chance. Or maybe, better yet, she'll forget about her obsession with going to groovy places and having money spent on her and realize I'm such a stud that it's better to be with *me* and half a pint in a pub than with Tony in the hottest place in town. And *maybe* we'll get on a better level now. Maybe she'll stop gossiping and giggling, and we can discuss things, we can get close, we can talk. . . .

Or maybe we don't really *need* to talk if we

can connect physically like that. Maybe talk's irrelevant.

It's with that low thought that I let myself in my front door, and I know from the minute I walk in the hall that there's an Atmosphere. All the lights are on for a start, and they're never all on unless something's up.

"Hey, Mum?" I call.

No answer. I can see Sam through the open living room door in his usual sprawl on the floor in front of the telly. He looks round at me with an expression of disgust on his face, then returns his gaze to the box. "What the hell's up with you?" I say, and he shrugs, carries on watching.

So I go into the kitchen. Mum's up against the sink with her back to me and she won't turn round right away, and when she does, it looks like she's been crying. And Dad turns on me and says, "Didn't it occur to you to phone, tell your mother you'd be missing dinner?"

Jesus, don't tell me all this is about me missing my sausage and mash.

"Bill," Mum starts up, "I've said it doesn't—"

"It does matter," snarls Dad. "It matters a lot. It's not just the dinner. It's his whole bloody attitude. His arrogance. You're part of this family, son. We're not just here to do your washing and dish your grub up."

He's not going to get to me. Not tonight. Not

when I feel this fantastic. I ignore him and turn very deliberately to Mum and say, "Sorry, Mum. I should've phoned. It was just—that girl I was telling you about, Portia, she let me sketch her, and then I took her out to dinner and—"

"Took her out to dinner?" snaps Dad. "What with? Oh, I forgot, you're in the money now aren't you? You come home drunk Friday night, drunk Saturday night, you sleep all day Sunday, and you miss dinner Monday *and* you miss it tonight without even the decency to phone and let your mother know."

I can feel my chest going tight, like it always does when he goes on at me. It's the scorn in his voice. The *judgement*.

"Look—I've been busy—"

"Sure you've been busy. We had a phone call from your college today. Why are you missing lectures, why are you not turning up for classes, why are you late turning in assignments in *all four subjects*—"

"Oh, for God's sake, Dad. Everyone gets those phone calls, it's no big deal. . . ."

"No big deal? You arrogant little shit. Nothing's a big deal to you, is it, apart from what *you* want. We've worked hard to support you in college, and you just swan around, working when you feel like it—"

"Jesus, will you *get off my back*. You don't pay for me to go to college!"

"*I don't pay for you?* Who the hell d'you think's paying to keep *this* show on the road? What do *you* contribute?"

"Dad, how *can* I—I'm doing A levels—"

"Are you? You don't seem to be. You seem to be spending your time doing just what the hell you like. And you live here, free board and lodging, nothing in return—"

"Oh, great. That's how you see me, isn't it—a fucking *parasite*—"

Suddenly, shockingly, Mum bangs down both her fists on the edge of the sink and yells, "Oh, for Christ's sake stop it, the pair of you!" She turns and faces us, eyes wet and glaring. "I hate hearing this! I hate hearing you fight. It makes me feel *ill*."

Dad shoots a look of focused malevolence at me, like it's all my fault Mum's upset. She's turned away now, back to the sink. So I walk out of the kitchen, stomp upstairs, shut myself in my room, slam my headphones on. Then I pick up my folder and pull out my drawings of Portia, and find the last two I did, the ones where I really got her. I prop them up at the end of the bed, and while I stare at them I relive kissing her, I relive the way her face looked as we started, as we finished, I go over every second of it. Until I'm so turned on I can't move.

I can hear Dad's voice raised, coming from downstairs, Mum's shrill answer, and I turn the volume up on my tape deck. I'm not going to let all that shit in. I'm not going to let it get me. And I'm more determined than ever now about tomorrow night.

I stare at Portia's face and I think—I've got to make money. I've got to get out.

And then my hands move down and I'm out of my head.

Chapter 18

I go into college next day early mainly to get away from my house but I can't say I learn much. I'm roaming around tense, waiting for the night, and inside my head I'm practising my authentic teen presence and teen-culture attitude. I only see Portia once, passing in a corridor. She doesn't stop, just gives me a conspiratorial spy-movie smile from under hooded eyes, which gets me off worrying about tonight and straight into sexual reminiscing and fantasy for the whole of the General Studies session that follows. I'm brought out of this pretty abruptly as I leave the room, though, by Chris shouting, "Hey—*shithead* you deaf or something?" and banging me across the shoulders so hard I'm practically skidding down the corridor.

"Fuck off, Chris, you nearly smacked me into the *wall* then!"

"Sorry, mate. We're getting a game together outside. Five-a-side. Come on."

"Oh . . . nah. Not up for it."

"Did I say you had a choice? Come on. Ollie's in, and Andy and Ryan. . . . We need you, mate. It's against those engineering bastards."

"Chris—leave it, OK? I've got that dinner tonight. The big one."

"Well, a game of footy is just what you need then. Unwind you a bit."

"Yeah, well, I don't want to get knackered, do I, before tonight."

"Playing as crap as you do, Rich, that isn't likely. Now come *on*."

And I find myself being hauled down to the pitches by the sports hall. The engineering bastards are already there, lined up like angry heifers, booting the ball about. They've all changed into their footy gear.

"Oh, shit," I announce smugly. "Haven't got my kit."

"You can borrow my spare," says Ryan.

"You mean the one you never wash?"

"That's it," he says. "Now come *on*, or it won't be just those bastards giving you a kicking."

In the end, it's quite a good match. We start off crap, and they get one in, but we don't let it get to us. Once I've got warmed up I feel all this energy powering through me and I really go for it, and I get our first goal from the sweetest possible pass from Ollie. We do the whole high-five *yee-ees* irritating triumph stomp just to wind the opposition up, and it works, 'cos only five minutes later Ryan smacks in another one. And at full time, we've actually beaten the engineering bastards three–two.

"You did all right there, Rich," says Ollie approvingly, as we troop into the changing room. "Once you'd stopped pratting about."

"Yeah," says Ryan. "You should turn up a bit more often. Practise with us."

"Got other things on his mind, haven't you, mate?" says Chris. "Fame, fortune. Portia McCutcheon."

"Ah," says Ollie knowingly. "You pulled her yet?"

"Maybe," I murmur, all smooth.

"That means he hasn't," says Ryan, who has a bit of a thing about me being more attractive to birds than he is. "What about you, Chris? What about Natalie?"

I feel a bit guilty when he says this, because *I* should've remembered to ask, shouldn't I, but the guilt evaporates when Chris's face splits in a grin and he says. "*Oh*, yes."

• • •

I leave college at about three, head home, and stake out the bathroom. I'm so nervous I can see my hand shake as I squirt shower gel onto it, and my breathing's coming out like I'm dying of pneumonia or something. "It's your drawings that count," I keep muttering to myself. "They're on trial, not you. As long as you don't actually fall over or throw up on your plate, you'll be OK."

I get The Shirt out, and seeing what it does to my eyes as I slide it over my shoulders boosts my confidence immediately. The jeans are OK, the loafers sort-of need a polish, but I don't want to look like I tried too hard, my hair still looks great.

I'm going to go. I'll be early at Nick's but I'll crack up completely if I hang round here too much longer. If I hang around at Nick's maybe I'll absorb some of the positive successful energy in his house. Maybe it'll rub off on me.

I leave a pointedly neat note for Mum who isn't back from work saying *I shan't be in for supper, I have my Marley-Hunt dinner.* It oozes self-pity 'cos it's uncharacteristically neat and polite and just the act of leaving it implies she might be so uncaring she's *forgotten* that my huge future-deciding night is tonight. I head for the door and then I stop. Coat. I haven't got a coat. My old pelt just won't do. If they see me in that at the restaurant door, they'll bar me. Possibly for life.

I peer out of the front door and see it's not actually raining and make a top-speed decision. I'll go without one. It's just about acceptable now at five-thirty on a fine May evening and if I shiver like shit on the way home, who cares, it's all over.

When I get to Nick's Barb opens the door to me with both the lurchers, who snuffle appreciatively up my legs. "Hi!" she says, warmly. "You look great, Nick! That shirt is brilliant!"

"Thanks," I say, smiling. "Look—I'm sorry I'm so early. I just felt so twitchy and nervous I—"

"No worries. Course you feel nervous. But you relax and leave it to Nick, yeah? He's the salesman. You're the—"

"Product?"

"Artist," she laughs. "And don't you forget it. Don't get carried away by all this commercial crap, will you?"

"No," I say.

"Well, come on, come in. Come and have a drink."

I follow her into the hall, and she says, "Um—I can't help noticing that fabulous shirt is all you have on. Won't you get cold?"

"Oh, I'll be great," I gabble. "It's warm out."

"Not that warm, Rich." She's opened up a

cupboard door set into the side of the stairs, half disappeared inside it. "And Nick said he's planning to walk to the restaurant. It's only twenty minutes or so away, but—Ah! Here it is!" And she emerges with this wonderful worn-looking black leather jacket. "Try it. It's a bit eighties. It's a bit Duran Duran. But you're tall, you'll carry it."

I put it on and I feel fantastic, like a Russian spy. "Oh, that looks *good*," she says. "Wear that. Honestly, Rich, you'll freeze otherwise."

I'm dying to see what I look like but reckon it would sound too vain to ask directions to a mirror, so I just thank her and follow her on to the kitchen. Freddie's rolling noisily about on the floor with the two dogs and a big rubber bone, and Scarlett is at the table, painstakingly spooning red jam into a tray of pastry cases. "Queen of Hearts, eh?" I say.

"What?" she says crisply.

"Um—Queen of Hearts, she made some tarts, all on a summer's day—"

"I don't think they were *jam* tarts," says Scarlett sniffily.

"Yeah, they were," says Barb. "Strawberry jam. Just like that."

"H'm," says Scarlett, unimpressed, continuing to spoon.

Scarlett would be a brilliant Queen of Hearts,

I reckon, like in *Alice in Wonderland*. Going around executing people like me.

Barb hands me a beer from the fridge, and Nick bursts through the door, looking sharp in what must be this season's black suit. "Hey, kid!" he yells. "What you doing in my jacket?"

"He's borrowing it," says Barb, and she walks over and turns the collar up under my ears. "Actually I think he's keeping it. It looks better on him. It's too scruffy for you, Nick."

"Bollocks," says Nick. "I want it back."

"You can't afford to look scruffy, babe. You're too old for scruffy."

"Bollocks!" bellows Nick happily, and he shoulder-barges Barb so she collapses sideways, laughing, onto the bench that runs along one side of the kitchen. Then she lobs a cushion at him, hard, yelling, "Getting *old*!"

This couple don't treat each other with anything like what my parents think of as respect. I love it. Their kind of disrespect is a whole lot sexier.

Nick claps me on the shoulder. "So, mate," he says, "just how nervous are you?"

"Um—twelve on a scale of one to ten?"

"Good, good. You'll be fine. Pass us a beer."

We sit and drink the beer, in more or less edgy silence, then Nick says "Let's get going. Thought we'd walk. Calm the nerves—"

"And work off some of that fat you're piling on, pooch," says Barb.

We get to Harvey's a good fifteen minutes before the Marley-Hunt barons are due to arrive because it's important, Nick says, to check out that the table's OK and be there *in situ* to meet and greet our guests.

Harvey's is a modern building, and they've gone for the over-the-top film-set look. The door is huge, crude and wooden, like King Kong might come bursting through at any minute. Nick twists the great brass ring, and the door swings open, and a waiter swoops on us before we've so much as taken two steps inside. He takes Nick's name, and relieves me of the fabulous leather jacket. I hate handing it over. It made me feel brave, wearing it—kind of heroic, and safe too. But still—I've got The Shirt on underneath. I'm fine.

There's a bar in the entrance. It's all dead classy. Wood floor, brass rails, like the deck of a ship. And filled with green light, like the *Titanic* going down. Farther in the restaurant, it turns into a space ship. Lines of white lights set into the walls, shiny doors, and these hologram waiters moving around.

On a table at the side is a huge crazy vase of flowers, filling the place with scent. Those flowers must've cost the earth, I think.

And I think again—money is style. Money is beauty.

Our table is a great oval-shaped one up against the window. I count six chairs. "I thought you said there were two, maybe three people coming?" I hiss.

Nick shakes his head. "Three, maybe four. Now let's wait at the bar."

Perched at the bar, I have another beer, which on top of the two I had at Nick's house is maybe not such a good idea, and we wait mostly in silence. Nick pulls out a packet of fags and automatically offers one to me and I'm so edgy I almost take one before I remember I don't smoke. I can see Nick mentally scrolling through his sales pitch as he inhales and I try and do the same but I end up just working on breathing.

Actually, I'm not as scared as I thought I'd be. I pulled Portia last night. I can pull this off too.

And then the Marley-Hunt barons are here. The door-waiter is kind of fanning them towards us, and Nick leaps off his stool, all welcoming enthusiasm and dynamic energy, like a big power switch has just been pulled inside him.

There's three of them, three guys. They're graded in height and (differently) in age, but they all have the same kind of classy suit and glossy, moneyed sheen. I'm introduced to them and their names pass out of my head like vapour. They decline Nick's offer of a drink at the bar, and then all five of us are being herded towards the table.

We're still getting ourselves sat down (me opposite Nick, a Marley-Hunt guy on either side of me) as two ice-filled buckets on stands, with gold-foil-wrapped bottle-necks sticking out are plonked beside us. "What's this, Hanratty?" growls the oldest Marley-Hunt. "Celebrating already?"

Nick smirks, and says, "Oh, you know me, John. I like to get in the mood." Then he and a waiter dish out the bubbly and they're all ra-raaing about how good it is to meet up, how this new campaign is going to make marketing history, etc, etc, and I'm smiling like I've got rubber bands hooking the sides of my mouth to my ears.

It takes me only five minutes to realize I'm only a very small part of this deal. I'm like an addendum, a PS. They're all talking strategies and financing and stuff I haven't got a clue about. What goes on the alcopop bottle itself is just a very small part of the picture, evidently. And then suddenly Nick says, "Hey. Before the table gets overridden with food, let me show you Rich's stuff, yeah?"

And the folder's out on the table, and my pictures are being fanned across the white cloth. I feel like I'm going to pass out, my blood's pumping so hard. The youngest of the barons goes "Wow," but apart from that there's silence.

I'm going to die.

And then Nick says, "You see? Solid impact. They're raw. You don't know what the hell to say, do you?"

"Well, you've got talent, Rich," says the middle baron. "I'll say that for you."

"These images are speaking to the id," says Nick. "They're speaking to something deep down, that's their power."

"They're different," says the youngest baron. "I'll say that for them."

"He's seventeen and a half," says Nick proudly, like he's announcing my birth weight.

"But aren't they a bit . . . nasty?" says the oldest baron tentatively. "A bit gruesome? For something you're going to drink out of?"

"We wouldn't use these drawings," replies Nick. "We'd make something new, something more positive. But keep that energy in them, that basic young raw energy. And more, guys. I'm thinking ditch the label. I'm thinking etching."

There's a kind of minor explosion round the table. "Etching?" "Etching on glass?" "D'you know how expensive that would be?"

"There're new processes now," says Nick eagerly. "Kind of fake etching. Just think—you ditch *labelling*. You ditch this thing that gets torn, dirty, washed away. You make something as simple and permanent as the bottle itself. *Part* of the bottle itself. How cool is that?"

And they're off. Talking costs, practicalities, and something called *guerrilla marketing*, and I'm an addendum again. I pick up a couple of my pictures and shift them around on the table a bit and think, Is that . . . it? Is that all I have to do?

The middle baron has fixed me with a studied, sincere look. "I'm intrigued by this youth thing, Richard," he says. "That's where the analysts tell us the money is nowadays. Low responsibility equals high disposable income, hmmm?"

Not in my case, I think. Low responsibility maybe, *nil* disposable income a dead cert. But I nod thoughtfully back at him, and he goes on, "Thing is, I think we need to take this whole marketing research deal very seriously. I contacted Youth Monitor the other day—"

Nick snorts with jovial disgust. "Martin, plea-*ease*! Those kind of youth marketeer outfits make me laugh. They're like, adults *stalking* kids, *spying* on kids, trying to check out what makes them tick over. But you can't do that. The world of the teenager is vague, guys. It's ever changing. It's elusive. And the minute you've analysed something, got it down, it's gone, OK? The kids've moved on."

There's an impressed pause around the table,

then the youngest baron says, "OK. Point taken. But if that's the case how the hell are we going to—"

Nick lunges across the table and seizes my arm, raises it in the air like I'm a prizefighter. "By coming up with the genuine article. That's how."

All three Marley-Hunts turn and look at me, and I cringe my arm away from Nick's hand and *blush*. Possibly as uncool as you could get. Great timing, Rich.

"Rich is an original. He's not *targeting* youth, he's youth itself. Just think what the trade'll make of it! Think of the exposure!"

"But it has to look good too," ventures middle baron. "It can't work just as a gimmick."

"Martin, it will look *fantastic*. Trust me. I've been around long enough to know talent when it smacks me across the kisser. We get some ideas together, we commission Rich, we decide on an *image*, a *creature*, Rich's creature, and we go from there."

There's a kind of positive lull in the conversation then, with all three barons smiling and nodding and raising their eyebrows at each other. Nick looks straight at me and winks, smiling determinedly. There's an aura of adrenaline round him, like a hunter just before the kill. I'm infected. I can feel my heart thud in excitement.

Maybe it can, maybe it's going to *happen*. . . ?

Then the waiter, who's come up to the table and been driven away by the intensity of the conversation about three times up till now, arrives yet again and hands out huge menus.

"Guys—choose," says Nick. "Let's eat. Let's relax." You can tell from his face he thinks the meeting's almost over. He's done his work.

I exchange one last hopeful smile with him and look down at my menu.

Shit! What *is* this stuff?

Chapter 19

Banana Leaf Wrapped Kingfish, Citrus Achiote Marinade, Plantain Crisps.

Navajo Stuffed Vegetables, Corn Tamale in Swiss Chard Leaves, Stuffed Squash, Flat Mushroom Bread.

I'm not even sure it's *food*. Jesus, what am I going to pick? Not the *Fresh Raw Oysters with Red Onion and Coriander Relish* for a start. My head's spinning from the incredible excitement and the beer and champagne and just the sight of the words on the card makes me queasy. Nick and the barons are anticipating, selecting—rolling the names round their mouths like they're tasting the food already. In a panic I go for *Caesar Salad, Parmesan and Anchovy Wafer* to start with 'cos I have dim memories of eating a Caesar salad before, and *Seared Spiced Filet of Beef, Sweet*

Potato Tamale, and Spring Greens (spring *greens*?) to follow.

Then Nick gets stuck into the wine list, and heavy discussions with the barons on what would go with what. Meanwhile, the waiter brings up five frosty water glasses and fills them. Thinking re-hydration, I grab mine and down it in a couple of gulps, and the waiter refills it again. I pick it gratefully up again, and sink half, and he walks over, very slow, very deliberate, and tops it up once more.

He doesn't like me. I can tell. He sneered when he wrote my order. I reckon he doesn't mind being servile to old rich gits 'cos they're old, but faced with a young stud like me in a top-rate shirt, and he's all eaten up by envy. I'm tempted to take another slurp, just to watch him being forced to pogo-stick forward again, but I'm basically nice so I don't.

The food arrives, and I find I can put it in my mouth. I even enjoy what it tastes like. I work on eating nicely, with my gob shut, finishing each mouthful before I fork in another. I'm doing OK I reckon. I'm even starting to relax a bit. And then the oldest baron twists towards me and says "So. College life."

I stare at him glassily.

"What's it like?" he goes on.

And I have the horrible realization that my

work's just beginning. Nick's sold them the blueprint, now I have to come on all authentic, the kid straight up from the streets.

But I go for it. I start talking, stream-of-consciousness stuff. I use lots of hip words I wouldn't normally be caught dead using. I go through alienation, despair, anger. I describe being crushed by soul-dead zombies paid to teach. I dip in and out of the drug scene. I toy with disconnected sex.

And I've got 'em. I can see middle baron licking his lips, oldest baron shaking his head, youngest baron smirking, all "Yeah, I was part of that too." And then reminiscing takes over, and I can sit back a bit while the three of them tell college stories, and Nick shoots me another triumphant look over the plates and glasses.

There's only one really, really bad moment. I'm describing Huw's art classes, making Huw sound like an insane unreconstructed Welsh wildman (pretty accurate stuff) and Nick interrupts and I seize the opportunity to fork some more beef in my mouth. But before I've got it chewed down someone asks me another question and as I try to talk and swallow at the same time I chomp into the side of my fucking *tongue*.

I'm so boozed up I can hardly cope with the pain. It's shocking, surreal, like being stabbed, and for one cliff-hanging moment I think I'm going to pass out or be sick or both. I blink furiously, breathe, reach for my water, and Nick, bless him, covers for me, and then when I think I can risk it I stand up and say, "Excuse me," and weave my way towards the biggest door I can see.

"That's the kitchen, sir," sneers the snotty waiter.

I slow down, stop.

"There's the Rest Room," he goes on, pointing. "There."

I change directions, concentrating on not puking up. I'm not going to give the snotty waiter the satisfaction of acknowledging I've heard him. Safe inside a cubicle, head tipped forward, I realize just how much alcohol I've put away. But I'm OK. The pain's gone off. And I'm going to stand up in a second and head for the water fountain and then I'll be *fine*.

The nausea's receding too, and in its place comes euphoria. Thank *God*. I'm not going to puke—I'm cool—I'm coping. I stand up, and turn to take a piss, and notice this little glass box inset into the wall. It's a sculpture I guess. Inside it is a chrome clamp and fixed in the clamp is a green pepper, going very wrinkled at the top.

Intrigued, I button up and check the other two cubicles. Same box in each. One has a clamped aubergine, and one has a sagging leek. Weird.

I take a big pull of water, and walk out. Snotty

waiter's there, asking unpleasantly, "Everything all right, sir?"

"Fine!" I bark. I head on, experience a moment's panic when I forget where our table is, stop as if I want to enjoy the view for a bit, then spot it and saunter over.

I can feel that waiter sniggering at me behind my back.

I hope it's his job to change the vegetables in the bogs. I really do.

As I sit down I see that coffee has arrived plus these little dishes of posh chocolates that the oldest baron calls "petty fours" and I realize we're nearly through it, we've nearly got there. I'm looking forward to being on my own with Nick and talking it over, like you rehash the best bits in a football match. Nick offers brandy, gets no takers, and calls for the bill. When it arrives I scan it upside down across the table and feel like my eyes are crossing in disbelief. It's *well* into three figures. Add a bit and double it and it'd be *four* figures. Jesus. Unreal. And the tip line, I can see that too. Massive. How come they think they can charge more for the same act of laying down a plate of food just 'cos that food's grossly over-priced?

Nick, however, seems unconcerned. He does the business with the gold credit card, and then we're all shifting about and standing up, ready to go. The little silver tray with gold card and receipt comes back and Nick picks them up and stows them in his wallet and then he pulls out a twenty quid note and lobs it down as though the snotty waiter's been such an all round great guy he deserves something a bit extra.

No *way*, I think. Waiters are fetching our coats and easing us into them, and as I slip mine on I hang back a bit and let my hand trail over the table and then I *sli-ide* that twenty quid note up into the lovely long concealing leather sleeve.

And I'm solvent again.

Chapter 20

"You did good, kid," Nick's crowing, as we leg it back to the centre of town. "Real good."

"Yeah? I felt like a total phoney half the time."

"S'OK. That's selling."

"And I got all fucked up with my words, you know, when I was trying to tell them about how shit it was trying to draw to a curriculum. . . ."

"Look—you were an authentic teen oik! That's what they wanted. Not some smart-arse smoothy. I knew we'd got 'em when John started on about how underneath nothing had really changed for the young, blah blah, just on the surface, blah. That's what those guys wanted to know—that they weren't complete corporate dinosaurs. And you delivered."

"But Nick—I want them to want me for my

art, not 'cos they think I'm part of some fake hip teen scene. . . ."

"Just want them to want you. Who cares why."

There's a pause, then I say, "So—what d'you think the odds are?"

"For the account? Eighty per cent."

"*Yeah?*"

"Yeah. Look, Rich—I have to be straight with you—I could get the account and them not want to use you. But I think they liked your stuff. I think they thought it was different enough."

"So—do I start creating a new *creature* then?"

"No. Wait until they've thrashed it through. They took your drawings off with them and they'll get some ideas. Then—if they go with it—they'll give you directions. Specifications. OK?"

"Blimey. Specifications?"

"Yeah. Nothing too exact, don't worry."

"OK. How long will it take? For them to decide?"

"No idea. Weeks. Don't be impatient, darling. Put it on a back burner in your brain."

"You're joking. No chance. It's all I can think about."

"Keep busy then. Keep your mind off it. You can come and finish those bloody storyboards for a start. I need them by the end of next week."

I stop in my tracks and wail, "You said you weren't in a hurry for them!"

Nick keeps walking, and I hear, "In this business, that *isn't* a hurry. Now come on."

By the time we've reached the place where we split to go our separate ways, I've agreed to skip college next day, turn up at Abacus Design, and work flat out on the storyboards. I shouldn't do this, 'cos I'm in trouble for skipping so much college anyway, but I don't give a shit and I may as well be hung for a sheep as a lamb.

And I might get to take Portia out again, so I really need the money.

Oh, bugger. That reminds me. I need to transfer that stolen twenty from the pocket of Nick's loaned leather jacket to my jeans before I hand it back to him, and I need to do it fast 'cos we've both stopped walking and we're about to say goodbye.

Nick claps me on the arm and says, "Great stuff, Rich. Thanks for coming." I grin and delve unobtrusively in my pocket with one hand while I'm starting to pull the jacket off my shoulder with the other.

"Here," I go. "Thanks for lending it to me." I stow the twenty safely in my fist and hand Nick his jacket.

He puts his head on one side and says, "Oh, sod it."

"What?"

"Keep it. Keep the jacket. Barb's right. Too scruffy for me now."

I can't believe it. I feel my jaw drop open like a cartoon character. "You're joking."

"Nah. You have it. Prize for being such a little arse-licking star tonight. I really think we've done it, darling. And it's huge. I can afford ten new jackets if we land this one."

"But . . . but it's your *jacket*. . . ."

"Yeah. I'll get a new one. I've seen the one I want."

"You have? How much?"

"About seven hundred quid."

"JE-sus!"

"Barb'll go crazy. But it's her fault. She made me give you that one, right?"

I don't actually sleep in the jacket, but I don't take it off for a good hour after I get home. I stand in front of my old bedroom mirror with the collar half up, and I turn my head sideways and put one eyebrow up and mouth, "Hi, Portia. All right?" Then I drape it over the chair and lie down on my bunk and look at it. Sam wakes up and I tell him I'll break all the bones in his puny little body if he goes anywhere near it. I ignore him at first when he asks me where I got it from and then when he pesters on and on I go, "Drug running."

His eyes get enormous and I can tell he's about

to go and wake Mum up and tell her, so I say, "Only joking, you little jerk. Jesus, have you *got* a brain? Now shut up, I'm thinking."

I'm thinking about Portia just about dying with lust when she sees me in that jacket.

I get to Abacus Design nice and early the next day and get stuck straight into the Chiccy Bits storyboards. I'm working as fast as I can go, and I find I've speeded up a lot now I've got used to sketching the characters. It still takes the best part of an hour to do one frame but I'm working on it. I've got the werewolf-pig dog off the fastest, and I'm getting bolder and more economical with the backgrounds. It's a bit dull, to be honest, the same thing over and over, but I press on till lunch time when Camilla appears with a whole stack of cellophane-wrapped filled baguettes and kindly chucks me one and even more kindly doesn't ask me for the money for it.

No one seems to be taking a break. Everyone stays at their desks, tipping themselves back in their seats to eat so they don't splat mayo on their work.

Blimey. I'm dying for a change of scene. I think about Nick's rubbish-filled flat upstairs, how much I'd like to go up there, throw those huge windows open and sit and stare at the rooftops. Or go downstairs and sit on the edge of the canal. I think of the college cafeteria, having a chat. I think maybe college isn't such a grind after all.

Then I think of the money. I've done three frames, I'm into the fourth. Nick gave me thirty quid a board, thereabouts. Hope he'll pay me in advance again.

When everyone's packing up at about six o'clock I am just about on my knees with exhaustion, but I have two complete storyboards to take into Nick's office and hand over. Nick gives them a quick look, says, "Great. Ta. Bung 'em over there." I bung 'em, but I stay in the office, and he glances up, pained. "What you want?"

"Well—I'll let you off the VAT if you pay me cash now."

"Ha bloody ha. Go on then." He sighs, rummages in the wooden bowl in front of him, finds a key, and unlocks the tiny drawer at the edge of his desk. I've seen this before. I'm like a Pavlov dog, panting. And then he's flicking off three twenties and a ten and flipping them towards me. I make this ten pounds over the odds but I'm not going to complain.

"Ah, shit," he mumbles, locking the drawer up again. "I've had enough. It's a great evening. I'm going home early."

Early? What the hell's late then?

"You want to come back with me?" he goes on.

"Barb was asking about you the other day. Said she'd like to see you again. God knows why. We're having a barbecue, if the weather keeps good. Get some friends round. Why don't you come?"

I grin, pleased. I think about supper waiting for me at home, dried out macaroni and cheese and simmering tension, and I think about Nick's place and a hot steak and lots of cold beer.

"That'd be great," I say. "If it's OK. Just got to phone home first."

Chapter 21

Money. That's the reason Nick and Barb are so sociable I reckon. They can afford to be. There're half a dozen people standing around in the large garden behind Nick's house, and a few more sitting chatting in the conservatory, and there's a whole stack of wine and beer and a great platter of steaks waiting to get slapped on the barbie. Me and the lurchers (who are sitting near by, quivering from nose to tail with greed) are drooling at the sight of them. I wait, a beer in one hand, a fistful of corn chips in the other, while Freddie kicks a ball against my legs.

"Oy," I say, cheerfully. "Cut it out."

"Cut it out yourself," he says, and slams the ball into me again.

I want to slap the little brat round the head, but you don't do that to the son of your hosts. You're nice to him, then your hosts will like you.

"Give you a game?" I say, heartily. "Down at the end of the garden?"

"*Yeah!*"

He jumps off, and I follow. He's got a little goal thing all set up and we spend fifteen minutes or so trying to save each other's shots. I let him put a few past me and he goes through the whole triumph-stomp thing, running about screeching "*YESSS!*" He's OK, Freddie, I decide. He's a laugh. I show him a bit of fancy stuff with the ball, and then Barb appears, all smiling and approving 'cos I'm playing with her kid, and says, "Come on, boys. There's a whole load of steaks nearly done."

I walk up to the house and nearly do a fast about-turn to the bottom of the garden again. Tigger—the up-herself vampire from the party on Saturday night—is standing there nose to nose with Nick. She's all in white this time, jeans and T-shirt—sort of studied look-at-me casual. I find myself glancing round for her daughter, but Bonny's nowhere to be seen.

And then Tigger spots me. She lunges at me, claws waving, earrings swinging. "I hear it went *well* darling!" she gushes.

It? Went well? What went well? My plan to pull Portia? The Big Dinner? Since when has she kept track of my life?

"Nicky says they were very *taken* with you,"

she gurgles on. "He thinks he's got the account!"

"Well . . ." I mumble. "He said he thought—"

"You must be *so thrilled*!"

"Yeah, well, if it comes off I'll—"

"Darling, it will come off! It will! I've got a sixth sense about these things!"

Just then, *thank God*, Barb joins us, a steak on a plate in one hand, a basket of bread in the other, and Tigger focuses on her. "Your daughter's dragged my baby upstairs with her!" she squeals, half jolly, half accusatory. "Said she was going to give her a *make-over*!"

Barb quails visibly. "Ah. A make-over, eh? That's very—er—*sporting* of Bonny. Scarlett's dead into make-up at the moment. Here—Tigger—have a steak."

"Oh, not *red meat*, darling," shrieks Tigger in disgust, as though Barb was offering her a dog turd. "I absolutely never touch it!"

"I'll touch it," I say, and Barb grins and thrusts the plate into my hand.

"Oh, you *cavemen*!" coos Tigger. "You're all the same!"

I don't know how Tigger stops herself gagging on her words half the time, I really don't. I preserve a dignified silence and collect two hunks of crusty bread from Barb. I'm just easing my steak between them when Scarlett—shimmering in a glittery nylon catsuit and a puce feather boa—appears at our side. She's towing Bonny along behind her who's looking a bit over the top around the eyes but on balance pretty glam and sexy. She's got rusty-coloured lipliner on and it makes you notice what a good shape her mouth is.

But Tigger takes one look and shrieks, "Oh my GOD, darling! You look FRIGHTFUL!"

Scarlett's face crumples like she's been punched.

"No she *doesn't*!" Barb turns on Tigger, showing all her teeth, like a lioness protecting her cub. "She looks absolutely *wonderful*!"

Then she turns to Scarlett and says, "It's great, darling! Really great!"

"It is," agrees Bonny fervently. "I love it, Scarlett, honestly."

"Oh, for heaven's SAKE," guffaws Tigger. "I only meant— well, it's like Hallowe'en make-up, isn't it? I mean—it's *meant* to be frightful?"

At this Scarlett's face collapses completely, Bonny gives out a little high-pitched moan, and Barb's fists clench like she might take a slug at Tigger. And I hear myself saying, "I think she looks dead horny. Really sexy."

All four faces swing towards me. I fix my eyes on Scarlett's and repeat, "*Really* sexy."

"There you are!" crows Barb, triumphantly. "Rich should know, he's a boy! Tigger's just scared you've made her daughter look too sexy and she'll have all these guys running after her!"

Tigger sniggers out this sarcastic little superior laugh but she's too intimidated by the ferocious maternal energy coming off Barb to say anything else. There's a kind of intense pause, then Tigger spots a fresh victim who's just arrived and heads off, shrieking, "Hell-*o*, darling, haven't-seen-you-for-*yonks*!"

You can almost reach out and pat the pleasure we all feel at her departure. Barb grins like she's been left victorious on the field of battle, then she says, "Just going to check the meat," and wanders away.

"D'you really like Bonny's make-up?" asks Scarlett, directing a watery smile at me.

"Yeah, I do. I think you're very creative."

"D'you really think she looks horny?"

"You bet. Totally."

"What does horny mean exactly?"

"Um-aah . . ." Beside me, Bonny's sniggering, and I shoulder-barge her just a touch and say, "OK, *you* explain."

"It's a special type of boy-sexy," Bonny says.

"But you're a girl."

"Um—yeah. You know, Scarlett? I bet Rich'd like you to make *him* up too!"

"No he bloody wouldn't," I growl.

"He just said how creative he thought you

were," Bonny goes on, mercilessly. "And I'd love to see what you do with him."

"Lots of boys wore make-up in the seventies," Scarlett puts in eagerly. "I'm really interested in the seventies."

"So I see," I mutter. "That cat-suit is—"

"They wore glitter round their eyes and eyeliner. And sometimes lipstick. It was quite dramatic."

I pick up my steak sarnie and munch into it, hoping to let this particular conversation die, when Bonny breaks in with, "Rich wouldn't mind, would you, Rich? It'd be a real laugh."

"I don't think he wants me to," says Scarlett mournfully.

"*Yeah* he does. Look—he's had streaks put in his hair. He's cool about that kind of thing. Only uptight inhibited guys who are really anxious about their lack of masculinity mind about putting make-up on."

I gawp at Bonny, scouring my brain for something crushing to say in reply, when she says, "Finish your steak, *caveman,* and let's go."

Oh, what the hell. I'll look like a raving queen but I can wash it off, can't I, and it's better than having to make chat with all the grown-ups. I bolt down the rest of my steak, grab another bottle of beer, and let Scarlett haul me up to her room, with Bonny giggling in close attendance.

Scarlett's room, like you'd expect, is a make-believe palace. The head of her bed is a great gold-painted crown shape, complete with jewels on the spikes, and she has another crown above red velvet curtains half-drawn across a rack of clothes. There are two lamps that ought to be in a harem, mock leopard-skin on the bed, fake tiger-skin on the floor. The top of her dressing table cannot be seen for all the shiny baubles and bangles and beads strewn across it.

"Sit there!" she orders, pointing me towards a little purple throne. I sit down, and she directs a reading lamp straight at my face, like I'm about to get done by the Gestapo. Then she picks up a very frightening-looking pot with a big pink powder puff sticking out of it.

"Not *too* much," I whine.

"Don't be a baby," says Bonny.

"You're a bloody sadist, you are," I mutter, and shut my mouth just in time to stop it getting filled with powder. Then I shut my eyes too, and let them get on with it, Bonny acting on Scarlett's strict instructions. They're like a couple of witches, whispering over me, dabbing at my face with pencils and brushes, smearing potions on my skin. It's a weird, scary, sensual experience. I can smell Bonny's perfume, and I think I know which hands are hers as they move across my face.

And then Scarlett says, "Da-*da*! You can look!" And I snap open my eyes and head for her mirror.

Well, it could be worse. It could be a lot worse.

My skin's been whitened, my eyes have been ringed in black and splattered with silver, and I've got whitish ghoulish lips. But I don't look too much like a raving queen. More like a mime artist or something minor from a horror film.

"Great," I say. "That's quite a skill, Scarlett. Now how do I clean it off?"

"Give you two quid to go downstairs like that," says Bonny.

"Sod off."

"Go *on*!"

"No."

"Coward. I went down."

"You're a *girl*!"

"Well *spotted*! Three quid."

"Five." I'm weakening.

"Four."

"Done. But I still say you're a sadist. You're paying me to give you pervy thrills."

Bonny tips back her head and laughs at that, and I can't help it, I join in. Then she links her arm through mine and we go downstairs, Scarlett following on.

And no one really notices my face. I get the odd second glance, the odd double take, but that's it. "No one's taking the piss out of you," says Bonny, disappointed. "I'm not giving you four quid just to get *ignored*."

"Oh yes you are," I say. "A deal's a deal. Scarlett's my witness."

"You should only have to give him two pounds," pronounces Scarlett, like a judge. "And you should be allowed to take a photo of him."

"Oh, Sca, that's a brilliant idea," says Bonny, greedily. "You got a camera?"

Barb whisks by with a salad bowl the size of a laundry basket. She glances at me and says, "Oh, Rich, you are a *sport*. Want another steak?"

"Yeah!" I call after her, then I turn on Bonny and crow, "She noticed! She noticed! Four quid!"

"Barb doesn't count. Barb's *sensitive*."

"All right, you cow! I'll get myself noticed!" And I march into the kitchen, tagged by the girls. I simper my way past two blokes deep in conversation and wink at them. They ignore me. I walk stiff-legged and splay-armed like a zombie into the garden, eyes rolling. No one looks up. I collect my second steak from Barb at the barbie and stare about me but no one stares back. I head over to a garden bench and on the way I just about jam my face between Nick and a fat guy he's chatting to but Nick just bats me away.

Scarlett and Bonny are in fits by this time, and I give up. I sit mock-grumpily down on the bench and attack my steak, while Scarlett fetches the camera and Bonny takes two photos of me. Then they lead me upstairs again and Scarlett puts on a *Greatest Hits from the Seventies* tape and they're dancing about and cleaning my face off with girly face-creams. I feel a bit like a sultan being fussed over, in that harem room and all. It's quite nice.

After I've checked my face in the mirror and scraped a bit of glittery goo from the corners of my eyes, I check my watch and find it's nearly ten o'clock. "I ought to go," I say. "I've got stuff to do."

"Homework?" asks Bonny.

"Yeah, homework," I say. Not that I'm planning to do any, I just feel I ought to go. Fact is, it's getting all too easy to be in this big, stylish house with all its happy evidence of easy-come, easy-go money. I'm feeling the contrast to my home more deep and painful every time I come here.

"Bye, Scarlett," I say. "Thanks for the transformation."

"Any time," she says.

I go downstairs and call bye and thanks to Nick and Barb, and Bonny kind of follows me out to the door. She watches me as I pull Nick's—*my*—leather jacket on and says, "Aren't you going to claim your debt?" And she shows me the two pounds in her hand, ready.

"Nah," I say.

"Go on." She leans forward, and as she slips

the coins in my pocket she says, "Can I see you again?"
If it wasn't for the fact that she goes very very red I'd think I'd misheard her.

Christ. I don't know what to say. It must have taken her a hell of a lot of courage, asking me that.

"Well, I—"

"Nothing heavy," she interrupts, breathlessly. "Just maybe—a film or something. I mean—I was thinking about what you said, you know, here last Saturday, about spending too much time with Mum, about . . ."

"Yeah. Yeah, right. It's just—the thing is, Bonny, I've sort of got a girlfriend."

"Oh." Her face looks like it's had a door slammed in it.

"I mean—it's all been a bit sudden," I gabble on, like my words—any words—can make it better. "It's only just really happened. And it's not exactly sorted yet but, you know—"

"You hope it will be."

"Yeah. Yeah, I do."

"S'OK," she croaks. "Bye." And she turns and heads back into the house and I feel like a complete shit.

I could've gone to the cinema with her. I needn't have come out with that crap about having a girlfriend. She's a nice girl. She's *really* nice—funny and intelligent, with a face that grows on you rather than stuns you first-off.

It's just I'm infatuated with Portia.

I'm going into college tomorrow. Thirty-six hours without seeing her in the flesh is starvation, OK?

Chapter 22

I was pretty sure my black leather jacket would have a positive effect on Portia but if I'd known quite how dramatic that effect would be I swear I'd have worked myself into the ground to get hold of one before this. There I am, sitting in the canteen, mulling things over, minding my own, when two soft, slender hands with highly manicured lilac-coloured nails slide over my shoulders and make their way down my chest and this voice (Portia's) is cooing, "*Where* did you get *this*?"

I turn to look at her, which means our mouths are so close I could slip my tongue in, only I don't of course.

"I just *lo-ove* animal skins," she's going. "I know you shouldn't but I *do*. I used to have a fur coat, but my mum made me throw it out when she was on one of her animal right's bashes—she said it made her feel sick just to have it in the house."

"Why? What was it made of?"

"I dunno. Cat? I *lo-ved* that coat. You know what?" She gets closer to me, practically wedges her mouth inside my ear. "I used to like to wear it with nothing else. *On*. *You* know. In my bedroom."

Oh, God, oh *God*, I'm on meltdown here. How can I offer to let her repeat the experience with my jacket without sounding like someone out of a bad porn film?

I clear my throat lengthily, and meanwhile she's got her hands down inside my collar and she's slowly sliding the jacket off my back. I kind of undulate, helpless. "Can I try it on, Richy?" she wheedles.

Well, I'm hardly going to say no, am I? Seconds later she's stripped me and got my jacket slung round her own shoulders, and she's off prancing across the floor to where Jenny and everyone are sitting, goggle-eyed in admiration.

"How do I *look*?" she demands.

"Super," they say. "Fan-*tas*-tic." "Fab." They're all vying with each other to come out with the most syrupy superlatives they can think of. The jacket's far too big on her and she looks like a sexy biker chick. Then I act on one of my hunches. I stand up all macho and say, "OK, McCutcheon. Gimme my jacket back."

"Come and get it," she says.

Yes! I'm lunging at her before the words are even out of her mouth, and she's ducking away, giggling, and then I get hold of her, wrap both arms round her, and squeeze her to me, her back against my chest.

"Let *go* of me, Richy!" she squeals, and I mimic her with, "Give me my *jacket* back, Portia!" Part of me is cringing at acting like something out of an American teen sitcom but the other part is very, very happy.

"Can't I *borrow* it?" she demands.

"No. It's *mine*." I push my face into her hair and inhale. "Give it *back*!"

She wriggles round to face me, still inside my bear hug. "Do a swap?" she wheedles.

"What for? What have *you* got?" And then she's looking up, and I'm leaning down, and if this was an American teen sitcom we'd wind up in a snog and everyone would be going, *Aaaaaah*.

But it isn't an American teen sitcom, so we both pull back, awkwardly, and I let her get free of me. But she doesn't go far. And then she says, "So how did it go on Wednesday?"

She remembered, she *remembered*. "OK," I say. "Pretty good actually. They've taken my stuff away, they're going to think about it, talk it through—it's just like the first stage, this. All the financial guys have to have their say. But Nick's eighty per cent sure he's got the account."

She seems impressed. "Who's Nick?"

"You know—the guy I told you about. The ad agency guy." I linger on the words. Then I hear myself saying, "So when are you going to come out with me again?"

"I thought we were going to go out when you got the account."

"That's to Harvey's. This is an eighty per cent celebration, right? What about the Pitcher and Piano?"

God, I'm witty. Portia giggles, then floors me with, "OK. Tonight if you like."

"Yeah?"

"Yeah. Just for a quick drink. One condition."

"What?"

"You let me wear your jacket!"

"Deal," I say, and then I suddenly grab the jacket by its lapels and pull her back towards me. We're suspended cornily like that for a few seconds, her looking up, all challenging, me looking down, wanting to kiss her so bad I can't breathe, then I shuck the jacket off her shoulders down to her waist and she's trapped. She giggles, and struggles away, while I hold on to one leather arm and watch her slither free. And then I've got my jacket back, and I'm wondering if she's feeling half as turned on as I am, and whether she's disappointed I didn't go for it.

She's looking at me with mockery in her eyes. "*Bully,*" she says.

"*Thief,*" I reply.

"You said I could *borrow* it."

"You can wear it tonight. When we meet."

"Don't you trust me?"

"Not an inch."

She grins at me triumphantly, and says, "OK. Meet you there. Seven o'clock?"

"OK," I say.

"Inside or out?"

"Out. On the terrace. Then you won't look like an idiot wearing my jacket." And then—God I'm *good*—I just kind of raise my eyebrows at her and turn on my heel and smooth it out of the cafeteria.

I make it to my English class only minutes late. I put my jacket back on and sit there with my face turned sideways into the collar, trying to find Portia's scent there. And I sit through the next hour oblivious to all the chat going on about Shakespeare's dramatic irony because I'm replaying that sweet cafeteria scene over and over and over again in my head.

Chapter 23

"So—how's life in the arid world of commercial exploitation then, boyo?"

"Jesus, Huw, they don't still say *boyo* in Wales do they?"

"Only to English bastards like you. Now answer the question. You had a decision yet?"

"No. Course not. These things take time."

"Ha! They won't take their time when they chew you up and spit you out, lad. They'll be speedy enough then."

Huw's in an up mood 'cos it's nearly the weekend and he can escape to his shed where he sculpts and doesn't have anything to do with pupils for a whole two days. I know I won't be able to get away from him until I've let him bounce me around for a bit, so I say, "Look, Huw, why are you such a snob about art that sells stuff?"

"Art doesn't *sell* stuff, lad. Art doesn't exist to

sell. Art exists to help us recover the sensation of life, to make us feel things, to make the *stone stony*."

"*What?*"

"Over your head, that, was it, boy?"

Huw's eyeballing me, all victorious. I rally myself and say, "Look—art can be anything. I was at this restaurant the other day, they had these glass cases with real vegetables in little clamps—"

"That was not art, lad. That was some pretentious poser putting vegetables in clamps."

"They were in the bog."

"Ha! Well, maybe it was art, then."

"Huw—I gotta go. Got a date."

"Oh, *Duw*, *Duw*, caught between sex and money, what hope has the poor sucker got?"

And he walks off before I can come back with a reply. One day I really am going to lob something very hard at the back of his irritating retreating Welsh head.

I decide not to go home first. This is partly because I'm meeting Portia early, seven o'clock, and partly 'cos I don't need to change or anything, 'cos I don't want to look like I'm trying too hard, and mostly 'cos my house is such a downer I want to steer well clear of it.

I feel *so* good. I thought getting off with Portia

that night after Allesandro's might be a one-off, that she might go back to being distanced and cool and snotty with me once more. But no way. Our relationship has moved up a whole new gear. It's *revving*. All it took was me looking smooth and leather-clad, boasting about the Marley-Hunt account, and a bit of hard cash. And my formidable snogging technique of course.

And I'm rich again, and that makes me feel even better. I've got the best part of ninety quid left—seventy from the storyboards, and a twenty the snotty waiter never knew he was supposed to get. I've only broken into a tenner, to get lunch and stuff. I'm rich enough to take on whatever the night with Portia brings *and* go shopping next week. I want another pair of jeans, or maybe a shirt. And some more aftershave.

I count the change in my jeans pocket, and find it's more than enough for a round of drinks. Then I remember something and shove my hand in my jacket pocket and my nails tap against Bonny's two pounds. I pull them out and look at them and just for a minute they make me feel really sad. I think—I should've given them back to her. But I don't suppose that would've helped.

I'm not really scared Portia is going to stand me up, but I am pretty sure she's going to be late. I buy myself a bottle of beer and find a nice empty table outside the Pitcher and Piano, overlooking the canal. It's the same canal that the Abacus Design offices are on, but at this end of town it's wider, cleaner, and with much more green along the banks. It's a great place to meet a girl. Romantic. Classy. The evening's quite warm still, and there's even a bleary-looking sunset up in the sky.

I wait a long fifteen minutes, and I'm drinking fast, 'cos I'm excited, nervous. Then, just as I'm draining the bottle, wondering if I should wait for Portia or get another one in now, she makes her entrance.

God she is *stunning*. She spots me, but doesn't wave or smile. She just widens her eyes, all dramatic, and then she glances to each side, as if checking there's no one here she knows, and sashays over to me. And I know in a flash she's into some fantasy in her head, she's getting off on playing the role of the unfaithful girlfriend who just can't help herself, and I know what I have to do to take part in this fantasy is *pounce.*

So I stand up and grab her, like I just can't help myself either, and she wails, "I really should *not* be here!"

I land a kiss by the side of her mouth, then one on her lips, and I hug her to me and say, "Yes you should. Yes you should."

"No! It's stupid. I'm being a bitch."

"No you're not."

"I *am*."

"What did you say to Tony?"

"Nothing. I didn't have to. He goes to the gym Fridays. He always does. I never meet him till about nine."

"So it's OK. We have two hours. Or we would've done, McCutcheon, if you'd been on *time*."

She giggles. "Sorry. I just—I wasn't sure. At the last moment I was thinking I should turn around and go back."

"Shut up. What you want to drink?"

"Vodka and orange. Please."

I shoot into the bar to get the drinks like I'm racing against the clock, which I suppose I am. I want to wring the essence out of every minute I have with her. My blood's pounding and at the same time one side of my brain is very, very cool. It's set back, watching all this, watching Portia play-act. The game she's playing is kind of sexy and sickening, both at the same time. I ought to want her to stop playing it, I suppose, but I know I don't give a shit what she does as long as I get to look at her. As long as I get to watch her mouth as it moves, the way she shows her teeth, the way her throat arches back.

I arrive back at the table and lay down the drinks and she says, "Thanks." Then she gazes at me meaningfully and says, "I'm cold."

"Oh—right." I strip off my jacket and lay it

round her shoulders, tucking it into her neck, and this time I let myself rub my whole face against her hair. "You smell great," I mutter.

"*This* smells great," she echoes, nuzzling into my coat. "God—I *lo-ove* leather."

Portia is some sensualist, that much is clear. I force myself to move round to the opposite side of the table again, and sit down. What the hell do we talk about, that's the problem. What is there to say? Then the Steele go-for-it instinct rises to the fore again, and I murmur, "Dump Tony. Come out with me."

"Oh, *Richy*. I am out with you."

"You know what I mean."

"I can't just dump him. I can't. Anyway—I'm really *fond* of him."

"So why are you here now?"

"I told you. I'm a bitch."

"No you're not. And that's not a reason."

"You're fishing for compliments."

"Well give me some then."

"Oh, Richy. You know I like you. I always have. We've always had this . . . I dunno. *Connection*."

Yeah, I think. Sex. "I know. I know what you mean."

"And when you drew me . . . oh, I dunno."

"You liked me drawing you?"

"Yeah. Yeah, I did."

"I thought you didn't like those pictures."

"It wasn't that I didn't like them. They made me feel . . . *defensive*. Like you'd—I dunno—seen through me. They made me feel naked."

Oh, *wow*. Portia's getting heavy. Oh, wow. Maybe she has got a brain after all. I'm not sure if I'm pleased or not. But anything that makes her feel naked has to be on the right track.

"Let me draw you again," I say. "Now."

I don't wait for an answer. I get this pencil and bit of paper out of my pocket, and I smooth it out on the table, and I look at her, very slow, very sexy, and then I start to draw. "Stop it," she says. "Just stop it, will you?"

"What does Tony do?" I ask, sketching in her hair.

"He's a manager. Stop it, Rich. I mean it."

"What does he manage?"

"It's some kind of a computer shop. I'm not sure. *Stop* it!"

"And does he enjoy it?"

"He likes the money. Let me see that."

"Not yet."

Portia lets out a huff of mock annoyance, then she says, "You know—it wasn't just your drawings, Richy. That made me feel different I mean. It was—you know. After the dinner. As well."

I look up. If Portia was the sort to blush, she'd be blushing right now. She's gazing at me, expecting me to say something. I put down my pencil and lean towards her and we have this amazingly erotic kiss across the little wrought iron table, nothing touching but our mouths.

"Oh, *God*," she murmurs. "Richy, you really can—"

I pick up my pencil again, and carry on drawing, even though my hand's trembling like mad.

"Let me *see*!" she demands again.

"When it's finished."

There's a pause, then she says "Rich—why d'you like drawing me?"

"Now who's fishing for compliments? You know why. You're beautiful." I put the last soft shading round her eyes, and hand over the drawing.

"Oh, God," she says again. "That's *faa*-bulous. That's really good. Can I keep it?"

"*I* want it."

"You've got all those others."

"OK. Have it. But let me draw you again, OK? Some other time?"

"OK."

"Promise?"

"Promise."

I take back the picture, and write *Love R* at the bottom, then I hand it to her and say, "Artists like

Rossetti and people—they always slept with their models."

She bridles elegantly, eyebrows raised. "Oh did they?"

"Yeah, they did. And I can really see why. Why they wanted to I mean. Why they felt—when they were drawing a girl—they were halfway there already."

Blimey am I making an impact. Her gorgeous, hypnotic green eyes are fixed on mine. I leave an impressive pause, and this time she leans across the table, grabs me by the back of the neck, and pulls me towards her. I'm not sure if it's just me turning her on or if it's me drawing her or if it's 'cos she's all fuelled up by this whole exciting two-timing swept-away-by-passion bit.

And you know what? Right now I don't really care.

At ten to nine, after a bit more chat and lots of intense pauses and two more tabletop clinches she checks a little blue-strapped watch on her wrist and wails, "I have to go. I really do."

"Dump him," I say. "Go on. Phone him up and dump him."

"Richard—I couldn't be that cruel."

"Lie to him then. Tell him you can't see him tonight. Like you did the other night."

Bad move. She looks annoyed, and says, "I'm

not in the habit of lying to him you know. I mean—we've got a really, really good relationship. He treats me really, really well. It's just—oh, I dunno. He's so *predictable.* And he's kind of—he's not a bit creative, or anything. He's not *exciting*. Not anymore."

Then she stands up, and I stand up too, at top speed, and wrap my arms round her so tight she can't move. "Don't go," I plead.

"I have to."

"I don't want you to go."

"I know, I know. But I must. Honestly, Rich. I've got no *choice*."

It's like the script of a Victorian melodrama. I'm only glad no one can overhear us. She pushes me away and starts to slide my jacket from her shoulders.

"Keep it," I say, hoping like shit she won't say "Thanks."

"Don't be silly. It's yours."

I take it, drop it on a chair, and wrap my arms round her again, and we're kissing, longer, better even than before. She pushes me off, cries, "Oh, God, I don't know what to *do*!" and then she's gone.

End of Scene III.

All *right*!

Chapter 24

"I mean, it's fake. It's like a total game. But I don't care. Is that completely superficial of me?"

"Completely."

"She's just so *horny*. It's like—I didn't *care* what's going on in her mind. I don't care if *nothing's* going on in her mind. I guess that makes me a real shit."

"Yup."

"Well I don't care. I've obsessed over that girl for so long from a distance and now it's close up, *boy* is it close up, and that's good enough for me, I don't need to get all serious and analytical and—"

"Rich!"

"What?"

"Have you any idea how fantastically *dull* you're being?"

It's Monday evening and I'm up at Abacus Design. There's just me and Nick there; I'm ploughing through some more storyboards while he taps out a report on his natty portable computer. I want to talk and he doesn't want to listen but apart from that we're getting on fine.

"Sorry, Nick. It's just—God! It's 'cos I'm visual, I swear it. This whole thing is a total visual trip."

"That's an original way to describe being led by the dick, darling."

"Well, yeah, it's physical *too*, obviously. I mean—when we kiss, it's like, *Jesus*, it's like—"

"Spare me the details, OK?"

"I'm not even sure I want her to dump her boyfriend. I mean—*yeah*, I do, 'cos then I'll get to see more of her, but this whole trip at the moment, it's just so steamy, and . . . and *tense* . . . it's fantastic. Today, at college, she was going past and we just kind of *looked* at each other and it was so *hot*, it was—"

"Rich—for Chrissake—for the last *time*—shut up. Or you're going through that window."

"Oh, that's nice. I come to you—as an older man—for advice and all you do is threaten me."

"You're not asking for advice. You're wanking on about how hot she makes you."

I put my arms above my head and grip my hands together and stretch back, a long, muscle-wrenching stretch, savouring the pain. Then I say, "Don't tell me to break it off 'cos I can't. I want to take it further. I want to take it as far as it can *go*. Now I need something to . . . I need something *exciting*. She thinks Tony's got boring. She says he's not creative. She thinks I am, 'cos I draw and everything."

"*Hurgh.*"

"I can't just ask her for another drink. A meal maybe. I need something different, something swishy. I need something –"

"Oh, for *Christ's* sake!" Nick bangs both fists down on his keyboard, making it squeak. "OK. Problem solved. This Friday. Big agency do. Up in town. Barb won't come. Says they bore her stupid. So I've got a spare ticket. You can come, and they'll let your squeeze in too, specially if she's as gorgeous as you say she is. Lots of glamour, champagne, canapés, loud media types—in other words, *swishy*. Your rating will go through the roof, kid, OK? She'll be so impressed she'll probably let you shag her in the car park after." He glares at me. "*OK?*"

I'm gazing at Nick like he's Santa Claus. "You *serious?*"

In answer, he rummages furiously in one of his in-trays, comes out with two silver-edged cards and waves them at me. "Here. Friday, eight p.m., at Medici's."

I lunge out for the cards, but Nick wafts them out of reach. "Oh no you don't. They're going over here. And if you make one more sound between now and eight o'clock—I *shred* yours. *OK?*"

I'm too happy to answer.

The next day at college I spend the first hour just roaming around trying to track down Portia. I'm feeling so bloody brilliantly charged up and good that what I want to do is just take her by the arm and say something along the lines of, "Come on, baby. You know you want to," and she looks at me, all "Yes" and adoring, and I lead her out behind the college, and get into a big, big snog, where quite a few people can see us, but only from a distance, and then we wander over to the trees at the edge, and then—there'd be like this little dip, this hollow, all screened, and we'd just subside into it, and Portia'd be wrapped round me like an octopus, and wham, we'd just be *doing* it, brilliantly, no fuss or fumbling, and not much foreplay, and she'd come about a million times, and then we'd lie there for a bit and she's all over me, all adoring, and then we get up and wander back to college, and I've got one arm round her, and with the other I'm doing something casual and a bit indifferent like lighting up a fag, only I don't smoke so maybe unwrapping gum, no, that's uncool, anyway, something, then we meet all my mates, one after the other, and they all say stuff like, "Hey, what have *you* two been up to?" because Portia's got this *afterglow*, she's like this beacon, and she's looking at me all *adoring*, and . . .

"*RICH!*"

Christ, it's Portia. I turn to face her; I smile at her all openly like I haven't just been fantasizing about shagging her over on the other side of the playing fields and then impressing my friends with it.

"What are you up to?"

"Up to? Nothing. I ain't up to— I'm not—"

"You're looking all guilty, Rich."

"Am I? Well, hey—I don't feel it, Portia."

"Well I do. I feel awful about Friday night. I felt—when I was with Tony—I just felt *awful*." I stare into her wonderfully spooky green eyes, and she says, "We mustn't keep seeing each other like that, Rich. We mustn't let it happen again."

Very slowly, I put my hand in my leather pocket, feel it close round the ad agency invite. "You don't mean that," I say.

"I do. I have to. I can't keep cheating on Tony."

"You're not exactly cheating on him."

"I am, Rich. Inside, I am." And she gives me this look heavy with erotic meaning.

I smoulder back at her and say, "Well, that's a

tragedy, Portia. I was just going to invite you along to this." And I hand her the glitzy invitation.

In her fabulous cat-face, her eyes grow huge. "How d'you get this?"

"Nick Hanratty. You know, the—"

"Ad agency guy. Wow."

"It should be great. And it'll be *packed* with media people. Film people. *Magazine* people. Nick thinks I might make some more contacts. It's a real shame you—"

"Well, it's kind of work, isn't it?"

In what passes for her conscience, which as far as I can make out is about as developed as a buzzard's, Portia is squaring things up.

"Work?" I echo, innocently.

"Yeah. You know—it's like an opportunity. To make contacts, like you say. I won't tell Tony I'm going with you. I'll tell him I'm going with—oh, I dunno. Mattie or someone. I'll tell him her uncle got tickets. Then it'd be OK."

"You mean you can come?"

"Sure. I'd *lo-ove* to."

"And you won't feel too guilty?"

"Rich!" She gazes at me, all trembling reproach. "Don't tease me."

"Sorry."

"You know I want to see you. It's just I—oh, *God*! Let's not talk about it." And there and then in the media studies block corridor she flings her arms round my neck and plants her mouth on mine.

That woman is a real moral *acrobat*. You've got to admire her.

I skip college again on Wednesday and put in a whole day's work at Abacus Design. Nick has made it clear the last of the storyboards need to be on his desk by the weekend or I'm not so much toast as something smeared messily on toast. This threat, and the fact that the balance owed to me is, I reckon, a hundred pounds, keep me chained to my desk.

"You're in luck," says Camilla, passing by, tidying away the two storyboards I've finished since I've got here. "Nick's had as much as he can take from one of the guys he uses for storyboards. He's too unreliable. Looks like you can take his place."

"Isn't that a bit mean?"

She shrugs. "He had it coming."

I don't say anything, but inside I'm thinking—I won't need to do storyboards much longer. I'll be the new Sling look and I'll be so rich this hundred quid'll just be pin money. Nick wanders by, and I call out, "Any news?"

"H'mmm?"

"News. On Sling. You know."

"Oh, right. Well I did speak with them last

night, actually. They're still deep in discussions. Still sounds positive."

"Yeah?"

"Yeah. They're looking into the whole etching idea, which means using you."

"Oh, that's *great*! Oh, God, I hope they say yes."

"Well, don't worry, darling—you'll be the first to hear."

He meanders off and I call out, "Um, Nick?"

"Yes?"

"Friday—how you getting there?"

"Cab."

"But it's miles away."

"Expenses. There's no way I'm driving."

"Well—would you mind if . . ."

Nick groans. "All right, I'll give you a lift."

"Oh, thanks, mate. Back too?"

"Jesus Christ, Rich, remind me again—just when exactly did I sign your adoption papers?"

"Aw, come on Nick."

"OK, OK. But you be ready to go the minute I am, OK? I'm not waiting."

"Oh, great. Thanks."

"And don't try any sleazy stuff with this bird you're bringing when you're sitting beside me, OK?"

"Nope. I won't even hold her hand," I say, while I'm thinking—hadn't thought of that. Maybe I can afford to get a cab back on my own. . . .

Nick's about to move on again, when he turns and says, "Nearly finished?"

"Yep. Six more to go."

"You've done a great job on them."

"Thanks. Camilla said there might be more—said you'd fallen out with one of your regulars?"

Nick frowns. "She shouldn't've said that."

"Why not? You just said I was good."

"You are good. You're also still at college. You keeping up with your work?"

"Christ, Nick, I've already got my old man and my art teacher on my back. Don't you start."

Nick smiles. "OK. It's not just college work though. You getting any time to do your own stuff?"

"What own stuff?"

"You *know*—stuff for you. Like the pictures you sent me."

I'm kind of stumped when he says that. I used to spend hours doing stuff out of my head—every time I got hold of a sheet of paper, practically, I'd get something down on it. But lately there just hasn't been the time.

"Yeah," I say. "You know—a bit."

"Well, don't forget about it, Rich. That's what it's all about—doing the work. The real work I mean."

• • •

I leave with only two more frames to go, promising Nick I'll get them done Thursday evening. And he says he trusts me and settles up with me there and then, and I walk out a hundred quid richer. As soon as I've got home Chris is on the phone, telling me he needs to go out and get bladdered because he's had a great gut-busting row with Natalie. So I meet him and buy him lots of beer and listen and by the end of the evening we're agreeing women are off a different planet and nothing we do can change that fact ever.

I get home very late. Everyone's in bed, which is just how I like it. Living in shifts. I look for a note from Mum about dinner being in the oven or the bin but there's nothing. I make a sandwich and eat it standing up. I'm too hyped-up and pissed to sleep, and that stuff Nick said about doing the work is stuck in my head, so I pull out a couple of sheets of paper and try out some sketches for my Sling creature. Nothing I do is right though. I'm just not inspired. My drawings are either too nasty or too much like a cheesy super-hero off some kid's cartoon. I tell myself I'll have to wait until I get the *specifications* from the guys at the top, then I bin the lot and turn in.

I sleep late Thursday morning and amble into college for an English class but by the afternoon I'm taken over by the lust to shop. I want a new pair of trousers, something sharp and styled and better than jeans to go with The Shirt for Friday night.

As I riffle through the racks of stuff I find myself wondering what Portia's going to wear to the party. Something completely jaw-dropping that's for sure. In my mind, I put her in something short and tight, then something long and low cut, something bright, something moody, something that will make every guy in the room shrivel up with envy.

Only just over twenty-four hours to go.

Till Scene IV.

Bring it on!

Chapter 25

Nick has told me to be outside the Blackbird at seven-thirty Friday and he'll pick us up in the cab, so I get Portia to meet me in there at seven. She's only ten minutes late this time. She's got a long loose glamorous cardie thing over her gear so I can't really check out what she's wearing, but I love her face and I like her wedgy, slightly Oriental-looking shoes and I do get a heart-pumping glimpse of cleavage as she holds out her arms to me.

"*Richy* this is so *exciting*!" she squeals. And then we're wrapped round each other and she's throwing back her head like an opera diva. I go for her throat fast as a vampire, and kiss the whole length of it. She pulls away just as I'm moving in on her lipstick and yelps, "Aren't *you* excited?"

"Yes," I say. "Extremely." I am, too. So excited I have to pull my jacket round me as I turn towards the bar. "Vodka and orange?" I ask.

"Spritzer, please."

This sounds to me like something you drink for a gut complaint, but the guy behind the bar doesn't query the order, just sneers a bit as he checks if she wants ice. When I get back to the table, Portia's firing from all cylinders. "So—this party. What d'you know about it? Where is it exactly? How many people are going?"

"Well—a hundred or so. Clients, and people the ad agency want to keep in with. Nick said there's gonna be a band, dancing and stuff."

"How *faa*-bulous!"

"It's being held in this real swishy restaurant. Nick said there's some kind of roof garden."

Portia's rolling her eyes in ecstasy. "God, I can't *wait*!"

I check my watch. "You won't have to, much longer. We should go outside and look out for Nick. It's nearly seven-thirty."

When we stand up, Portia reaches out and takes my hand, and together we leave the pub and stand at the edge of the busy pavement. I've got no idea what kind of car to look out for. I'm feeling a bit edgy, hoping nothing goes wrong, when a black Merc with smoky windows purrs to a halt alongside us. Then the passenger door opens and Nick peers out. "All right, Rich?"

"Hi!" I'm beaming all over my face with relief,

and with thinking how impressed Portia will be. "Might've known you wouldn't go for a normal cab!"

"Nothing but the best, mate." Then he clocks Portia, and clambers out of the car, all charm and flattering enthusiasm. "*Hi!* You're Portia!" He swoops in on her, grabs her shoulders, and pivots her—first left, then right—in the direction of his mouth, planting a big luvvy kiss each time it makes contact with her skin.

God, I'd never *dare* do that to a woman I'd only just about said hello to. But Portia's glowing. "Hi!" she giggles. "Thanks for saying I can come tonight!"

"A pleasure, Portia. A total pleasure. Hope you enjoy it." Then he opens the rear door of the car and ushers Portia inside. As I slide in after her, Nick pulls a comic, approving "You done all right there, my son!" face at me, and shuts the door on us.

Nick gets back in next to the driver, and the car smooths off from the kerb. Portia settles like a pampered cat into the soft leather of the seat and turns to smile at me. She's done something extra-dramatic with her eyes tonight, and what with that and her black silky hair she looks like an erotic Egyptian priestess.

I wish it was my car. I wish I was paying for it and Nick wasn't there and I could do what the *hell* I liked on the back seat. Every tiny atom in my body, every fibre of my being, every quivering nerve ending wants to *jump* on her. I lean towards her and inhale her perfume and I feel like I'm aching with the need to get hold of her.

Oh, *sod* it. Nick's not going to turn round, is he? Right away? I slide towards her and start easing my arm round her shoulders, but I'm reckoning without Portia's pathological fear that her lipstick might get smeared or her dress creased. She snatches up my hand like it's a bug crawling across the back of her neck and lays it down on the seat between us, then she holds it there, keeping it out of trouble. Message understood: No messing about before we get to the party.

I'm disappointed but there's something sexy about that hand grip too. I concentrate everything I'm feeling on our linked hands, lying there like a barrier between us. I move our hands up on to her leg. I move them up and down. I massage her thumb.

The Merc goes like a spaceship along the motorway and it's not long before the driver announces we're almost there. My guts clench with nervousness. I've been so focused on Portia up to this point I've forgotten I've got to take *part* in this agency gig. I wish I'd grilled Nick a bit more, but it's too late now. There's no way I'm asking for etiquette tips in front of Portia.

We park, get out. Medici's is on the top floor of a very grand block of offices and other places (there's even a little art gallery tucked away on floor two). It's almost totally intimidating. We walk through the big, chilly, classy, picture-hung hall up to the desk and Nick hands over the tickets and we get ticked off the party list by an enormous doorman. Then Nick introduces Portia as "a very desirable extra" and they both ho-ho-ho together and the doorman says no problem, sir, no problem at *all.* Then enormous doorman's sidekick is whisking round the front of the desk and whisking our coats off our shoulders.

This is the moment of truth. I'll see what Portia's wearing. She's very, very aware that four men are staring as she slides her cardy thing off her shoulders—she even delays the moment, like some kind of subtle stripper.

At first, I'm slightly disappointed. Her dress is so *plain.* Olive green with wide shoulder straps, nice and low but that's all. And then Portia swivels round and I see what's so fine about it. It's understated, and elegant, and incredibly sexy because you don't really see it. You see *her.* It reveals her intensely. Not just her shape, although it does do that—but *her.*

I'm overcome by the need to draw her again, to get this down. I'm even glancing round like an idiot at the desk to see if there's any paper I can snatch. She's raising her sorceress eyebrows at me. "Don't you like it?"

"Your dress?" I croak. "I love it. It's completely brilliant."

"It better be. My credit card's so far in the red it's turning purple."

I recognize this as one of Portia's jokes, and crank out a laugh, and then Nick's ushering us into the super-smooth high-speed lift. "Bit of a contrast to the lift at Abacus, eh?" he says, as we rocket upwards. I feel like my guts have been left behind. Portia's studying the reflection of her gorgeous profile in the mirrored walls.

Once the lift stops, I take Portia's hand and we follow Nick along a short plushy corridor and through a door flanked with so many jugs of lilies we could be in a funeral parlour. A waiter all in white flourishes a glittering tray of glasses in front of us and Nick takes two, one of which he presents to Portia. "Cham-*pagne*!" she squeals in delight.

I manage to grab one for myself, and then Nick says, "Right, kids. I've got to go and present myself to about a million people. You're on your own, OK? Have fun."

I want to wail, "Don't leave us!" but I just nod and say, "See you later." And he's off into the crowd.

I am desperately, desperately keen to impress

Portia; to take charge, to seem cool, relaxed, up for all this. But everything's against me, the weight of all the conspicuous success and money in this place is landsliding against me. And I'm rooted to the spot, waiting to be buried by it. I take a gasp of champagne, and turn helplessly to her.

And she saves me. She places one beautiful hand flat on my chest, smiles up at me, and says, "Rich, this is am-*a*-zing! But I feel like a gate-crasher."

"Yeah? Me too."

She giggles. "They won't throw us out, will they?"

"Nah. Not if we act snotty and self-assured, like everyone else is doing."

"You think? Like this?" She raises her glass, takes a regal sip. Another white-clad waiter pivots in front of us, this time with a tray of little goodies.

"Madam?" he says. Portia simpers, and takes one. I take one too, and the waiter skates away.

"See?" I say, and I can feel my confidence coming back, flowing back into me, because we're turning it into a game. "We fooled him. We'll fool everyone. Come on. Let's tour."

She laces her hand in mine again, and we start weaving our way through the glamorous crowd. There's a lot of shouting going on, a lot of fake greeting and gushing. Portia's lapping it up. Her head's rotating like that girl in *The Exorcist*, checking everyone out. And while she's doing that she's lapping up the admiring looks she's getting. And so am I, if you want the truth. It's so good, strolling along beside her.

"They're all wondering who the hot new couple are," I whisper.

"Don't be an idiot," breathes Portia, loving it.

"I bet they think we're in the latest art film. We're the new discovery."

Portia laughs happily, and we reach a bar, all shiny glass and cocktail shakers. "I'd love another glass of champers," coos Portia. Manfully, I take her glass from her and put hers and mine down on the bar, and before I can even fret about what to say or whether I'm supposed to pay, they've been whisked away and the barman says, "Same again, sir?" and places two more brimming glasses on the polished wooden bar.

I'm feeling pumped up now, I'm enjoying myself. I hand her a glass, lounge back against the bar, and survey the scene. Portia moves in on me and kind of undulates against me, her face pressed against my chest. "This is brilliant," she breathes into my neck. "Thank you *so-oo* much for asking me." Two twenty-something guys walk by and ogle her, and as they do she pulls my face down and plants a slow kiss by my mouth.

And I realize she's off into another game. Directing stacks of sex towards me to make ogling blokes even more worked up about her.

I'm not about to complain.

I emerge from the kiss and ask, "You hungry yet?" I feel like I can provide it all, and I've just spotted a sumptuous looking buffet table over on the other side of the room.

"Not yet. Or maybe just for another of those little boaty prawny things."

As if on cue, a waitress trundles up to us with a whole tray of canapés, and Portia squeals pleasurably over these for a few minutes, sampling one of each kind. Then she says, "D'you have to go and talk to anyone, Richy?"

I shrug. "Wouldn't know where to start. I've seen a couple of people I recognize. From Nick's place. Maybe later, yeah?"

"But what about making contacts?"

I leer down at her. "Right now, making contact with anyone but you seems really unimportant, Portia."

I cringe when I hear that exit my mouth, but Portia loves it. She nestles herself right under my arm and says, "Shall we go for another little wander?"

"Yeah. Let's."

"I think the roof garden's out that way. Look—see those plants? Let's go and check it out."

Wound around each other, we walk towards all the greenery and step through a wide glass door into a wonderful roofless space. It's a beautiful evening, and the night air is a fix after the smokiness of the party room.

"Oh, isn't it *gorgeous*!" Portia gushes. "So sweet. And *romantic*."

It's a bit over the top, to be honest. Like someone got a job-lot on exotic pot-plants and pseudo Greek statues and Ali-Baba pots and nifty trickly little water-features. But if it makes Portia feel romantic, it's OK by me. We start to waft down the little tile-paved path, over to the edge of the roof. There's a wall coming up to waist height, and then a trellis on top of that, heavy with climbing jasmine.

"*Mmmmm,*" breathes Portia. "Smell that. Isn't it *heavenly*?"

"Mmmm," I echo dutifully. If you crane forward and look through the trellis, you can see down to the street. It's like, *miles* away, and the cars look like little toys. It reminds me a bit of being in Nick's shag pad, gazing out of the great open window.

"Wow," I say, "look how high up we are."

"Oh, don't," whimpers Portia. "I can't bear heights. I can't look down, I'll get dizzy."

This is the perfect excuse for me to steer her away from the edge, and down a side path to the end of the terrace, where a little bower-type place is waiting for us. It's all droopy with roses and hanging baskets, and Portia just about goes into orbit with delight. "Oh, it's *sweet*! Oh, Richy, come on, sit down. Just for a minute."

I don't need asking twice. I throw myself down on the twee little bench inside it, and pull her down beside me. I put my arm round her, but I figure I should make a bit of conversation before I follow this through, so with cutting-edge originality I ask, "You enjoying yourself then?"

"It's *fa-abulous*!" she sighs. "And what's so amazing, Richy, is, if you get that account and everything—this'll be your life."

"My life?"

"Yeah. You know. This kind of do, mixing with these kinds of people. You'll be doing this *all the time*."

I don't think it quite works like that, but she sounds so impressed I don't want to enlighten her. And anyway—it could be true. If they use me for Sling it really could be the way I'll be spending Friday nights from now on. I let myself salivate over that thought for a few seconds, then I say, "I wish they'd confirm it. I really do. I feel like everything's hanging in the balance."

"Me too," says Portia, soulfully, and turns her luminous, sexy cat-face towards me. I move down towards her, silently asking, Can I? And she hesitates for a moment, then she lets me go for it. Passing through my mind is the unworthy thought that in the moment of hesitation she was thinking, "S'OK, I'll let him, I'll go to the bog on the way back, fix my face again," but I push that aside. What does it matter anyway?

We're well hidden inside the flowery bower. We kiss once, my hand on her shoulder, her fingers in my hair, then we wind our arms round each other and start seriously snogging. It's amazing, we're so sure what to do now, we're almost used to each other. Not in any boring way, but in a great way, a way that says, Move on. Move on to the next stage.

I come up for air and mutter, "Oh, *Portia*, I want you so much it's making me ill, I swear it."

"Don't," she says.

"You have to ditch Tony. I swear I'll burn up, I will, I really will." My hands are moving down from her hair to her neck, then lower, and I'm thinking—this is it, go for it, *move on*. I open my eyes quickly and scan the terrace, making sure we're still alone. And over the top of her head I see two eyes watching me from behind this great lush palm. I kind of freeze rigid, then I glare back angrily. And it slowly dawns on me through my shocked and revved-up state that the two eyes belong to Bonny.

Chapter 26

My eyes lock on to Bonny's, and there's no way I can just unlock them and pretend she isn't there. I know I've got to speak to her. And the weirdest thing is, one of my first thoughts is how shitty it must be for *her*. To see me and Portia like that. After she'd asked me out and all.

"Bonny," I croak.

"Sorry!" she wails. "Oh, *God* I—I just came out here to get away, I—*God*, these parties are so incestuous, if I'd known you'd be here I—*look*, I'm going—you carry on—Oh, *Christ* I didn't mean that I—"

"Who's *she*?" demands Portia crisply, in her total snot-queen voice. Under my hand her back goes all rigid, like the hackles on an indignant dog.

"It's Bonny," I say. "Friend of Nick's. Well, her mum is. She—"

"Bonn-EEE!" Tigger's unmistakable sing-song siren voice ricochets among the urns of plants, bounces off the front of my head. "Where *are* you?"

"Oh, *fuck*," mutters Bonny, frantically, retreating back behind the palm.

"You're hiding!" I say.

"Spying," hisses Portia.

"You came out here to get away from Tigger?"

"Yes," says the voice from behind the palm. "Her and the total phoney idiots she keeps introducing me to. Oh, *fuck*."

"Charming," mutters Portia.

"S'all right," I say. "Your mum's gone over the other side of the terrace."

And then suddenly there's a kind of wailing explosion from behind the palm. "I didn't want to come to this shitty phoney party in the first place! I told Mum I wasn't coming and she made a huge fuss, started *crying*, said we were growing apart, said this party was major and she needed my *support* . . . *real* moral blackmail . . . and then the minute we get here I'm just trailing round after her like a spare part, and everyone's all, *Oh, Tigger, aren't you wonderful, running your own props company and STILL finding time for your daughter, such a close relationship, how DO you do it*—it's all such a LIE, it's—" then Bonny stops short with a sob, as if horrified at what she's let burst out of her.

I don't know what to say, what to do. And at my side Portia is still stiff with indignation. You can tell she feels absolutely no sympathy whatsoever for Bonny's plight. "Are you going to introduce us, Richard?" she asks, icily.

"Um, yeah. Bonny, this is Portia."

Bonny peers nervously out at us, then she shuffles round from behind the palm. Portia assesses and dismisses her with one flick of her eyeballs.

"Hi, Portia," mumbles Bonny. "Um—sorry about that. It's just if I have to go back in there I'll—I'd sooner jump over the edge of this roof!"

"I think it's a fabulous party," Portia says coldly.

Bonny looks helplessly at me, and I say, "It's the deal with her mum that's the problem."

"God, I wish *my* mum could get me invites to parties like this. I really do."

"But I don't feel it's *me* being invited," Bonny whispers. "I'm just like this—*appendage*."

"Well, I came as Rich's appendage, didn't I, darling?" Portia lays her hand possessively on my arm. "We had to chat up the doorman to let me in. What does it matter how you got here?"

Bonny looks like she might start crying any

minute, so I come to her rescue again. "If you had Tigger as a mum you might—"

"Oh, my mum's *awful*. Most people's mothers are *awful*. You just have to deal with it."

"I do," croaks Bonny. "Usually. It's just all the fake crap in there, I got upset and—"

Portia's clearly decided to take issue with everything that comes out of Bonny's mouth. "I don't think it's fake, *or* crap," she retorts scathingly.

"Portia—butt out," I mutter. "You don't know what her mum's like."

"She can't be *that* bad," Portia hisses back—and as if on cue, Tigger's hunting cry booms out again, this time heading our way. Bonny looks so forlorn I have this urge to jump up and give her a hug, but I don't. And then Tigger appears through the foliage. She's wearing a staggering slinky black dress with silver tasselly things hanging off it, and very high silver sandals. She has terrifying and undeniable *impact*.

"Oh, *there* you are! Darling, I've been searching *every*where! The dancing's just about to start, and I thought I really have to have the first boogie with my little girl. . . ." Tigger clocks me and Portia in the bower and trails off. Then she shrieks, "*RICHY!* It is you, isn't it?"

No escape. I stand up, and Portia stands up with me. "Hi, Tigger. This is Portia."

"Portia, hell-*O*! Lovely to meet you. So

Richy—you *dark horse*—is this your girlfriend?"

I cough non-committally, and glance at Portia, who's looking superior.

"Oh, *I* see," gurgles Tigger. "Mind my own business, eh? Well, all I can say is, *lucky Richy*, if you are! What a completely divine dress. That sexy green—it's perfect with your lovely dark hair. Oh, it's *super*. You look *gorgeous*. It's *you*."

Portia's smirking, really lapping this up, and Tigger goes on, "I'm Bonny's mum. In case you hadn't realized."

"Well, no, I hadn't," simpers Portia. "You look more like sisters!"

Over Portia's head, I see Bonny looking like she's in the last stages of drowning. I pull a silly face at her—eyes crossed, mouth down—and she gazes at me like I've thrown her a life-line.

"Oh, you're *sweet*!" Tigger's braying. "Saying that! Oh, everyone says that, don't they, Bonny darling!"

"Well, it's true!" Portia squeals.

"Oh, darling!"

"And I lo-ove *your* dress! It's stunning!"

"Oh, sweetheart, thank you! I was *so naughty* to buy it, I can't really afford it, but you know what it's like when you find the *perfect thing*—"

"Oh, absolutely!"

"You don't think it's too young for me?"

"Oh, absolutely not!"

"I walked out of the shop at first, told myself no, but then I turned round and went back and bought it."

"Well, good for you!"

"My bank manager is going to be *very cross* with me but—"

"Oh, sod *him*! He's a man—what would he know!"

Then they both go off into hideous peals of girly laughter. Something very like horror is sweeping over me. "Shall we go back inside?" I croak.

On the way back through the garden terrace Tigger and Portia kind of magnetize together. Tigger's gushing over Portia like she's the daughter she wishes she had, and Portia's gushing back like she's the mother she wishes *she* had. Bonny's walking beside me. She's still looking pretty upset but there's something else there. It could almost be laughter.

"She's your girlfriend then?" she whispers.

"Yeah. You know. Sort of. There's someone else."

"For *you*?"

"Nah. Her."

"Oh." This time I'm sure she's laughing.

The band have started up: we can hear them before we get through the big glass doors. "Come on!" brays Tigger. "All four of us! On the dance floor!"

What happens next is too grisly to deal with, and I kind of block it out as it's happening. Tigger grabs two more glasses of champagne from a tray, thrusts one at Portia, and tows her on to the floor. There, they both start swaying seductively about and within seconds they have three admiring male onlookers.

"Come *ON*," shrieks Tigger to me and Bonny. "Get on the *FLOOR*! Stop being such *WIMPS*!"

As if we've been choreographed, Bonny and I simultaneously take two steps backwards, and I turn to Bonny and mutter, "You want to go get another drink?"

Chapter 27

Bonny is ashen-faced but determined as we stand against the gleaming chrome bar. "I've had it," she says. "I've got to get out."

"From here?"

"From home. From *her*."

"Oh. Right."

"I don't do my A's until next summer. I don't think I can hang on that long, honestly. She's started to bitch about me working, you know. *Already*. She knows, if I get good grades, I'm off to uni. She doesn't want me to leave her."

A big, shiny tear collects in each corner of Bonny's eyes. "It's OK," I mutter, putting my hand awkwardly over hers.

"I know it is. I know it's OK. It's just starting to be OK. I'm just starting to see straight. See it through *my* eyes, not hers. Most parents nag about work and not going out too much. She has loud dinner parties and drags me out and wants to join in *my* life all the time and tells me to ease off 'cos I'm overdoing things and tells me . . . tells me . . ."

"What?"

"How boring I'm being. Get me that drink, will you?"

I want to ask her how it got like this, how long it's been like this, whether there's a dad involved, but I don't. I get us a couple of beers and we lean against the bar and look glumly at the party raving all about us.

"I feel really sorry for her in a way," Bonny suddenly says.

"Yeah?"

"I mean—the way she pressurizes me to go out with her and stuff. It's sad. It's 'cos she hasn't really got any friends."

"I'm not surprised." It's out of my mouth before I can stop it.

Bonny turns to look at me. "You hate her, don't you?"

"Oh, come on. I'm not involved enough to hate her. I just—*huuurgh*." Suddenly I'm too raw and wound up and pissed off with the way things are going to be anything but honest. "Look, Bonny, when I first saw your mum—when she turned round—she made me think of a vampire."

"A *vampire*? Why, for heaven's sake?"

"Oh, she turned round and it was like she was a helluva lot older than her clothes and her figure and everything. It made me think of vampires, when they suddenly lose it and age."

Bonny's half-groaning, half-laughing. "You're *right*. . . Oh, God Mum would *die* if she heard you say that."

"Anyway, it was weird I thought of vampires 'cos everything I see about her and you've told me about her—well, she is one, isn't she. A real living breathing human vampire. She's feeding off you."

There's a long, long pause and then I say, "I shouldn't've said that."

"Yes you should. You think it."

"I mean—she supports you too. But not really *you*. Just her image of you. What she wants you to be."

Another long pause, then Bonny says, "It's so hard. It's like—if she feels I'm moving away, she hangs on tighter."

"I know."

Bonny's looking into her glass and blinking, fast. "Change the subject for God's sake," she mutters. "Let's talk about you."

"Me?"

"Yeah. You really hooked on her, are you?"

"Portia? Yeah."

"Well don't sound so depressed about it."

"*Huurgh*. Change the subject, OK?"

We don't, though—there's nothing to change it to. Portia and Tigger are filling our minds. We stand there in silence, just watching everyone. Then Bonny says, "Have you had anything to eat yet?"

"Nah. Only poncy little titbits."

"I haven't even had those. Want to go over to the buffet table?"

"Yeah, why not."

The table's been pretty decimated but there's still some good stuff left. We pick out the best bits in companionable silence, then Bonny says, "Won't Portia be pissed off you haven't gone and danced with her?"

"I can't dance."

"Well, you know. Found her."

"She could come and find me."

Bonny goes into that silence that could be laughter again, and I'm pretty relieved when Nick suddenly pitches up beside us, kisses Bonny hello, and barks, "Ready to go!" It's an order, not a question.

"Sure," I say.

"Lost your girlfriend?"

"She's dancing."

"Go and get her. Five minutes, by the entrance downstairs, OK?"

I say a muted goodbye to Bonny and head for the dance floor. There's a great, homogeneous mass crowded on to it now, and I can't see either Portia or Tigger. I squeeze my way through all the bodies and then I see Portia's back view.

With two great masculine mitts plastered across it.

And the music isn't even especially slow.

I have a decision to make. I pile in now all indignant and possessive, or I play laid back sophisticate, and tow her off in a relaxed fashion when the current song comes to an end. I decide on the last one, mainly 'cos I'm a coward, although I'm not all that relaxed as I put my hand on her arm and say "Portia—we gotta go."

"Al-*ready*!?"

"'Fraid so. Nick's got the car waiting."

The guy she's been dancing with kind of evaporates away, and Portia smirks at me. "Were you jealous?"

"No. Should I have been?"

"Where's your little grey friend?"

"Grey. . . ? You mean Bonny? She's not grey."

"Oh, *you* know what I mean. Drab. Boring. Her mum's a lot more fun."

There's nothing I can say to this. I get Portia a bit frigidly by the hand. I'm filled with a sense of disappointment that the night hadn't turned out like I'd hoped it would.

"What's *wrong*?" she snaps, as I tow her towards the exit.

"Nothing. Just, it would've been nice to spend the rest of the party with you."

"Well, you could've—"

"*Alone*. Not with that freak of a woman."

"Oh, Richy, she went off after five minutes! After some man!"

"So why didn't you come and find me?"

"*Find you?* Why the hell should I come and find *you*? You were with that boring girl, anyway."

"And *you* got asked to dance. And I didn't notice you saying no." Then I realize I'm sounding like a jealous boyfriend so I shut my mouth and sulk like one instead.

Going down in the lift Portia's not speaking to me, but once we get in the back seat of the Merc she comes over all amorous. She sidles across the leather seat and cuddles up to me and says, "You're not cross, are you?"

"What's there to be cross about?"

"Oh—I dunno. Me dancing with that guy. He was in *films*."

"Well, wow."

"I didn't tell him I was at college. I said I was—"

"An actress."

"Oh, don't be so sour, Richy! Come on—

lighten up!" And she starts schmoozing these little breathy kisses up the side of my face. I can't resist it, not for long. I start kissing her back, and soon we're into a really heavy session. I'm having these unreconstructed male thoughts like—she went to that party 'cos of *me*, she *owes* me. I glance at the front seat—Nick looks like he's collapsed with exhaustion. There's no way he's going to turn round. I'm bending Portia further and further back as we neck and then I kind of topple over on top of her. And then we're stretched out together on the plushy seat as the Merc speeds through the night.

Chapter 28

The Merc driver, being a total salt-of-the-earth gent, coughs very loudly as we get near the Blackbird and enquires can he drop the young lady off first or is she accompanying the young man home? Portia pushes me off her and husks out her address. We're there in five minutes: the driver glides to a stop and says, "I'll wait while you see the young lady to her door, sir."

I slide out of my side of the car and Portia slithers out of hers and then we fasten together again as we walk up her path. She turns her face up to mine and I can tell it's anguish and tragedy time. "We've got to stop this," she says. "We've got to. Before it gets out of hand."

I suppose by that she means before we end up having sex. Which is where everything in me is focused and aiming and trying to go.

"Um," I say.

I covered just about her entire body on the backseat of the Merc. Through her dress, but even so.

"Don't you think?" she pleads. "Honestly?"

"No," I say. "I don't." I want to ask her if she's sleeping with Tony but I don't feel I can. And I sort of don't want to know, anyway.

"It's not that I want to. Stop seeing you. But—"

"So don't. Stop seeing me."

"Oh, *Richy*—"

"Oh, *Portia*. Come on, don't get so heavy. We had a great time tonight, didn't we? Most of the time."

"Yes."

"Especially the last bit."

We exchange a lengthy kiss, nostalgic for the last bit. "I have to go in," she breathes.

"I'll see you at college," I say.

And our mouths home in for one last kiss, and she's gone.

Back in the Merc, the driver says, "You next, sir?" Beside him, Nick's snoring peacefully, so I say, "Yeah. Yeah, that'd be great," and give him my address. For some reason, I'm feeling really flat, really tired. Too many late nights, I think. Too much booze.

Although I'm not all that pissed tonight, so it's weird that when I get to my front door I can't get my key to open it. I think the lock's stuck so I pull the key out and try again, and this time I ram my shoulder against the door and heave, and it dawns on me that the place the door's stuck isn't the keyhole but right at the top where the big inside bolt is.

And then it dawns on me that they've bolted me out.

Before I want to think about this I've grabbed the knocker and I'm hammering it down, checking my watch at the same time. It's only twelve-thirty. What are they on about, locking me out?

A light goes on in Mum and Dad's bedroom at the front and glares down at me on the doorstep. I can hear voices—Mum's voice getting shriller, sounding upset, Dad's voice getting louder, more determined.

I decide not to bang on the door again. I wait.

And then there's the sound of two sets of feet coming downstairs, almost as if they're in a race, and the bolt's drawn back and the door's opened and there's Dad frowning out at me.

"What's up?" I say, fake-casual. His frown still makes me quake. "It's only twelve-thirty."

"Let him *in*, Bill," says Mum. "Don't just keep him on the doorstep for heaven's sake!"

Dad stands aside a bit and I push my way past him into the narrow hall. "What d'you lock me out for?" I say.

"I didn't think you were coming home," says Dad. I can sense all this anger banked up behind his eyes, his words, waiting to burst out. "It's not like you've been around much in the last few weeks."

"Oh, for Christ's sake—I always sleep here!"

"Yes—and that's about all you do, isn't it?"

"Oh, not *this* again—look, I'm tired, OK?" I turn and start to head up the stairs when Dad says, "Just you hang on a minute. We want a word with you."

"Bill—now is not the time," says Mum.

"When else do we see him?" snaps Dad, and he stamps into the kitchen.

"Come on," mutters Mum. She won't look at me. We both follow Dad through.

He's standing by the table, holding a letter from my college. I recognize the tired old bits of heraldry at the top, the pompous lettering. "You didn't care about the phone calls," he says, meaningfully, "maybe you'll be a bit more concerned about *this*." And he thrusts it towards me, triumphant—*pleased* even.

I take it and scan it. It's a serious warning, signed by the principal. It lists all my "unauthorized absences" from lectures and lessons. It lists my failure to turn in assignments, course work, essays. It winds up reminding me of the contract I signed when I enrolled, promising to fulfil the requirements of the college, and ends up threatening to kick me out at the end of term if I don't rectify things very, very fast.

My stomach's contracting in panic. "Shit," I mutter.

"Yes," snarls Dad. "Shit."

"Look, I—"

"You wouldn't listen, would you? You wouldn't take warning."

"I can turn this around. I can get an extension on the time. I can go to the principal, and—"

"Wriggle off the hook. You're good at that, aren't you." And suddenly his anger bursts out, like I knew it would, like I've been waiting for it to do. "You've *wasted* it, for Christ's sake, Richard! You've wasted your chance! You won't be able to turn it round now—you'll have to redo the year. *If* they let you. I wouldn't. God, you make me *sick*! You're given a place at college that loads of kids would give their eye teeth for, and you're so *arrogant* and *stupid* you let it slide, you just can't deal with it, you can't be *bothered*, can you?"

Somewhere in my head this red pulse starts up, beating. "Look—I can sort it—"

"*Sort it?* You sound like a smalltime crook. *Sort it*. You make me sick. What about making the best of something, really working at it?"

"Dad, I—"

"It's too *late*! You've wasted your chance. Thrown it away 'cos you're lazy and arrogant and—and someone tosses you a half-baked promise about as likely as winning the lottery. I warned you about this whole advertising thing! I warned you to keep your feet on the ground, but no, you have to put all your trust in some . . . some *stupid*, *corrupt* little outfit promising you everything, giving you nothing—"

"Corrupt? Where d'you get corrupt from?"

"Don't give me that. I know what goes on in these outfits. I've seen the state you get home in half the time."

"Oh, right. You think I'm on drugs."

"Are you?"

"Yeah, Dad, yeah." My voice is two levels higher than normal and still climbing. "I go round to Nick's place and the coke's just lined up on the kitchen counter, waiting to get snorted up."

He takes a step towards me and for one crazy second I think he's going to slug me. "They're not like you think they are!" I shout at him, like my voice might be able to push him back. "They've been giving me work—look!" And stupidly, suicidally, I put my hand in my pocket and pull out my fat roll of money.

Dad gawps. "*More* money! Where the hell did you get that?"

"I earned it. Doing storyboards. For Nick."

"How long has this been going on?"

"A couple of weeks. That's why I've been missing college. But I'll plan it better next time, I'll—"

He stops. It's like he's seen me for the first time. "Where the hell did you get that fancy coat?"

"Nick gave me it."

"Oh, I see. *Nick* again. Presents, money—didn't it occur to you to offer your mother some housekeeping, from that great stack of cash?"

"Bill, I don't care about housekeeping!" shrills Mum. "I care about him getting thrown out of college!"

"Well *I* care about housekeeping," snarls Dad. "I see you come in every night from your shift, worn out, having to cook for everyone, and then I discover that that selfish little shit—"

"Don't you *DARE* try to pin that on me!" The red pulse in my head explodes, splits up like atoms. I'm yelling now, moving towards him, fists clenched. "It's not my fucking fault Mum has to work so hard! *Jesus!* Why d'you think I'm sticking my neck out on this account, eh? Why d'you think I'm pinning everything on it? 'Cos I want to *make* something of myself! I want to *get* somewhere! I want this chance! I don't want to end up a *sad loser* like you in a dead end job where you can't even afford fish and chips on a Friday night!"

I've said it. It's there in the room like a rock, like a wall, and it can't be unsaid.

The kitchen feels like it's swaying, shaking, like all the air's been sucked from it. "Richard," whispers Mum. "You *apologize*, you—"

"I don't want him to apologize," Dad grits out. His voice is full of disgust, loaded with it. "His apology would mean *nothing*."

"I'm going," I choke out.

"Yes," says Dad. *"Get out."*

I stumble out to the front door. I can hear them talking, shouting, arguing behind me but I don't care. I get out the front door and I slam it behind me and as I reach the end of the path I swear I hear the door being bolted against me again.

Chapter 29

"*Chris!* Chris, mate!"

I feel like a total idiot, stooped over on Chris's doorstep, hissing through his letterbox. I'm not going to knock though. I'm not knocking on any more doors, not tonight. The red pulse is still in my head. I want it there, filling my skull—I don't want it to stop, I don't know what'll take its place.

There's no answer. I go to the side of the house and clamber up and over the tall side gate. I've done this lots of time before and so far no one's called the Bill on me. I drop to the ground and make my way, crouching low, to the kitchen window, and there's Chris—all on his own, thank God, pouring boiling water into a coffee mug and smirking to himself. He turns to get sugar from the cupboard, exposing this great jagged lovebite on the side of his neck.

I reach out and tap on the window. He looks up, shocked, then he clocks me and his face relaxes. Then he's over at the back door, unlocking it, letting me in.

"Thanks, mate," I say. "Can I stay here tonight?"

"Sure," he shrugs. "Lost your key?"

"Nah. Big row."

"Your old man?"

"Yes. I've had a letter from college—"

"Kicking you out?"

"All but."

"Shit."

"I'll sort it."

Chris shrugs again, gets another mug out of the cupboard. He's not that bothered. I've walked out on a big row before and kipped down with him. He's got laid-back parents, and this huge old sofa in his bedroom. And he's a great mate. I realize that now, looking at him, thinking how much he puts up with from me. I want to thank him, but I can't.

"So the shit hit the fan did it?" he asks.

"Yeah," I mumble. I don't want to talk about it, so I say, "How d'you get that hickey on your neck?"

Chris grins, mouths "Natalie," and then tells me the story of their big reconciliation.

Stretched out on Chris's sofa an hour or so later, I can't get to sleep. I shut my eyes and try to relive the horniest bits of my evening with Portia but all I can see on the back of my closed eyelids is Dad's furious face. All my life I've disappointed him. Not good enough at exams. Not good enough at sport. And what I was good at, he never really valued. I feel like he's pitched against me, dragging me down.

I'm up early the next day, stowing away two big bowls of Shreddies. Chris's mum plods serenely into the kitchen just as I'm finishing off and says, "Oh, hello, Rich. OK?"

"Yup," I answer, through a gobful.

"Good. Chris not awake yet?"

"Nope. Um—gotta go now." I stand up. "Thanks for having me."

"Any time," she smiles.

I remember to stow my bowl in the dishwasher, then I make my escape. I'm on a mission. There's no way I'm going back home. It's official—I've left.

"Oh, God—you again?" groans Nick, still in his dressing-gown on the doorstep. "What the hell d'you want?"

"I need to talk to you," I say. "Please."

"It's Saturday *morning*."

"I know, I know. I'm sorry. It won't take long, honest."

"Bloody hell. OK, come on in."

He stomps through the house, and I follow. "Where's the family?" I ask.

"Out," he says, "with the dogs. I was having a lovely bit of *solitude*. Till you bust in."

We go into the conservatory, where the morning sun is streaming in and mixing with the steam from a pot of coffee. He's got toast and the morning's papers all laid out on the table and for a minute I feel a real shit for barging in on him. But I have to do this.

Nick sits down, picks up his cup of coffee, opens the paper, sighs, and takes a sip. "Go on then," he grumbles. "Spill."

"I had a huge bust up with the old man last night," I mutter.

"Why?" he says, eyes scanning the newsprint.

"Oh—it doesn't matter. Tons of stuff. Thing is—I've had it. All of it—it's a downer. I want out. I can't stand living with his disapproval anymore. Or his penny-pinching. Or his—"

I want to say "failure" but I don't. I want to tell Nick what I said last night, the real reason I can't go back home, but I don't.

"You should try and make it up."

"He locked me out last night."

"Oh. Well—you can kip here for a bit if you want." He turns over a page of his paper. "Till it blows over."

I seize on this piece of casual generosity and

lean across the table excitedly. "It won't blow over. It won't. Nick—I've got a plan. Your shad pag. I mean shag pag. Shit. Your flat. Let me move in. I'll caretake for you. I'll stop burglaries. You said there were rats—I'll kill 'em."

Nick sighs, and turns another page.

"Go on, Nick. Say yes. I'll clean, in lieu of rent. I'll clean your fucking office *toilets*, Nick."

There's a long pause, and finally, finally, he looks up from the newspaper. "Jesus, calm down, mate. This is not a big deal."

"It's not?"

"No. You can move in there any time you want."

I feel my jaw clang wide. "Nick—why didn't you say this before?"

"You didn't ask, darling."

It's easy getting the office key and the flat key off Nick there and then. I get the feeling he'd do anything to get rid of me. He makes noises about the flat being too dirty to move into and I brush them aside, I say no problem, I'll deal with it. Then he tells me how to de-activate the burglar alarm and I leave, calling out thank you, thank you.

The next bit's the hardest. I need to go back home, get my clothes and stuff. It's about midday now and I know if I hurry I'll get to the house before the regular-as-clockwork Saturday morning trip to the supermarket returns to base.

So I get a cab. It's the first time I've ever got a cab on my own in the daylight. It pulls up outside the door and I say, "Wait five minutes, will you?" Money no object.

Five minutes are all I need. I hare upstairs, pull out my old rucksack from under the bed, yank the battered leather case from the top of the wardrobe. Then I'm jamming them full of stuff. Clothes, a few tapes, college stuff, nothing else, nothing sentimental. I hurry into the bathroom, snatch up my toothbrush, aftershave, razor. Then I tip the dirty clothes basket out over the floor and grab everything I recognize as mine. I cram it all in, buckle up the rucksack, sling it on my back, pick up the case. I'm just legging it down the stairs when the door to the living room opens and I get a glimpse of Sam's open-mouthed face as I slam the front door behind me.

Chapter 30

It's weird, being in the flat on my own. I was completely hyped up as I paid off the cab, got the main office door open, turned off the burglar alarm, rattled up to the top floor in the lift, and wrestled the door to the flat open. And now I'm here I feel like I'm in total collapse.

I sit hunched up between my case and my rucksack, looking at the great grimy arched window, and I don't even have the energy to open it. I don't know what I'm doing. I'm scared. It's like I'm falling, waiting to hit the ground.

Oh, shit, what have I done? I've not so much cut all ties as ripped them off and shredded them. What happens when my money runs out? What'll happen Monday, at college—how am I going to fix it? What'll happen to the bills here? How am I gonna *eat*?

It's all hanging on the Sling account. I've got to

get it, I've got to. Then I'll be soaring. I'll fix this place up, I'll say to hell with college, I'll leave, I'll be on my way in the ad world, I'll *make* it.

If I don't get the account I'm stuffed.

Not going to think about not getting it. Oh, shit. Why haven't they confirmed yet? Why don't they *phone*?

I sit there like I'm waiting for a blood transfusion, staring at the sun trying to break through the filth on the huge panes of glass in front of me, when this low, irregular banging starts up, somewhere under the floorboards. My first thought is rats but I reject that because they'd have to be operating hammer-drills to make that kind of noise. The banging gets louder, more frantic. I can hear weird, gurgling noises from one of the rooms to the side, then another room—it's the bathroom, the kitchen. Jesus, what's going to happen—is something going to explode? And then a voice calls "Ri-ich! You there?"

And Barb pokes her head round the flat door. I'm so surprised and pleased to see her my throat chokes up. "Hi!" I croak.

"Can I come in?"

"Course! Course you can!"

"I've just turned the water on," she says, walking over towards me. She's got a bulging carrier bag in each hand. "Nick told me what'd happened. *Typical.* Sends you off here without telling you where the water main is. That guy is—" She breaks off, dumps her bags down, and looks at me. "Rich, are you sure you're doing the right thing? Shouldn't you go back and make the peace with your folks?"

I shake my head.

"OK," she says. "OK. I'm not going to interfere." She sits down beside me, on the dirty floor. "It's just—moving out after a big row, it's not really the ideal way to leave home, you know?"

I shrug, keep silent.

"Will you at least tell them where you are? Your parents?"

Another long pause. I want to talk, I want to be a grown up, but somehow I can't speak. Probably because what I deep down want to do is throw myself in her arms and howl.

"Oh, Rich. I just want to help, OK?"

"I'm all right, Barb," I mutter at last.

"Sure you are. It's just—look. I've got some old sheets in the car. And some towels. And things."

I stare at her. Sheets and towels. Stuff like that hadn't even crossed my mind. "I can get stuff," I say. "I've got loads of money left."

Barb's blinking very fast. She reaches out a hand towards me, then suddenly she's scrambling to her feet saying, "Let's see if the water got through, OK?"

I follow her through into the bathroom, and watch her as she flushes the bog and twists the taps. It helps, somehow, just watching her do ordinary stuff like that. There's a lot of banging and rattling as the air fights the water in the pipes, then there's a clear stream into the sink, which she leaves to run for a bit.

"The electricity control is out here," she says, "on the wall. Look." She presses a few buttons. "There! You'll have hot water in no time. Nick had it all checked when they did the office below."

She bustles past me, into the kitchen. "Yuch, it's filthy. Let's see if that kettle still works. Yup You're in luck. And the cooker. Yup. Look—I've brought some cleaning stuff—you want me to stay for a bit, help you get things straight?"

I want her to stay so much I know I've got to get her to go. She's being so kind it's killing me. "Barb, you're really great, I just want—I want—"

"To be on your own for a bit? Course you do. I'm off. I'll just bring up the stuff from the car, OK?"

"OK," I mutter. "I'll come down with you."

We ride the lift in silence, and as we walk across the car park Barb points across to a couple of rubbish dumpsters. "If you want to clear out the old carpet, get rid of some of the rubbish—

just leave it by those. In bags. We can tip the bin men a bit extra to clear it away."

"Thanks," I croak.

"You can get rid of everything. Chuck it all—you'll be doing us a favour," Barb says, as she loads me up with sheets and towels and a pillow and a duvet. "Can you manage? You want me to help you carry it up?"

"No. No, honestly."

"OK, kid." She reaches up, ruffles my hair. "You'll be due for another haircut soon. Just call round, all right? Any time you want feeding or anything. OK?"

"OK."

"Promise?"

"Promise."

And she gets in the car, shuts the door, and drives off, before I've even had time to thank her properly.

I go straight back to the flat and dump the sheets and stuff down on the floor. A great grey cloud of dust rises up, choking me. I head for the kitchen, find a glass in the cupboard, rinse it under the tap, fill it, and drink. It tastes cold and good. It makes me realize how hungry I am, so I wander over to the bags Barb brought up with her. One is all J-cloths and Flash, the other is food. Bread. Cheese. Choccy biscuits. Apples. Packed into a big shiny saucepan. I sit there like a half wit and tear bits off the loaf and the hunk of cheese, and eat an apple and eight biscuits, and as all this hits my stomach I start to feel OK again.

I think about what must've happened an hour or so ago, when Barb got back home with the kids and the dogs to find Nick had given me the keys to this place. I think about her dropping everything, gathering up food and sheets and coming straight here. I think about the way she was just here for long enough, the way she knew I needed to be left alone. The way she made me promise to call round and get fed.

Then I stand up, unfasten the bolt on the two great arched windows, and swing them back against the walls.

Chapter 31

"All right, you bastards. Chinese *and* beers. But only if you get the whole lot cleared, OK?"

I slam the phone down, exit the phone box, and leg it into town. In three-quarters of an hour or so I'm back at the flat with a red plastic bucket, a scrubbing brush, a broom, a dustpan, three six-packs of Fosters and a big roll of extra-strength bin bags.

Right. I'm not touching the floor and all the junk, not when I've just negotiated hard for Chris, Ollie, and Ryan to do it. The kitchen. I'll start with that.

It's pretty easy, really, 'cos it's dead small. First I empty the skinny little cupboard on the wall and the larger one under the breakfast bar. All the eighty-year-old dried pasta and pre-war salt and stuff I bung in a bin bag; anything like a mug or a plate that can be scoured clean I shove in the sink. Then I sluice out the cupboards. They're quite wet and soapy by the time I've finished, but they're dead clean. Then I wash what's in the sink, and put it back in the cupboards; and then I open the fridge. It's very, very nasty inside. It's also warm.

Before I even think about cleaning it I decide to check it still works. At the back I find a plug, and when I've plugged it into a socket on the wall a light comes on and the fridge whirrs. So I scrape it out and scour it, and then I put the cheese and the bread and beers inside.

I'm on a roll. I launch myself at the tiles on the walls, the breakfast bar, anything I can see, and then I get some newspaper and mop up the floor, and then I scrub that. I'm sweating when I've done, and when I check my watch I see it's taken me over an hour and a half. Bloody hell. I never realized cleaning up could take so long.

I'm just pulling the ring on a can of Fosters when there's an aliens-contacting-earth crackling from over by the door to the flat. I head over and find it's coming from a little oblong box.

Hey—I've got my own intercom!

"Yes?" I shout into it. "Hello?"

"We're here, you prat!" crackles a voice that could be Chris's. "Let us in!"

I push the black button at the top, then the red

button at the bottom. "Anything happened?" I shout.

"Nothing!"

I push the buttons again, then I finish the beer, leg it down in the lift, and open the door to the guys in person. They're really impressed. They're firing questions at me left right and centre—Whose is it? Why'd he let you move in? How long can you stay?—and when we get up to the top floor and into the flat they just about go into orbit. It makes me feel great. I can't believe how good I feel when only a couple of hours ago I sat there on the floor, so down in the depths I couldn't move.

Ollie's brought along a cassette player; he dumps it on the floor and plugs it in and soon a loud beat is filling the flat. "Great acoustics!" he says approvingly.

"What's that shit you've put on?" grumbles Ryan.

"You could have an ace party here!"

"Where's the beer?"

"You ain't getting nothing till that floor's cleared," I say, taking control. "Come on."

"Not yet, you nonce! Give us the tour first!"

So I show them the other rooms. My clean kitchen first ("Man, it's *dripping* in here! What did you do? Hose it down?"), followed by the bathroom, where they all make puking noises over the aubergine-coloured bog and basin and Ollie discovers to his cost that the creaky-looking shower is actually very, very powerful. We bypass the rubbish room, and head for the boxy bedroom, where there's lots of obscene comments about the mirrors and they agree with me that I should drag the big low bed out into the main room and sleep in front of the huge window.

"Imagine what's gone on on that mattress, though," says Ollie. "Blimey."

"Yeah," says Ryan. "Still, it'll get a rest with Rich, won't it. Impotent git."

"*Yeah?*"

"Yeah!"

This provides me with the perfect chance to goggle all three by bringing them up to date with what's gone on with Portia. Chris interrupts with what's going on with Natalie, and we start tearing up the nasty pink shag-pile, and by the time I've got to the snogging session in the back of the hired Merc and Chris is saying he thinks he might be in love we've got a good third of the floor cleared.

"All right," Ollie's crowing. "This is gonna take no time!"

"Unlike Portia," jeers Ryan.

"You wait, mate," I say, all superior. "Now

I've got this place, what's gonna stop me?"

"Bastard," mutters Chris. "You gonna lend it out?"

"Depends," I say. "Keep working."

And we all set to again, pulling up the carpet. It reminds me of an old dried-out turtle shell I had when I was a kid. I used to try and stop myself tearing leathery chunks of skin off the outside but it was difficult to stop 'cos it was just so damn satisfying. The skin came off just as easily as this carpet's coming up now.

Ryan's examining the floor underneath. "This is OK, man. Clean it up, it'll be OK."

"Yeah," says Chris. "Real swanky *Ideal Home* stuff."

They're right. It's filthy, but it's good, solid, stained wood. "I bet this was how the floor was, when it was a mill," I say. "It's all worn smooth."

The wooden floor looks so great compared to the sad old shag-pile, we all pitch in with renewed enthusiasm. I fetch the roll of bin bags, pull off half a dozen, and shake them out. Then I come on like a foreman, organizing Ryan and Chris to carry on carpet ripping while I get Ollie to help me bag up the strips of carpet and shift it all out to the lift. We work like slaves for the next forty minutes, with the wind from the open window helping counteract the fug of dust. When I can see an end in sight I leave the three guys to it and start in on the heaps of storyboards, props, and bulging rubbish bags piled all round the room and outside the door of the flat, heaving them down to the dumpsters. Some of the better stuff—op-art faces, blown-up photos—I leave piled against the wall. I'm thinking I might nail them up for decoration later.

We have a short break when Ollie discovers some dodgy looking photos showing almost naked women cavorting artistically with shiny-skinned guys in weird codpieces and big, beaky bird masks. "H'm," says Chris. "Think that'd turn a girl on?"

"Nah," I say. "Who wants to get laid by a pigeon?"

"Right," says Ryan. "Unless you're an egg."

I shove Ryan hard, and he topples over, then we all have another look through the photos, then we get back to work. Before too long the last strip of grungy pink has been torn up, and the last loads of bags are on their way down in the lift with Ryan and Ollie. Chris turns to me, grinning. "All right—where's the beer?"

"Aw come on mate. We haven't swept up yet."

"Sweeping up was not part of the deal."

"But I bought a *broom*!"

"I don't give a shit if you bought a feather duster. Come on—where's the beer? In the fridge?" And he heads towards the kitchen.

"OK, OK," I grumble, 'cos I know when I'm beaten. "You go down to the phone box near the garage, order up the Chinese. No more than twenty quid, OK? Or you pay the extra. You'd better wait for it downstairs."

Chris continues on to the kitchen, collects a Fosters, then grabs the two tenners I'm holding out. "Deal," he says, and walks out of the door.

With just me in the flat I can get a really good sweeping session in. I've got a half-baked idea I ought to sprinkle water down to keep the dust from flying up, but I'm scared of all the dirt turning into mud. So I just sweep, shifting all the muck to one side of the door then scooping it up and bagging it. Dust is fanning about as I work, coating the windows in an even thicker layer of grime, and I think—I'll clean those last of all.

Ollie and Ryan clatter in from the lift, admire the floor, and head straight for the fridge, pleased when I tell them the Chinese is on its way. We sit and down our beer in satisfied silence until Chris gets here with the food. As we open all the little cartons up I'm pretty sure it must've cost more than twenty quid—it's a real feast—but Chris doesn't ask me for more. He holds up his beer can, clangs it into mine. "Here's to your new pad," he says, grinning.

"Yeah," says Ryan. "When can we come back again?"

"Soon."

"You gonna have a party? It'd be great for a party."

"If I get this alcopops account," I say, "I'll throw the biggest fucking party ever."

Pretty soon, the three of them get up to go, because everyone needs to take a shower and get on the phone and make arrangements for Saturday night. I'm all evasive when they ask me if I want to meet up later, 'cos what I really want to do is stay here. I give them a sort-of promise I'll see them in the Rose and Crown, and they head off

Then I go and fill my new bucket with hot water, and add detergent, and I shift an old chair over in front of the window. I open both sides wide against the walls, and wash down the outsides and polish them. Then I shut the window, and work on the insides. And as I clean from top to bottom the setting sun breaks in through the glass and shines along the empty wooden floor.

And I feel great. I can't tell you how great I feel.

Chapter 32

That Saturday night, I'm like a recluse. I clean the bathroom, I haul the bed in front of the window and make it up with the sheets and stuff Barb gave me. I hang up my clothes on a hook in the wall on some old hangers I find in the bedroom, and have a mild panic attack when I realize I'm going to have to negotiate a laundrette from now on. At around nine o'clock I make myself a cheese sarnie and pull the ring on the last can of Fosters, then I stretch out on the bed and watch the night come in and think about Portia stretched out beside me. As I start to feel drowsy I think—it's OK. I can just sleep. I can sleep and wake up when I want to now.

Sunday starts off weird. All I wanted when I lived at home was space and silence—well, not silence, but noise that I made, not noise from Mum nagging and Dad grousing and Sam and his slimey little friends beating each other up and yelling. But this is like a vacuum, like being in limbo, like outer space. It's sort of good, but it's weird.

I make myself some cheese on burnt toast (the grill heats too quickly) and tea, and as I'm drinking it I get washed under this great wave of guilt about Mum not knowing where I am, not knowing if I'm safe or not. She'll have phoned Chris and– *Jesus.* I have to contact Chris. I have to tell him not to tell her where I am. I realize that's the last thing I want, right now, that however weird it feels I want this space, this silence, it's what I've got to have.

I pick up the flat keys and head out, locking the door behind me. It's not the first time I've done this but suddenly it feels like ownership, suddenly it gives me a real buzz. It's not ownership, of course. Me staying here is just a blip, it's squatting, hiding out, until I can get some hard money, and I can do a proper deal with Nick.

I race down to the phone box and dial Chris's number. His mum answers, and says he's still in bed, but she says she'll wake him. She sounds really friendly, even more friendly than usual, which makes me think Chris has put her in the picture about things.

Chris picks up the receiver. "Wotcha, mate."

"Chris, has—"

"Yeah. I told her you were OK."

"Did you say where I was?"

"I said you were in this place Nick owned. She sounded really upset, Rich. She said to remind you she gets back from work early tomorrow—she wants you to phone or go round, you know, when your dad isn't there."

"She say anything else about him?"

"No. Not a thing. I told her to phone me again, if she wants to get in touch with you."

"Oh, thanks, Chris. That's perfect. Thanks, mate. I mean it."

"So are you going to?"

"What?"

"Go round?"

"I dunno."

All I want to do this Sunday is be alone or see Portia. But I can't phone Portia—I haven't got her mobile number. I meant to ask her for it Friday night but too much else was going on. And she hasn't offered it to me, probably because she sees giving me her number as yet one more betrayal of Tony.

So I spend the rest of the day alone. I'm nearly through Barb's food, so I make a foray out to a little Spa shop and get more bread, more milk, more chocolate biscuits, two tins of baked beans, and some bacon. When I open my wallet and see the fat frill of notes I still feel absolutely loaded, but I know I've got to watch it, I've got to pace myself.

You won't believe this but I spend a good proportion of the rest of the day scrubbing the wooden floor. I'm lugging bucket after bucket of hot water in from the kitchen. All this grime and muck comes up, and as it dries you can see the wood grain beneath, and it's beautiful. I don't bother to clean the creamy coloured mucky walls 'cos when I know I can stay here I'm going to get the guys round and have a painting session. Sharp white. Or that burnt-earth colour maybe.

In the end I don't nail up any of the art boards I've saved. They're so big they look good just propped against the walls. They make the place look like a studio, like a lot of serious work goes on here. There's a couple of display stands that would make great easels and for a few minutes I think about actually sticking on some paper and doing some drawing, but I don't.

It's so quiet here. I should've grabbed my little cassette player when I was picking up my stuff from home. Maybe I'll go round tomorrow, like Mum wants, and pick it up.

I get an early night. I'm going into college first thing. Mum would laugh if she knew how dedicated I'm being. I'm not going in to sort out the whole mess of them threatening to kick me out, though. I'm going in to see Portia.

Chapter 33

"Steele! You little bastard! Stop right there, boy, I want to talk to you!"

Oh, shit. Huw. Just the person I most want to avoid as I slink through the college doors at ten past nine. And he doesn't mean he wants to *talk* to me. He wants to yell at me about five millimetres from my face.

"You've had the letter then?" he demands.

"Yeah, I've had it—"

"Don't you *DARE* take that bored bloody sneering attitude with me, lad! I spent forty-five minutes with the board of governors last Wednesday afternoon listening to their bloody nitpicking list of clauses and rules, trying to convince them not to kick you out right now on the spot!"

"Huw, I—"

"Just you shut up and listen to me. I've been

to see your Graphics teacher. He agrees with me that despite being a bone-idle arrogant little bastard you've got talent and like me he's prepared to fight for you. *If* you pull your weight too. Now—here's my list of what you've got turn in. Here's his. You can have four weeks, maybe five, to get it all done." And he rams two sheets of papers, with about a million things written on each, into my chest.

"Huw, I—"

"Shut up. Your English Lit teacher is not nearly so enamoured of you. She's quite happy not to have your face in her class ever again. In fact she's delirious with pleasure at the thought. However. I twisted her arm and she gave me a list of the essays you have to make up. Your General Studies—*ha!*—teacher had to be reminded who you are, it's so long since he's seen you. But he gave me a list too." Two more thickly written lists crack against my ribcage. "Christ knows how you'll do it in the time. Neither of 'em cared. All I can say is you'll have to do it somehow. Make a start. Take along two essays—one even—prove you're determined, and they—and more to the point the principal—will have to listen. Which brings me to him. The principal. You have to go and see him."

"Huw, look—"

"I can't do everything for you, lad. You go along with that letter of summary execution and you *grovel*, and promise to *work*, and then maybe the axe won't fall. Right? *Right?*"

"Huw, for fuck's sake *listen* to me! I'm going to hear this week if I've got that account. I know I am."

"Oh, for God's sake, you still on about that? What difference does that make?"

"You know what difference it'll make."

"You still want to get snapped up and chewed to bits and spat out again do you lad."

"Look, Huw—"

"No, *you* look. Of course you're good enough to get siphoned off by some agency. Of course you are. But that'll be it, if you fail this here. This is your payment for art college, Richard. And I want to see you with that chance, three years at art college with the time to do *your* work, not somebody else's, not jumping through some cretinous commercial hoop, not twisting your mind round what they want before you've developed your own—oh, what's the use!" He stops, both fists raised, clenched, then he turns on his heel and walks off.

"Huw!" I shout after him, but he's gone.

I look at the four lists and they make me feel so sick I can't even read them. I don't care what he says, they're part of my past, I'm leaving all this grind and shit behind, I'm moving on.

And right now I'm going to find Portia.

It's not too difficult, running her down. I collar one of her sycophantic girly friends and find out she's in a textiles art class. I wait outside the room it's in and when she emerges at around eleven o'clock I haul her off to the cafeteria for a cup of coffee.

Portia is now officially two-timing. That's clear from the first, from the way she says "Richy darling, I've *missed* you!" and the way she starts off on a *mmmwaah* kiss on the side of my face and then slides straight over to my mouth and starts chewing it. I'm pleased about this but less pleased that we now have to discuss the moral implications.

At length.

Because I must share the burden of her guilt.

"Oh, *God*, Saturday was weird. Being with Tony I mean. Oh, God, what a mess. I felt so *guilty*. And I couldn't get you out of my head, Richy."

"Yeah?"

"Yeah. Don't smile, it was awful. It made me feel even more guilty—and so then I'd be extra nice to him—and then he'd get all happy and tell me he loved me—so I'd feel even *worse*—and we just kind of sat there and I'd start to think about you again. . . . Oh, *God*!"

There's a pause, and I feel I should contribute to the conversation, so I ask, "What did you do?"

"Oh, nothing much. The pub. That's the thing about Tony, he never wants to do anything really good. *So-oo* boring after Friday night. Friday night was *so-oo* good."

She scrapes her nails seductively up my arm and I wrench my brain back to Friday night, because it's aeons away now, after everything that's happened over the weekend. "Yeah, it was good," I agree throatily. "God, it was good. And you looked fabulous in that dress. It was just a pisser we had to leave so soon. I wanted it all to go on and on."

"Me too."

I gaze masterfully into her eyes. "Portia, I've got something to tell you—"

"Don't tell me to finish with Tony. I couldn't hurt him like that."

"No, I—"

"He's so sweet. And he's so in love with me."

"Yeah, look—"

"It'd be easier if he was awful, but he isn't. He's just—you know—a bit *dull*. If I'm off with him he goes all kind of pathetic. And he tries *so* hard. He's not like you, Richy."

I'm trying, I think. Right now I'm trying to get a word in edgeways.

"I actually think he was hinting about getting married last night. Seriously. He—what are you looking like that for?"

"Like what?"

"Like—horrified? I mean—it's not that weird an idea. Is it?"

"No, of course not. Well—yes actually it is. Tying yourself down when—"

"You see, he doesn't think that way. He's *totally* in love with me. He wants to be *sure* of me."

Poor bastard, I think. Short of manacling her to your side how could you ever be sure of Portia? Even then you couldn't be that sure.

"He was talking about needing more time together—he wants to *live* with me."

"Has he got his own place?"

"No. Not yet, of course not. But he's—"

"I have," I say.

"What?"

"I've moved into my own place." I wish there was a longer, more impressive way to say it. Or that maybe you could say it twice without sounding like a dickhead.

"What?"

"My own place," I repeat, so casual the words sing out of my mouth. "Wanna come and see it?"

When Portia has got over her excitement and I've been through the whole story and described it in detail (with lots of lingering on the sheer romance of the huge cloud-level window), we fix up that I'll take her there tonight. Then we talk about what a betrayal of Tony this is. And from the way our legs are wrapped together underneath the table and our arms are tangled up across it I have strong hopes it really will be.

Chapter 34

"Mum? Mum? You there? It's me."

Silence. Maybe she's not back yet. I know Dad won't be back yet and I really really hope Sam won't be back yet either.

"Mum? Mum?"

There's a noise from upstairs, a little, unsure stirring noise. And then Mum appears at the top of the stairs trying to look like she hasn't been crying.

"Hello, luv."

"Hello, Mum."

"I phoned Chris. He—"

"Yeah, he told me."

She starts down the stairs towards me. "You want a cup of tea?"

"Yeah, that'd be great."

We go into the kitchen. "Thanks for coming," she says as she fills the kettle, and then there's a long, long silence. I'm standing near her, leaning against the counter. She turns and glances up at me, and I realize I'm towering over her now. When I was about twelve or so, I'd drive her crazy coming up to her and measuring myself off against her. I was about her height for what seemed like ages and then I suddenly took off and shot up and left her behind.

I stare across at her as she spoons tea into the teapot. I can see the faded parting in her hair where the grey's growing through the rinse stuff she uses on it, and I'm suddenly filled with such sadness and love I can't bear it.

"Are you OK, Mum?" I croak out.

She nods, says, "Are you?"

"Yeah, I'm all right. Honestly. Nick's place—it's great. He's been great, letting me move in. I know Dad thinks he's some kind of drugged up smoothy but he's straight, he's kosher, seriously."

"You know you can come home, don't you, Richard."

"What?"

"Any time. You keep your keys, and you can come home."

"Unless the old man bolts me out again."

"Oh, Rich. Don't go holding that against him. He was so angry when he got that letter from your college . . . I've never seen him that angry. And those things you said to him—"

"He said stuff to me too."

"I know, I know. He's—he really does want the best for you."

"He's disappointed in me."

There's a silence as she carries the teapot over to the kitchen table, gets a couple of mugs out of the cupboard, milk from the fridge.

"Isn't he, Mum."

"It's not *you*. It's what you've done. What you haven't done."

"Well, that's me. Isn't it?"

She doesn't answer. We both sit down at the table. She pours out the tea, and I say, "Look, I can see that he's pissed off about college and everything. What I don't understand is why he's so down on this chance I've got."

"I suppose he doesn't trust it. He doesn't trust easy money."

"Mum, that last load of cash I made—I *earned* that."

"I know you did, luv. But—" She heaves a great sigh, then takes a sip of tea. "Money's never come easy to him. You know that. When he was a kid he survived doing a paper round in the morning and collecting glasses in a pub at night. He was in his first real job when he was your age and he didn't move from it for ten years. He had friends in and out of work, running scams and things, sometimes with lots of money, sometimes with none—I know he felt jealous when they were loaded, but I think at the end of the day he wanted to know where he was, know he had an income he could rely on."

"You reckon he thinks I'm like one of his dodgy friends, then?"

She smiles. "Not dodgy. Risky maybe. I don't know—maybe he's scared for you. Maybe he's a bit jealous, too. All he's ever had extra has been a tiny annual rise and a stingy Christmas bonus. And it's too late for him now."

I feel kind of cold when she says that. She reaches out and squeezes my hand and says, "Richard, I don't have to tell you we have never, ever had enough money. Well—enough to manage, but not enough to be comfortable. It's hard. And it's been hardest of all for him."

"But if I pulled this off, I could help you out, I could—"

"And you think *that* would be easy for him?"

I think back to how hard he seemed to find it to swallow the fish and chips I'd bought, and shake my head. "I can't win, can I."

"Yes. You can stick at college and get the foundations laid. You can finish your education. That's so important to him. He can't bear to just stand back and watch you risking your future, your security."

"Or maybe risk really making it."

"That's not fair."

We drink the rest of our tea in silence. Dad's attitude to me, his mind-set—we can't solve it just by talking about it. After a bit Mum asks, "What's this place you've got like?" and I tell her, but I don't give her the address, and she doesn't ask. She knows I don't want Dad to find out where I am, so it's better she doesn't find out either. Pretty soon I check my watch and say I'd better go.

She smiles, sadly. "So you're not here when your dad gets in?"

I shrug. "I've got a date tonight."

"That girl you were after?"

"Yeah."

"She's interested in you now you've got a bit of cash is she?"

"Don't be cynical, Mum."

We go out to the hall together, up to my room. I pick up my cassette player and a few other bits of stuff I'd forgotten, and Mum hands me a towel and a beautifully ironed white shirt I'd left behind dirty.

And it's time to go.

We go downstairs, stand by the front door. "You can bring your washing back, you know," she says. "If you like."

"Thanks, Mum. I might take you up on that." There's a pause, then I reach out and put my arms round her and hug her.

And she won't let me go.

"I never thought it'd be like this when you left home," she whispers. "I thought I'd have a bit more time to get used to losing you."

When she says that this great shuddery choking invades my throat and I want to *howl*. It comes from a place so deep inside me I hardly knew it was there.

"You're not losing me, Mum," I croak. "You're *not*."

"Don't let all this drive you off, Richard. Don't. I couldn't bear it if you stopped seeing us, if you . . ."

"Course I won't stop seeing you. *Course* I won't. Look—we'll give it a week or so, yeah? Let things calm down. And then I'll come round for Sunday lunch or something, and we can talk. Yeah?" I'm casting about wildly for ways to make things seem better, to make her smile. "And I'll get college sorted out. Before I see Dad again."

"Will you?" she squeezes me tight. "Are you going to see your principal?"

"Yes," I lie. "I'll sort it, don't worry. And the flat—I can really work there, Mum. It's going to be great to work in. You know there isn't really the space here."

"Yes, I know."

"You'll have to come and see it."

"I'd like to."

"It'll work out, Mum. It will."

Then I put my hand on the door handle, and somehow I pull myself away from her, and I'm gone.

I've told Portia I'll meet her at eight o'clock at this pub about ten minutes' walk away from the flat. Which means I have just under two hours to get back and get myself and the flat ready for what I hope will be the seduction scene of the century.

I stop at a supermarket on the way back, and pick up some white wine and some very posh-looking crisps and put them in my wire basket. Then I add some beer, and stand there in the middle of the aisle wondering what else to get. I wander towards the tills and find myself distractedly eyeing the bins of flowers by the exit.

Pull yourself together, Steele. Buying flowers would be insincerity on a major scale. Even Portia isn't corny enough to get taken in by them.

So I just pay for what I've got, and head back. The knitwear people have all gone home, but Abacus Design is still up and running. They don't notice me as I slink by. I hope they'll all be gone by the time I bring Portia back here. Particularly Nick.

As I let myself in through the door I am struck

that what the flat consists of is a big floor space and a double bed dominantly positioned. Not exactly subtle. Shit.

If only I had a bit more time I could buy a rug or something to throw over the bed and try and make it look more like a sofa. But there isn't time. I pull some of the art boards I've got leaning up against the walls up nearer the bed, to try and distract the eye, and then I shift the two display stands over behind it. Then I get out my two favourite portraits of Portia and prop them up on the stands. Then I immediately take them down and put them up against the wall, one a bit behind the other, and put another of my old sketches up on one stand, with a couple of pencils next to it, as though I've been working on it. On the other stand I rest a blank sheet of paper. What a poser.

Then I stand back to admire the effect. It still looks as subtle as all hell. I might as well write "Let's shag" on the blank bit of paper, and have done with it.

Too late, too late, too bad.

I leg it into the shower—my shower. I put on The Shirt. I'm ready.

Chapter 35

I order a beer as soon as I get to the pub and down a good third of it while I'm still standing at the bar. And the alcohol mixes in with my empty stomach juices (I've forgotten to eat since breakfast) and does a double rush up to my jangling brain and I get this lump in my throat and—what the hell is this?—I feel like I'm going to start blubbing right there and then.

Jesus, Steele, sort yourself out, mate. One, two hours from now you could be in the sack with Portia and you're crying? I call the bar man, order one of the dodgy-looking cheese sarnies they've got stacked behind a smeary glass case, and start wolfing it down, hoping to God Portia doesn't sail in and see me with it crammed in my face. I finish it, wipe my mouth, head over to an empty table.

You're all right, you're all right, I tell myself.

Everything that's happened over the weekend's getting to you and also—you're nervous as hell. It's—how long since you slept with a girl?

Nearly four months, that's how long. In fact if you want the truth my sexual career has not exactly been star studded. I tell other blokes I lost my virginity at fifteen, but I'm not sure if it counts if you're so drunk you don't know what's happening. And you ejaculate almost as soon as you get the damn condom on and sort of get in the right place.

Not that that's the limit of my experience, no way. Just before my seventeenth birthday I got into a Relationship. She was called Emma, and we met at the kind of party where it seems like everyone but you is in a serious clinch. We spent the last half of the night hunched up together on a sofa while people writhed randily around us, discussing how sordid it all was and how superficial one night stands were. I was impressed by how open she was, how ungiggly, and though I didn't fancy her all that much I asked her to see a film with me. And then somehow we were Going Out. She was the first girl I'd been able to discuss adult things like sex and feelings with and it made me feel majorly mature.

But you can only talk objectively about that stuff for so long without wanting to get subjective, too. We were both running on a huge desire to find out what sex was all about. It was only after we'd actually gone ahead and slept together that I got round to realizing we had virtually nothing but this huge curiosity in common.

Still, during the next couple of months we learnt a lot. And we acted out the boyfriend/girlfriend thing, phoning and dating and even buying each other presents. But it never got good. I was beginning to be appalled by it, the flatness between us, the functionality, the lack of any kind of spark. I was the one who broke it off, and I can still see the look of hurt on her face. I think she'd got a bit into me by then. But I was too separate from her. Apart from her. Even when I was inside her.

When I dumped her I made myself a promise not to sleep with anyone unless there was a real link there, a real vibration. Trouble is, the kind of girls who really turned me on generally turned me down. Still, apart from a couple of alcohol-fuelled binges, I kept to my promise.

And then along came Portia. Totally, obsessively *right*. OK, she's an idiot half the time, OK, she's got a boyfriend– she's still *right*. And now the green light's shining. *Go, go, go*. So why am I all wobbly inside? It's sorted, with Mum, with Nick, with everyone, it's sorted, *I'm* sorted. Stop being such a mincer, Steele. *Go*.

I check my watch. I've waited ten minutes so far. Which is average for Portia. Tonight, I expect to wait longer. Fifteen, maybe twenty. As a kind of payment. But then the door swings open, and it's her.

I've got used to gauging the scene Portia's playing from the way she walks in, and this time it's no different. She's all raised chin, bold eyes, raunchy swagger. She's fantastic. Playing the role of cheating girlfriend right up to the hilt.

She doesn't say a word, just comes over to my table as I stand up and gives me this kind of aggressive kiss on the mouth that goes straight to my groin. We peel apart and I offer her a drink. As I limp up to the bar I cop several jealous glances and I reflect on how Portia is so unashamedly drama queen. It makes me cringe but something in me really gets off on it too.

"So," I say, as I put our drinks down on the table and take my seat, "you meeting Tony tonight?"

She looks at me coolly. "No."

"But you haven't finished with him."

"No."

"You look great, Portia."

"Thanks."

After that the conversation kind of dwindles. We drink our drinks fast and she asks how near the flat is and I say, "Why don't I just show you?" and then we're standing up and on our way.

We hold hands as we walk along the canal bank and it's like all my senses are on overdrive, like the weedy, reedy smell from the water's flooding me and the twilight's overpowering my eyes. I can feel my blood pulsing round my body. Then this image of my bed floats into my head, all soft in the fading light, and me and Portia lying there, tangled up together. . . .

I stop and pull her in towards me for a kiss, but she's as strung out and taut as a bow string just before it lets fly. "Say something," I mutter.

"Something," she says.

We walk on. I let us both into the building, and pull open the iron lift gate, and suddenly I'm sharp again, I'm focused.

"Is there anyone else here?" she whispers.

"Don't think so." As we ride past Abacus's floor I peer out. "No. All gone home."

Then the lift clangs to a stop. "My floor," I say, and I turn and smile at her, wanting her to realize just how cool this is.

She smiles back, and I'm just reaching for the gate to pull it open when she says, "Lifts like this are kind of sexy, don't you think?"

I stop dead. That was an invitation. What am I

waiting for—a card with RSVP at the bottom? I turn back to her. She fixes me with a weird look, then she lifts her left arm, and takes hold of one of the iron rails of the lift cage behind her.

It's hard not to stare at her chest. Which must have been part of her intention. I move closer, start sliding my hands round her waist. I'm waiting for her to put her arms round me, too, but she doesn't. She lifts her other hand, and takes hold of another black bar. Blimey. My knees kind of judder. What's this—bondage without the bonds? Her hands on the black bars look like they're fastened there. She still has her feet on the floor, but apart from that she's hanging there, gorgeous. Like a ship's figurehead. Or a crucifix.

Fine, I'm up for it, up for anything. If you want the truth I'd been up for it for the last half-hour and I'm beginning to feel a dull pain in my crotch.

I squeeze her in tight to me. She keeps hold of the bars, and kind of writhes against me. I bring my face down to hers and kiss her mouth, then her neck. And then I slide my hands round to the front, and she doesn't stop me. All right! I kiss her again, doing all the fancy things I can think of with my tongue, and I work my hands up under her jumper, and then, and then . . . and then I hate to admit this, but I start to feel ridiculous. I begin to wish she'd—you know—interact. I begin to wish she'd let go of the sodding bars and put her arms round me and hug me or something. *Hold* me.

God, what does she expect? Just what is expected of me here? Should I go for it, or what? And isn't she going to *help*?

Suddenly those weird photos we found in the flat beam into my brain and I have this flash-thought that I'm in a cheesy soft-porn film and then even more suddenly, God help me, in sheer panic, I laugh.

Into her mouth.

She jerks her head back.

"What?" I whine.

"You—*laughed*!"

"I didn't! I didn't! I just—it's the dust here, I coughed, I—"

"You—sodding—laughed!"

"Honest, Portia, I didn't, I—" and then it's like my mouth has a nervous seizure. I laugh again.

It takes two seconds for her to wrench open the clanking lift door and high-heel her way down the stairs, shouting "Loser!" back over her shoulder.

I stand there limp as a gutted fish. Oh, Jesus *Christ*. I can't *believe* what I've just done. What I *haven't* done. Then I throw myself after her, hanging over the stair rails, shouting "Portia! Hey—come on! Come back!"

I can hear her shoes stabbing down the stairs, but there's no answer. I start racing down the steps, practically airborne at each bend, and catch up with her just as she reaches the bottom.

"Portia—I—*Jesus*. I'm sorry. Don't go."

She's going. She's refusing to look at me as she yanks open the big main doors. I reach out, grab her arm, and she shakes me off like a terrier tosses a rat.

"Portia! Come on. I just—I freaked. I've had—I've had a weird time recently. Moving out, and . . . and everything. And—*Jesus*—I'm not used to one-sided making out. You know?"

She turns, slowly, and gives me one long look. Crushing, condemning. Humiliating. Then she turns once more, and slams out of the building.

I limp over to the lift and ride up in it with my eyes shut because I can't bear to look at the bars she was hanging from five short minutes ago. I let myself into my flat. I walk over to the far wall and drive my head into it, twice, very hard, and the strobe lights that appear behind my eyes take a bit of the pain and shame away. I try not to think what I might've been up to at that precise moment if I hadn't behaved like such a total inadequate. I bang my head into the wall once more, then go over to the fridge and pull out a beer.

Two hours later I'm still sprawled on my bed,

horribly alone, looking at the dark sky. I'm trying to excuse myself, telling myself she and I were just in different places, playing different scenes, she was all risk-seeking and erotic and I just wasn't up to it right then, I needed it to be *mutual*, and I panicked, I freaked, 'cos underneath I just wanted to be *held* like the great useless soft git I am. I'm an idiot, a eunuch, and my life can't get any more shit.

Little do I know.

Chapter 36

I know something's up the minute I open the door to Nick at eleven-thirty the next morning a) because he's not the sort to make the effort to trek up here in the normal run of things and b) because of the way he's smiling. Like someone's just died.

I stand back, and he walks in, and we're both kind of hovering, and I look away, out of the window, and I feel like my insides are slowly setting in lead. Then Nick says, "Rich—I've spoken to John Hunt."

"Yeah?" I mutter.

"Yeah. Just now. On the phone."

"And they don't want to use me." I make myself say it.

There's a longish pause, then he says, "They thought you were terrific, Rich. Martin Wood—

the one who was most up on the whole youth marketing thing—he thought you were great, he's asked to keep your sketches."

"But."

"But—*shit*, I feel awful about this. Your drawing gave me the whole idea for doing away with a label and etching straight onto the bottle, and in the end it's that they really went for. And they looked into it, and it's significantly cheaper with a simple design. So that's what they've gone for. A simple design. Here."

He shoves a fax at me, with a sketch on it. And it is very simple, like an upside down tick, like a weird letter, like a dagger. "They're having purplish-coloured glass," he adds, as though that might make me feel better.

"So you've got the account?" I croak.

"Yeah. They want me to handle it."

I look back out of the window and think about throwing myself through it. I'd pinned so much on this. Everything. Now it's dead.

"Come on, sit down," Nick says. "I'll go and put the kettle on."

He hurries off to the kitchen and I sit down on the edge of the bed in a kind of sick daze. Thoughts are worming into my mind, like—it's over, it's all over, I'll lose the flat now, I'll be skint again, I'm being chucked out of college,

I've screwed things up with Portia.

I wish I was dead. I'm homeless, broke, jobless, loveless. I may as well be dead.

Nick comes back and puts a mug of tea into my hand. "You all right?"

"Yeah."

"You weren't banking everything on this, were you?"

"No. Look—congratulations. On the account I mean."

"Thanks. Look, mate, don't be so despondent. I know this is a blow. A big whammy, right to the solar plexus, yeah? But all is not lost, Rich, really it is not."

I try to look at him, but I can't.

"Fact is—they liked your stuff," he says. "Fact is—they're not going to forget you, and they may use you later, or even pass you on to someone else. Fact is—*I* like your stuff. I really do, Rich. And I can still give you hack work, storyboards and things, and that is bloody excellent training for this business and I might have other, bigger jobs for you sometime soon. And the *biggest* fact is I have no doubt whatsoever that you're going to make it one way or another sooner or later. You are, Rich. You're class. You can wait. You're still at college, for Christ's sake, Rich. You're still learning. Fact is it would be downright bloody obscene if you pulled this one off and made megabucks even before your eighteenth birthday. Everyone'd hate you. I'd run you down in my car. Come on, mate, cheer up. Drink your tea."

I smile, all watery and dejected, only half taking in what he's saying. Then Nick just about jams the mug up to my mouth and says, "I've got the account. And it's kind of down to you. You were part of the input, part of the buzz. So I owe you. Barb says I owe you. So I'm not going to be hassling you for rent, OK? You can stay here, and keep the rats away, and . . . and clean the stairs or something. I don't care."

I'm aware I should feel glad about this, but I don't feel anything. I make myself croak, "You mean—rent free? Still?"

"Yeah, yeah, rent free. No one else'd want it."

"Thanks, Nick. Really—thanks." There's a pause, and then I say, "I'm being thrown out of college."

"No you're not."

"I am."

"You're *not*. Jesus. There's always a way back in. Now come on—Barb says you've got to come over for lunch."

And he stands up, and like one of the walking dead, I stand up too and follow him.

As we walk up the path to Nick's house a weird howling is filling the air, coming from inside.

Nick seems unconcerned, and I in my zombie state just feel it's kind of appropriate. We go through the hall and I look into the main room and see Scarlett sitting cross legged on the floor, eyes shut, chin raised, howling. She's flanked by the two lurchers howling with her.

"She likes to do that," says Nick. He plods on into the kitchen, where Barb is doing something at the stove. Barb comes straight over, puts her arms round me, and hugs me. I kind of collapse inside when she does that. It's all I can do not to start howling along with the trio up the corridor.

"Come on, Rich, sit down," she says. "Shall I get you a beer? No? Tea? Coffee?" She's being very, very kind to me. I still feel like I'm six feet under but even down there her kindness is getting through. She stomps to the door and shrieks, "Scar-LETT! Cut that out now, OK?" And gradually, the howling stops. "You know, it's probably for the best, Rich," she goes on. "This let-down. If they'd used your picture one thing would've led to another and you'd end up being taken on by some big agency before you'd even finished college."

I'm silent, because that's exactly what I was hoping would happen.

"These ad agencies—they've no conscience. I've seen it again and again. They snatch up some promising student, suck him dry, and then kick him out, wasted."

"Barb, leave it out," mutters Nick. "We've been through this."

"Yeah, right," she snaps. "Just look at how gutted he is."

"Look, he knew it wasn't a sure thing. . . ."

"Yeah, yeah. At seventeen you really understand these things."

"If it'd come off, it would've been great."

"Well it hasn't come off, has it."

"And he was the one who sent the damn pictures to me in the first place—"

"Which you used."

"Yeah, I used them." Nick spreads his hands. "I think he's brilliant. It just didn't come off this time. But it will one day. He's gonna make it."

Barb's face kind of softens. "He is. You hear that, Rich? You are."

"I've told him he can stay in the flat, doll," adds Nick. He's looking at her, gauging her reaction.

"Good."

"And I'll have other stuff for him to do."

"Good. As long as it doesn't take too much from his time at college."

There's a long pause, then Barb shouts "*Lunch!*" and turns to the stove and starts dishing up this pasta stuff. Scarlett appears in the doorway, looks at me, and announces, "I'm not at school 'cos I have a cold. In case you were wondering."

"I was," I say. "Is howling good for colds?"

"Yes, clears the tubes," says Nick.

"Don't be disgusting, Daddy," snaps Scarlett. "I do it for the dogs. So they remember their roots."

"Oh," I say. "Right." We all sit down to eat. I find myself wolfing down the delicious pasta even though two minutes before I would've sworn I couldn't swallow a thing.

"Have you made it up with your parents yet?" asks Barb, after a while.

"Yeah. Well—my mum." Then it crosses my mind that she wants me out of the flat and I say, "Look—I can move back home if—"

"Only if you want to," says Barb, firmly. "You stay in the flat if it's good for you. It's good for the building to have someone in residence at night. Security."

"I'll get you a badge," says Nick, glancing at Barb again.

"I'm not bothered about the flat," says Barb, ignoring him. "I'm bothered about your relationship with your folks. I dunno. You kids. It must be something in the air. We had Bonny round here the other night, crying her eyes out."

"Bonny? What was up?"

"Need you ask?"

"Oh. Tigger."

"Yeah, Tigger. The poor kid's had enough. She's finally starting to stand up to her, and it's causing all kinds of trouble. Tigger's turning on the emotional blackmail at full power."

"It's deadly, that relationship," says Nick. "Dead unhealthy for the girl."

"I told her she should move out and stay in my room," says Scarlett.

"Did you, darling?" says Barb. "Well, that was sweet."

"So can she?"

"Well, she can *visit*. But Tigger would get really angry with me and Dad if she actually moved in."

There's a depressed pause, as everyone thinks about Bonny. Then I say, "I'd like to stay on in the flat, if it's really OK. There's not much space at home, and I can really get some work done there—" I break off, because I remember about getting kicked out of college. I let my fork slide out of my hand and clatter down on the plate.

"What's up?" asks Barb.

"Um—"

"He's in trouble at college," says Nick.

"I'm behind on all these assignments," I mutter. "They've threatened to sling me out if I don't catch up."

"Well, *catch* up!" blazes Barb. "How much stuff have you got to do?"

"Oh, I dunno—six, seven things for graphics, not so much for straight art, 'cos Huw gets on at me—"

"Well, you get down to it, Rich. Christ. You shut yourself away in that flat and *get down to it*. Don't fall by the side this early in the game whatever you do. One picture at a time, one step at a time. And don't do any more storyboards, you hear?" She glares at Nick. "You spend your time on your work, till you've caught up. If you run out of money, Nick'll give you an advance. *Won't* you, Nick? Considering how it was you helped him get the account in the first place. In fact he probably owes you anyway, now I come to think of it. For your input and inspiration and everything. *Right*, Nick?"

"Right," says Nick, gratefully. You get the feeling he'd agree with anything Barb said.

"The art's not the real problem," I say. "And General Studies—I can wing that. It's the English that's the real bastard. Jesus, I'm so behind. I've got all this reading to do—"

"Reading is *fun*," says Barb.

"And I've been stuck on this essay on *Macbeth* for, like, *years*—"

Barb's face lights up. "Yeah? I love *Macbeth*. What's the essay title?"

"Dunno. Some crap about the influence of the supernatural—"

"Oh, Rich, what a *doddle*. It's practically written for you. All the imagery. And the prophecies. And the witches. You do understand about the witches don't you? They don't actually do anything. They're just—what is it—'juggling fiends . . . that palter with us in a double sense.' In other words—wankers."

"They are?" I gasp.

"Yeah. You bring your essay round, I'll help you."

Nick gives me a lift back to the flat. As we're speeding along I'm aware that I don't feel quite so dead and leaden anymore. The grief is still there, the disappointment, and it feels like a great stone, weighing me down. But somewhere at the edge of my consciousness, a thread of hope is creeping back.

"You all right?" asks Nick.

"Yeah. Thanks for lunch and everything."

"No problem. Barb meant what she said, you know. About helping you with your essays."

"I know. She's—she's just *great*."

"Yeah," he says ruefully. "She nearly had my balls off this morning, when I told her about the account falling through for you."

"It's not your fault."

"No, but it was my fault I gave you thc hope, set you up to get let down."

There's a long silence, then I say, "Well, I don't wish it hadn't happened, Nick."

He smiles and pushes up a gear, and I realize that despite everything I mean it.

Chapter 37

As soon as I get back to the flat I start getting ready to go out again. I'm not going to let myself stop and think about the weight on me, because then I won't move. I'm going to act, I need to act, just as fast as someone hanging off a cliff by one hand needs to act. If I give up and let go now, that's it, it's over.

I wash my face, change my clothes, and one hour thirty-five minutes later I'm in the college principal's office. He's not particularly pleased to see me, nor is he especially encouraging. He listens to my inarticulate spewings about family problems/need to earn money/storyboards/moving out/general pain and suffering. He says: "It's neither my intention nor my wish—nor the intention or the wish of the governors—to have you leave the college if it can possibly be avoided, Mr. Steele." He asks me if I've drawn up a timetable whereby I can make good my outstanding work and I waffle through this, making it up as I speak, and together we come to the conclusion that I need another two months on account of keeping up with current work at the same time as making up the deficit.

He opens a big file, makes a few notes, processing me. Then he makes me promise to bring in some kind of plan on paper by the end of the week.

Then he stands, shakes my hand, dismisses me.

"So I've got another two months then?" I say, just to be sure.

"You have," he says. "But please be aware that it's not that long, and it's the last extension I can give you."

I leave.

I get out of college just as fast as I can. I don't want to see Portia, or anyone who might know Portia. It's because I've got my head down so low when I'm crossing the car park that I nearly get run over by a battered old Morris Minor.

"Richard, you blind bastard! I'm asking you if you want a lift!"

It's Huw. For some reason, I don't mind Huw. For some reason, I'm actually glad to see him. I pull open the passenger seat and climb in and announce, "I've just been to see the principal."

"And—?"

"Two months."

Huw grates the gears triumphantly, and bumps us out of the car park. "Well *done*, lad! Well done! I thought we'd lost you! I didn't see you for a couple of days, and I thought you were a goner—"

"I thought I was too. I wanted to be a fucking goner. I'm only not one because those alcopops people dumped me—it's OK, you can smile, you were right."

"I'm not smiling, boy. Well—not much."

"Smile. I don't give a shit, not anymore. In the last forty-eight hours or so my whole life has just—it's *shit*. I've lost all hope of making money. And I've split with my *family* and I've screwed things up with this girl who . . . *uuuurgh*. I came in here to sort out college 'cos otherwise I'd have had nothing *left*. I'd just slide down the fucking *drain*."

Huw reaches out and pats my leg. "Well done, lad," he repeats.

"Stop saying that. I don't think it's well done. Maybe I should just slide. I don't know if I can do that work. I feel like I'm dead. Maybe I should just go with that."

Huw laughs. "I always thought you had a bit of Welsh in you, boy. Now I know."

"What you mean?"

"You're a melodramatic little bastard, aren't you. Given to lachrymose overstatement."

"What the fuck does lachrymose mean?"

"It means you're a whiner. Where d'you live?"

I point out the turning, and he doesn't take it. "Huw, what you doing?"

"I never realized you lived this close to me, lad. Frightening, really. I'll take you back with me for a bit, show you my work shed."

"What makes you think I want to see your poxy work shed, Huw? I'm depressed enough as it is."

"Don't sneer at a privilege many have begged for and few been granted, boy. Here we are."

And he stops the car.

As we walk down the side alley alongside his terraced house, he's telling me I've done the right thing, that although it's crap that the world demands bits of paper as proof of progress, demand them it does and what I've got to learn is that beyond the acquisition of the bits of paper lies Freedom and the heady heights of Art College, which he knows I will love. Blah, blah, blah. He's just starting to tell me what a gas he had at Art College back in the seventies when we reach his shed. It's old red brick, like the house, half covered in ivy, and much larger than I expected it to be.

"What was it?" I ask. "Originally."

"A carpenter lived here," he says proudly. "It was his work place. It was why we bought the house." Then he unlocks the door and ushers me through. It's spacier than I thought it would be, empty and dusty, with clutter round the walls. Light is coming in from weird and brilliant angles, because he's knocked holes in the roof and the walls where he needs them to be.

"They safe?" I ask, pointing to the battered brickwork.

"Safe enough," he replies.

On a wooden platform right in the middle is a beautiful wild boar, half carved. I saw it the minute I walked in but for some reason my eyes slid away from it, avoiding it. Why do I say *for some reason*, I know the reason—it hits you, smack in the face, with its beauty, its brilliance, and it's so good, it's too much to take, I can't bear it. It's so full of life, struggling its way out from a great slab of stone.

A great sigh leaves my body, and I walk over and put my hand on its snout.

"I have to get the face right, see?" says Huw. "Some people say get the shape first, but I know if I've got the face the rest will follow."

I can't speak. I stroke the side of the boar's tusks, put my face up against its nostrils as though I might feel it breathing.

"What d'you think then, lad?" asks Huw.

"It's fantastic." I croak. "Fucking fantastic. You know it is." I put my arm round the boar's neck and look round me, at Huw's work shed. It's so humming with energy it hurts. And in the middle of all the old sheets and dust and grot and empty beer cans is this beauty emerging, this sculpture of a wild boar.

I think of Huw here, chipping away, hour after hour, inspired, content. "You should show this," I say. "It's brilliant. You should enter it for a competition or something."

"Give over, lad. You sound like the missus. She's always on at me to put myself about, get recognized."

"Yeah? Well, she's right. You should."

"All that takes time. If I got flogging myself about, when will I get time to come here, eh? Out to my shed."

I look at him and I realize that's all he cares about, getting time to come out to his shed and work. It makes me feel small, somehow, shabby, like I'd forgotten something important. What mattered was doing your work. Above all, that was what mattered.

"This is why I teach," says Huw softly, looking at his boar. "It's a bit of a crap job mostly, but it gives me some time. So I can keep a little bit of freedom. So I've got time to do what I want."

"What will you do when you've finished? Sell him?"

"Yeah. Got to. Make room for the next one, see? I've got someone who takes them off me, sells them on."

I bet you have, I think. And I bet his profit margin is way out of sight. But I don't say anything, because I know Huw won't want to listen.

He asks me if I want a lift home then, and I say no, I can walk, easy. He sees me to the end of the alley and says, "Go on then, Icarus. Get back to your place and get some paper out."

"Icarus?"

"Don't tell me you don't know who he was, you ignorant little git."

"He was that guy who—"

"Flew too near the sun. So his wings melted. He was an overreacher. Just like you. Now get back and do some work. And draw something *you* want to do. Sod the assignments."

Then he waves me off, and he's back to his shed.

Chapter 38

When I go in and shut the flat door behind me for the second time that day I'm so spaced out of it I don't know what I think or feel anymore. All I know is I'm exhausted. Part of me just wants to curl up and sleep, sleep for days, but I feel scared, superstitious about just closing down. Like if I fall asleep with my mind all skewed I'll wake up mad.

I sit on the edge of the bed and wait for the lead weight to settle on my shoulders and into my guts again, and although it's there all right, it's lost its power, it's fading. I sit there and look hard at the grief I feel, and my mind grows very, very clear.

It was just a dream of money. It was never real. The stuff I earned from slogging at storyboards was real, but not the other stuff, the megabucks alcopops stuff. That never was. Just vapour.

Like Portia. She was never real either.

Christ—where did that come from?

I stand up, walk over to the wall, pick up one of the sketches I've done of her, and I think—Portia pisses me off. She really, seriously, pisses me off. Not just some of the time, not just most of the time—on one level she pisses me off all of the time.

Yes, she's beautiful, yes she's amazingly, incredibly horny, but she's phoney, she's vain, she's treacherous. She's hard work. The kind of work I just don't want to do.

I prop the picture back against the wall. It's the best thing about her, the only thing I want to keep.

Whoa. It's like a solar wind's screaming through me, scouring my brain. I walk over to the windows, open them wide against the wall, and I get that scary, thrilling feeling of flying again. I remember how Portia hated heights, and I laugh. Then I pull the display stand with the blank sheet of paper on it over in front of the wide sky-space and I stand there for a minute, breathing in the air with its smell of canal. Then I fetch my pencils, and draw just what I can see. The rooftops and the clouds, the scrubby trees, the jagged light. It's good. I'm shading like a madman, getting the light.

The sky's changing, the clouds are getting mean, they've got monsters in them. I drag over the other stand, and put up some paper, and start on the monsters.

A while after that I've got a sheet spread out on the hard floor, and I'm working on the rooftops again, but the rooftops with rain sheeting down and scared, skinny people running.

I go back to the monsters. Then to my first picture.

This is fine. A few weeks back Huw was rapping on about this cubist guy who used to work on eight, maybe ten canvases at a time, just skating round adding to one after the other. Why shouldn't I have three on the go? Right now I've got the space for them. Space here, and in my head.

It's doing it, it's working.

I don't stop till someone knocks on the flat door for the second time that day. I don't know how much time has gone by, but it's getting really dark in the centre of the sky and I realize as I come to that I'm hungry.

I think: it's Portia. She's come back to sleep with me. Now I know she's not real and she pisses me off, does it mean I can't sleep with her?

I don't answer that, just walk over to the door with no expectations and pull it open.

And come face to face with Bonny.

On the floor beside her there's a big hold-all. I

look down at this, then up at her face again. Her eyes are starting to spill over with tears. "Rich?" she says. "I've . . . done it."

"Done what?"

"I've left home."

"Jesus—"

"The big doors were open downstairs," she whispers. "So I just came up. Is that all right?"

"It's fine, it's—"

"We had another huge row, and Mum stormed out, and while she was gone I thought, I can't live like this, I can't take any more, I'm going, so I just—I went upstairs and packed. And left."

"And came straight here?"

"No. No, I went to the Hanratty's first. Scarlett'd said I could share her room. It was mad, but it was all I could think of. *Anyway*. Barb and I were talking, and the phone went. It was Mum. She was hysterical, she said she'd phoned round everyone she could think of to find out where I'd gone. Barb wasn't quick enough. Or she couldn't lie, or something— Mum got suspicious I was there and said she was coming round and slammed the phone down and I—*God*!!"

Tears have started to spool down her face. "Look, come in, Bonny," I mutter, awkwardly. "Sorry. Didn't mean to leave you standing there."

She walks in and collapses down on the edge

of the bed, with her back to the light.

"Can I get you a drink or anything?" I ask.

"No. No, I'm fine. Well, I'm clearly not fine I'm just—oh, *shit*!"

I sit down beside her, put my arm nervously round her. "Look, I'm so *sorry* to do this to you," she's wailing. "When I heard Mum was on her way over, I just *freaked*. I *panicked*. I grabbed my bag, and ran out of the door, and Barb ran after me, and I was yelling about not being safe from Mum anywhere, and Barb shouted out, '*Go to Nick's office*.' Then she caught up with me and got hold of me by the wrist and said you had the top flat and there was a spare room up there. Then she said, 'Don't just wander around the streets, *promise me you'll go there*.' Then she *twisted my arm*, made me promise. Then she raced back inside. To get there before Mum, I suppose."

There's a long, long pause, and slowly Bonny stops gasping and crying, and I keep my arm round her shoulders. Then I say, "D'you think Tigger'll turn up here?"

"No. I really don't think Barb'll tell her. I think she knows that the one thing I need is not to see her right now." She looks up at me. "Rich—can I stay here? Just for tonight? Please?"

"Of course you can," I say. What else can I do?

She stands up then, turns, walks right up to

the open windows as though she might go through them. “Oh, wow,” she breathes.

“Don’t get too close to the edge, Bonny, Jesus! Aren’t you scared?”

“No,” she answers softly. “It’s fabulous. Like flying.”

And she lifts up her arms like wings.

. . . A GIRL BORN
WITHOUT THE FEAR GENE

FEARLESS™

A SERIES BY
FRANCINE PASCAL

PUBLISHED BY SIMON & SCHUSTER

3029-01